Praise for Meryl Davids Landau's
Downward Dog, Upward Fog

"Lorna's soul journey is the topic of Meryl Davids Landau's first novel, an inspirational gem that will appeal to introspective, evolving women."
—*Foreword Reviews*

"A lighthearted novel about a woman who just can't seem to stay on the spiritual path, something most of us can relate to."
— *Yoga Journal* Buzz Blog

"Women who loved *Eat, Pray, Love* have been hoping for another page-turner that reflects their spiritual goals . . . Meryl Davids Landau fills the void."
—*Natural Awakenings*

"Written for spiritually-seeking women like you, who want to see yourself reflected in the novels you read."
—DailyOM

"This book is light, but it's enlightening."
—Elephant Journal

"I really enjoyed *Downward Dog, Upward Fog* because it is fresh and different."
—Chick Lit Central

Also by
Meryl Davids Landau

Enlightened Parenting:
A Mom Reflects on Living Spiritually With Kids

Downward Dog, Upward Fog
(the novel that introduces Lorna Crawford)

Warrior Won

To Sheree — with appreciation + love — Meryl Davids Landau

WARRIOR WON

A NOVEL

Meryl Davids Landau

Alignment Publishing company

BOCA RATON, FLORIDA

Warrior Won/ Meryl Davids Landau. -- 1st ed.
ISBN paperback: 978-1-936586-48-6
ISBN ebook: 978-1-936586-49-3

Cover design by Mayapriya Long
Interior design by The Book Designer

For Gary, Richard, and Kelsey
the brightest lights in my life

and for Joyce and Joe
who sparked my own light in the beginning

Te hlada paritapa-phalah punyapunya-hetutvat

***Our actions determine whether we
experience joy or pain***

—The Yoga Sutras of Patanjali 2:14

1

I'm deep in my meditation when I hear a blood-curdling scream from the other room.

"Crap," I say, as I click off my cell-phone timer, glumly noting I've been sitting just four minutes. I heave myself off my cushion and scurry down the hall.

"What's the matter, little angel?" I coo to my shrieking daughter, standing on her twin bed.

"Hold me, Momma, hold me," she squeaks between ragged breaths, then flings herself over the guardrail into my arms.

I walk her into the hall, sobs ricocheting off the walls like a Grand Canyon avalanche. Lilah's been so hard to soothe lately, the silky teal comforter on my king-size bed the only thing standing a chance of calming her.

Entering the master bedroom, I place her on the blanket, a gift from my husband's sister when we tied the knot four years ago. She says Lilah is soothed because the fabric smells like us. Daria is a pediatrician, so she presumably knows. But these days, even it doesn't settle my girl. If she wails much longer, I fear the neighbors might call the cops with concerns I'm dismembering my two-year-old.

"It's okay, sweetheart," I lilt, even though I'm starting to wonder if maybe it isn't. Lilah was a dream as a baby, but now she's become so needy she's—dare I admit it— unbearable.

I rub her back, glancing longingly at the blue cushion on my floor, and at the Tibetan Buddhist altar rising next to it. Last year I finally upgraded from my scarf-draped end table to this two-tiered, antique, black number with gold-leaf designs. I got it from Craigslist; the sixties-hippie owner was moving to an assisted-living facility and wanted to find it a suitable home. I'm not Buddhist, but I promised to revere it as much as he did, so he let me have it for a song.

I've taken a cue from the Buddhists and placed bowls of scented water, flowers, and candles on the high shelf (out of reach of my inquisitive child), along with my gold figurines of the Chinese goddess of mercy Kwan Yin and of Jesus in meditation. A photo of the Hindu goddess Lakshmi (I'm an equal-opportunity spiritualer) and my brass Tibetan singing bowl sit on the bottom shelf. Each week I rotate in one new item: yellow daffodils picked from my little backyard garden recently joined the crew.

Sitting in front of these lofty items centers me when I *sujal*. Most people use the term *meditation*, but since I discovered this blissful practice several years back I rarely call it that. Even before I ever had a session where I went so deep I was nestled inside the egg of the universe—something that happens . . . well, not every time, but at least periodically—I knew I wanted a word that reflected my experience. I made up the name *sujal* because it sounded both soft and relaxing. I didn't realize until Lilah became unglued that the word *sujal* mimics the sound of *soothe*, which is what I desperately need right now.

I return my attention to my daughter, who has finally exhausted herself from her screams and is headed back to dreamland. "*Suj, suj, suj,*" I whisper. Knowing from experience not to stop rubbing, I keep a hand in motion as I reach towards my oak nightstand and grab the book atop my tottering pile. Despite reading many eclectic spiritual books in recent years, there are so many more I continue to encounter. This one is Sally Kempton's classic, *Meditation for the Love of It.*

I flip to a random page and read aloud, hoping the message will sink through to Lilah—and to myself.

"'Ever since the artists of the Indus Valley carved their famous statue of the horned god sitting in meditation—back around 5000 BCE—meditators have been grappling with the same basic scenario. We sit for meditation. We focus on the breath or practice mindfulness or begin repeating a mantra. We try to hold on to the feeling of oneness. Then the thoughts come. The thoughts come. Thethoughtscomethethoughtscomethethoughtscome.'"

I chuckle at this apt description of my own sometimes runaway mind, trying to keep the knowing laughter from disturbing my daughter. When I first took up meditation, I naively figured it would be akin to bridge or tennis—that with enough practice I could come close to mastery. I'm not sure why I thought that; I've tried baking for years, but my cupcakes still emerge dense as ball bearings.

My mind doesn't like to be tamed, no matter how often I gently request it. Whether a particular sujal is a great one or a "thoughtscomethoughtscomethoughtscome" seems to be unpredictable.

Still, I don't want to leave myself emphasizing the difficulties, so I flip to another spot: "'I like to think of meditation techniques as portals, entry points into the spaciousness that underlies the mind. The inner spaciousness is always there, with its clarity, its love, and its innate goodness,'" I read.

"Hear *that*, Lilah," I whisper. "This sums up the secret of life." She doesn't stir. I guess she's in the inner spaciousness that is also entered when we slumber.

I hear the front door open, and silently pray our nanny Erin doesn't slam it behind her. All I need is for Lilah to shriek again. Fortunately, it closes delicately.

Lilah finally dozing, I head downstairs to greet her. She's added a purple stripe to match the pink and blue ones in her red hair.

"Cute." I touch her curls.

"Do you think so? My mom says it's ridiculous." Her voice is charming even as she conveys the insult. Erin's sugary nature is the main reason I hired her. I want her effervescent glow around my offspring. Her personality suits those springy ringlets, warm green eyes, and gracious smile.

"Well I'm not old enough to be your mom; I'm more like a big sister, and a cool one at that." I silently do the math to be sure this few-years-beyond college grad couldn't be my daughter. *Let's see: I'm thirty-eight, she's twenty-four. Whew, nope. I'm good.*

"I *do* think of you as my second mom, Lorna." Her mischievous smile masks whether she's being factual or frisky.

"I'm happy to play the mom role. I *am* getting quite the experience." I place my hand around my growing abdomen, cradling child number two. We've taken to calling this baby *Deuxie,* for the French word for that number, although we jokingly pronounce the should-be-silent *X* and elongate the *U* more than a proper Parisian.

"How is Duke-sy doing?" Erin asks. "A lot easier to take care of that one than the one upstairs, huh?"

"Don't I know it."

"Still really fussy?" I'm guessing she was hoping between Friday and Monday, Lilah had gone back to her formerly peaceful self.

"Afraid so. Wish I knew what's going on in her head. Likely it's the pregnancy, but she won't say."

I glance at my watch—almost seven thirty—and excuse myself to shower. I'm already going to be late for work because I have an appointment with my midwife. If I don't move along, I'm going to be late for that too.

I vault upstairs, taking the steps in threes. I'm pleased I still have the strong leg muscles I developed from yoga, even if I haven't taken steady classes in a while; having a child has definitely cramped my yoga style. I try to do poses at home a few times a week, but it's hardly the same. This reminiscence of all those yoga classes I took while single, and even married without a child, saddens me as I gather my work clothes and head to the bathroom.

I turn on the shower and reach for one of the many techniques I use to raise my mood when it goes south, which lately it's done more than I'd like. I strip off my long tee and step inside. I begin by mindfully feeling the water flow over my body, how it hits my back and shoulders, then slides down my butt and legs. I turn to face the spout, chuckling as the liquid dances off my swelling belly.

I move my attention to what I appreciate about this shower: the massaging head's perfect pulses; the scent of my new ginger-lavender shampoo; and, best of all, that I get to shower when Erin's here, so I can fully immerse myself under the water instead of my typical one-ear-out stance, to hear Lilah if she wakes. Appreciation, I've learned, is another portal to the spaciousness that underlies my mind. "Mmmm," I sigh aloud.

By the time I exit the stall, I'm more upbeat. I grab my super-soft beige towel—another thing to be grateful about—and dab my body and short brown hair. My stylist finally convinced me to get this "mommy cut," promising it would be faster to get ready than with hair past my collarbone. I'd resisted her urgings since Lilah's first weeks, but now that I'm going to be a mother times two, something's gotta give.

I'd rather take minutes from my hair routine to have time for my morning meditation, even if it was only four minutes today. I comb my locks, still not thrilled with the look—too much Lucy from Charlie Brown. But it's lovely to scrunch my waves, pull on my shirt and pants, and toss on lipstick and mascara—the minimal makeup of mommyhood—since I'm already running late.

After I nod to Erin, grab my bag, and open the front door, Lilah screams. My heart plunges. If I could hold her for a minute before running out, I'd do it. But as her crying escalates, I know that's not how it would transpire. I take a long, slow breath through my nose—hoping this centering will keep guilt from rising—and slip outside.

My midwife's office is decorated like a cozy home, with comfy furniture, flickering candles, and walls lined with pretty canvases bearing uplifting sayings. ("Be brave, be bold, be authentic." "A mom's hug lingers long after she lets go.") An essential-oil diffuser spews a milky scent, which makes me crave coffee; I realize that, with Lilah's screaming, I forgot to make my cup this morning. Since Deuxie climbed aboard, I've been drinking decaf, even though it is nowhere near as satisfying.

I wait a few minutes before the receptionist calls "Lorna Crawford" in her bedroomy voice and I'm led into one of the midwife's warren of rooms—which could be mistaken for living rooms but for the exam tables. Sally's nurse Madison ushers me into the "Lavender Room," its striped purple wallpaper lending the name stenciled on the door. I hand her a box of artisan chocolates I bought at a farmer's market the other day.

"You shouldn't have," Madison protests, even as her smile says otherwise.

"Sure I should have. You love dark chocolate. And I want you to know how much I cherish you. And Sally—you should probably share some with her."

After a dozen thanks, Madison directs me to the fluffy, faux-fur red chair. She takes my blood pressure, then hands me the pee cup, letting me know as she leaves the room that Sally will be in soon.

After filling the cup in the adjacent bathroom and dropping in the stick to check my urine—this office believes in empowering women to know what's up for themselves—I step on the scale. The number startles me, but I dutifully record it on my chart, along with the results of my urine stick: Everything's normal.

Sally strides in a moment later, tall and regal. She glances at what I've marked on my chart. "Looking good, mama!" She measures my abdomen with the tape measure she always seems to whip out of thin air and consults my records on her iPad. "Beautifully on track for your due date, Lorna. Twenty more weeks. I don't have to tell you the time will fly by."

"You certainly don't. I feel like I was pregnant five minutes before Lilah popped out."

"But she *was* full term?" Sally suddenly gets serious as she combs through my chart.

I hadn't discovered Sally before I had my daughter, although I wish I had. Someone at my yoga center told me to select a midwife over an obstetrician, the latter highly trained surgeons who often view birth as a risky venture they must vanquish, rather than the natural process dogs manage without assistance. I found a midwife on my insurance plan and plowed ahead.

Only when I was well into my pregnancy did I discover that all midwives are not equal. In New Jersey, as in many states, midwives must affiliate with a physician, and some come to mimic those doctors more than you'd expect. When I tried to present that midwife with a plan for a natural birth, she blew me off with talk about needing to be flexible and open to whatever transpires.

Lilah was born with all her fingers and toes, so I'm happy for that. But in talking to other moms since, I realized that a healthy baby and a meaningful birth do not have to be mutually exclusive. *Meaningful* would not be the word I'd use to describe Lilah's entrance, what with the midwife inducing my labor (for no reason I can fathom except her scheduling convenience), resulting in contractions so intense I had no choice but to drug myself up.

All the granola moms I see at the park swear by Sally, and even though I consider myself only partially granola—more like a trail mix with M&Ms—I decided to use her when I got pregnant again. I'm thrilled to be in such loving hands.

"Yes, she was full term," I reply. "And she was so easy in the beginning. Lately, she's been hard to handle." Suddenly tears fall onto the red chair, pooling into a lagoon that flattens the fuzz. Red to symbolize menstrual blood and fertility, Madison once told me. "I feel like such a terrible mother."

"Oh love, you're a wonderful mother. I've seen you with Lilah. You treat her with such attention and respect. Children can be challenging because they're dealing with complex emotions they can't express—like being upset because her mom looks different, or that you don't have a cozy lap for her right now."

"Sorry." I reach for a tissue to blot the wetness. "I guess I'm more hormonal than I knew."

"You *are* hormonal—it's kind of the definition of pregnancy," Sally says, smiling. "But you're also a caring mother. Don't apologize for that."

"You're amazing."

"Just a teller of truths." She pauses, letting me compose myself. "Since you know pregnancy does go by fast, you know it's not too early to think about your birth. The biggest decision is where you want to have the baby. As we discussed, I work in several places: the hospital, which has a gorgeous birthing suite and lets me more or less do my thing. The birthing center, which has a kitchen and sitting room so you're extra comfortable. Or your actual home, which is the coziest and least restrictive."

"I think the home option's out. I know it's relaxing, and we wouldn't have to worry where Lilah would go when I'm in labor, but the idea makes me nervous."

"I understand. Plenty of mothers feel that way. But if you look at the literature I gave you, you'll see that for low-risk pregnancies it's as safe as the others. I had my three babies at home. And you don't live far from a hospital should the rare emergency happen. But I'm not pushing. Do what you think's best."

"How long do I have to decide?"

"About two months. If you're delivering in the hospital, you have to take their tour and classes and fill out all the paperwork and whatnot."

We discuss my diet—pretty good, except for my occasional craving for double-chocolate-chip cookies, ideally dipped in the fudge ice cream of my prior employer, Favored-Flavors. We talk about exercise and the fact that I don't get to the gym or yoga studio as much as I'd like.

Sally suggests subscribing to one of those online yoga streaming services so I can take classes at home. And she admonishes me to be kind to myself, something she believes is the most important thing a pregnant woman can do for her health and her baby's. *I love this woman!* We hug, in a deeper, longer embrace than one might expect from a health-care professional—I guess she really believes "a mom's hug lingers long after she lets go"—and I exit the office.

As I'm getting into my car, my cell phone rings. I glance at the caller ID and feel my sizable stomach drop. I thought at this point in my spiritual development I'd be more skilled at seeing the best in everyone and at maintaining my inner peace no matter what.

Like the sujaling, though, this has proven tougher than I expected. For a while after my initial awakening five years back, I perpetually floated on a cumulus cloud, all of my relationships unfolding perfectly. But over time, rain started gathering inside the cloud. I now know that maintaining this lovey-dovey state indefinitely is an unrealistic goal even for a monk or swami, but I did like when wafting inner peace towards everyone came effortlessly.

Although it doesn't elicit the same forceful "Damn!" it did before my spiritual opening, I'm still not happy to see who's calling: my verbally abusive mother. I should be kind to myself and let it go into voicemail.

Instead, I answer the phone.

2

"Hi Mom. What's cooking," I say, mustering the most chipper voice I can manage.

"I'm calling to see how my child's doing." *Wow. Maybe that generous mom I glimpsed a few years ago is making a comeback.*

"I'm fine, Mom. Thanks for asking."

"I meant Lilah." *Of course.*

"She's fine, too. Just a little unsettled, what with a new sibling on the way."

"Angelica wasn't unsettled when you were on the way, even though you made me sick through the whole pregnancy," she says, never missing an opportunity to ding me or, more important to her, praise my older sister. That used to rattle me, but now I've come to see the beautiful light my sibling is.

"It is true: Angelica is wonderful in every way." I love that I mean it.

"She's why I'm calling. I'm reminding you about the luncheon honoring her Saturday. You have a tendency to forget important things." I let this arrow fly high above my head. "Being named to that interfaith committee, or whatever it is, is a big deal, you know?"

"It sure is, so there's no way I could forget." I start my car's engine while taking a deep breath to maintain the patience I wish had more firmly taken root in my life. It's more like an air plant that blows in and out. "One o'clock at the Bimini restaurant, right? The three of us will be there. Bye Mom."

I hang up before she has a chance to say anything that sends the fern airborne. Angelica is an interfaith minister who has coached me to look for the good in someone even she agrees is far from the world's best mother.

Still, I know that the most important thing I can do is raise my *vibration*, in the parlance of my new favorite spiritual teacher, Esther Hicks, which basically means tuning in to my highest self. And focusing on Mom's good qualities is a prime way to do that.

As Hicks writes in *The Amazing Power of Deliberate Intent*, "Whenever you deliberately look for positive aspects of something, you are deliberately activating beneficial vibrations. Now, it is not important that you find the perfect vibration *[Thank goodness!]*, or the best vibration, but deliberately looking for the positive aspects of a subject will automatically get you pointed in the right direction."

One of the techniques Hicks teaches is to go through the alphabet summoning positive notions about the person. Driving to the office seems a good time to do this.

Mom is . . . *an ass,* I giggle, amused that I can't get through one letter without my negative feelings bubbling up. *Come on, Lorna. You're doing this for you, not her. Ridding your mind of hateful thoughts is being kind to myself, one of my midwife's homework assignments.*

I start again.

Mom is *an angel.*

No Lorna, to lift your vibration, you've got to say stuff you actually believe.

Learning about vibration and seeing how it works in my life has been powerful. Esther Hicks channels a higher consciousness she calls *Abraham*, although it has no relation to the Judeo-Christian forefather—and in any event, Hicks claims it's a stream rather than one particular dead guy. She says we continually send our thoughts into the universe, and only things that match their energetic level can come to us. It's a message popularized in the movie *The Secret* some years back.

When we feel like a loser, success can't follow. When we're angry, joyful experiences are impossible. I know that it was only when I started feeling better about my own worth that my extraordinary husband and wonderful new friends were able to come into my life. And when, a few months ago, I decided I deserved a new job with nicer people, my phone rang with the man who is now my great boss on the other end.

Mom is *adored* by my daughter. An excellent *baker. Candid. Delighted* by everything my sister does. *Enthusiastic* about her garden. A *friend* to animals. *Generous* towards her favorite charities. *Happy.*

Nope. That's one thing Mom certainly is not.

But *I* am. *I'm* happy I'm able to speak to my mother without needing a monthlong Tahitian vacation. I'm happy with the beautiful family I'm in the process of creating. And I'm happy I'm just about at my office, so I can spare myself from having to think of nineteen more words to describe my mother.

I pull my silver Jetta into the garage. I planned to replace this old car before my boyfriend and I decided to wed four years ago, but marriage led to thoughts of buying a new home. With Hoboken real estate prices in the stratosphere, we decided to put off a shiny auto until we saw how much house we could buy. Good thing. We paid a fortune for a narrow four-bedroom townhouse. That money would buy a mansion elsewhere in the world (okay, maybe not San Francisco or London, but still). Even after selling my little home, our mortgage is epic, so money is tight despite the good jobs both of us have.

My new position fell into my lap when Jason Sunders, the marketing VP, said he'd watched my work and wanted to meet me. I felt intimidated—*someone was watching?*—but also flattered. When you do special events for an ice cream manufacturer, they're either a public success or a very visible meltdown—pun totally intended. Fortunately, my events have been mostly the former.

Now I do special events for a medical app company, about as far from sugary sweets as you can get. Jason is a terrific boss, as is the company's CEO, Michael Mills, who brings in chair-massage therapists for everyone once a week and regularly stocks the kitchen with healthy snacks.

Recently, the company raffled off high-end headphones, and I won. (Because I was *vibrating* to win, I wanted to tell everyone in the office, but I refrained. No reason for them to think the new gal is nuts.) Sure, I sometimes gripe about my job, especially about being away from Lilah. But it does give me satisfaction—especially since our apps have been named some of the best in health care.

I walk down the hall to my office, waving to several employees. I inherited all of them from other parts of marketing when my boss created the special-events unit, but I would have hired every last one. The people at this company are terrific; no backstabbers or egomaniacs like at my last job.

The second I sit down, my cell phone rings. *That will be my husband*, I think, as I root around my purse for the phone. He's been away on business in a remote area of Colorado where cell service is spotty. I'm just as thrilled to discover it's my best pal, Janelle.

"Welcome to the yoga mission field," I say when I answer. This is our running joke, our way of reminding ourselves that we want to bring the inner peace we cultivate on our yoga mat and meditation cushion into our regular day, ideally by doing good things for others.

"Welcome to you too. I'm calling to say hi before the week gets going. And to check in to the 'mission field.' It's kinda hard to remember on a Monday morning."

"I'm in a pretty good place," I say. "Lilah's still an unhappy camper, but I'm hopeful she'll grow out of it soon. I spoke to my mom without crumbling. And I'm pumped about the interesting stuff brewing at work."

"Glad to hear. I'm doing great too."

I pause. "I was about to say, 'You always are,' but then I realized, so am I. I've got to start giving myself credit for my successes."

"Attagirl. Have a great day. Call me whenever."

I hang up and click on my desktop calendar. Several meetings are scheduled today, mostly to firm up our marketing plans for the medical app we quietly launched a few weeks ago; we wanted to debug it before making hay.

This skin-cancer app has the user take a cell phone photo of any moles on their body, which are automatically compared to the hundreds of thousands of images in our system. Then it alerts them to potential melanomas.

I'm sure the tech guys in these meetings are going to yammer on about machine learning and whatnot, which, frankly, I still don't have a clue about. But I do understand what a breakthrough the app is: Some ninety thousand Americans are diagnosed with this serious skin cancer annually, and one person dies of it every hour. If this app gets more people to their dermatologist early, when it's most treatable, that will be incredible.

And this is only one of the apps we've launched or are developing. One on the market analyzes sleep patterns throughout the night and rings your morning alarm when you're in a lighter stage, so you wake without feeling groggy. Another helps you regulate your breath so you fall asleep faster. I've been pondering special events to publicize these, including something with rock stars, since all their touring screws up their slumber.

One app in the works, which we hope to launch by the end of the year, detects the early signs of irregular heartbeat known as atrial fibrillation, or AFib. Our engineers have given it the playful, and accurate, working title AFab.

Right now I'm focused on the skin-cancer app, since we have a big public launch next month. What I've learned since joining this company is that medical products can't be shilled the same ways ice cream can. No cutesy promotions. No world-record stunts. Although we'll do something more creative this summer, the launch will be a relatively staid affair, with hot-shot dermatologists talking about cancer, and our CEO demonstrating the app for a group of media, influential doctor groups, and patient advocates. Michael is no Steve Jobs, but he'll do fine.

I do want to add some pizazz to the occasion. Maybe I can have a guy dressed like the sun, like in those stupid breakfast sausage commercials. *No Lorna, it's the costumed sun that makes the commercials asinine.* I've already decided to hand out bright orange lollipops that I found online for cheap, and also to serve platters of triangular-cut cheddar cheese set around a circle of grapes. I got both of these idea from people planning watch parties for that big solar eclipse that crossed the US a while back—thank you Pinterest!

My computer alerts me that I have ten minutes before my first meeting. The old me would have used that time to answer work emails. But the newer me knows I will be so much more productive today if I spend the time centering.

One of my favorite breathing practices is *nadi suddhi*, where you close off one nostril and exhale through the other, then inhale through that side and switch. I've been practicing it for so long I can do it without pinching my nose with my fingers. My brain tells one nostril or the other to seal, and it does.

I set my phone timer for ten minutes and lower my eyelids. I direct my attention to my left nostril and exhale slowly through it. I've worked up to a count of ten beats per exhale and five per inhale, since I've been told—by no less an authority than a Hindu guru—that the exhale should be twice as long. When I started this practice, I did six and three. *My progress is another thing to appreciate myself for, if I'm looking to be kind to myself.* I inhale through the left, then exhale right. The breath flows slowly and featherlike out that side.

When the timer chimes, I'm in a state as smooth as rose petals. That's the thing about deep breathing, or any form of inner practice, really—you never want to stop. The peace feels so good that leaving is like being pulled out of a warm bubble bath into icy air.

I remind myself that the goal isn't to exit this state, but to take the bubbles with me. And right now, that means to my meeting—after a quick stop in the restroom, that is.

Daniella is in charge of this gathering, I happily see through the conference room windows. She's the lead engineer on the project. That's another thing I appreciate about this company—they have women in key tech roles, where other firms would be a sea of testosterone. She's supposed to report on how the soft launch is going and whether there are problems with the app's performance, before we make public noise.

". . . so that's what I've been hearing from the field," Daniella says as I enter the room.

Darn. I keep forgetting that when they call a meeting for ten fifteen here, they mean it. In my old company, anything with the word "ten" wouldn't have started until the elevens. Everyone stares as I silently slink to my seat.

This reminds me of the faux paus I made at my girlfriend Sarah's wedding last year. Since Sarah is Jewish, I figured the wedding would start the late time that is customary for Jewish affairs. But Sarah married a Methodist. We got to the catering hall four minutes after the time the wedding was called for—right as they were playing "Here Comes the Bride." I had to duck so nobody spied me behind my glowing friend. Fortunately, I am steeped enough in spiritual teachings that I refrained from beating myself up, and I don't do so now.

I peek at the notes of the guy sitting next to me: "All systems go," he has scribbled. With the smiles on everyone's faces, I gather the product is performing well. Daniella talks about machine learning and how the app doesn't need to see the exact same mole or lesion on the person as what's in the database; it can learn from the sample and project beyond that. *Stated in a way I actually understand!* I jot a note to have Daniella describe this during the launch event. A few more speakers and the meeting ends.

My cell phone trills as I return to my office. Finally, it's Don.

"Hey love," I answer, closing the door behind me.

"Hey love to you." His voice is deep and sexy.

"How's your morning going?"

"Great. I got in some yoga and a sitting meditation this morning before my first meeting, the advantages of my body being on Eastern time when everyone else is on Mountain."

"Wonderful. And how are the meetings going?" I want to get insights into his work before he steers to the personal stuff, as is his wont.

"Great too. Colorado's rivers face the same issues as Jersey's, so teaming up is going to be perfect—not to mention it will save us tons of money with all the resources we'll be able to share."

Don is the public affairs director of an advocacy group for our state's rivers. It's inspiring to watch him give speeches around New Jersey on the importance of restoring the waters after decades of damage by the chemical and drug industries and government neglect. He recognized soon after getting this job that the environmentalists who'd long run the group needed to make common cause with people who don't consider themselves tree-huggers—fishermen and tourism executives, for example—but who also need a healthy ecosystem. Over time he also realized groups around the country, like the one in Colorado, were doing similar work, so why not pool their limited resources?

"How's my little angel? She calm down any?" Don asks, and I know the business conversation is over. "And how's my bigger angel?"

"I'm good. I saw Sally today—she's so wonderful. Lilah was a wreck again this morning, but I'm holding on to the vision that she'll be chill when I get home."

"Keep holding that and it will happen," Don says. He's a big fan of the Hicks stuff too, although he gets his fill from watching her on YouTube.

His support feels like a giant hug. "When are you coming home? I miss those blue eyes."

"Is that all you miss? Not other parts?"

"I'm . . . I'm not going there while at the office," I stammer, blushing. I look to see if anyone can see me through the internal window that makes my office less private than I would prefer. Fortunately, no one's around.

"I meant my hair," he jokes. Don does have gorgeous hair—black and wavy, like the evening ocean.

"Of course, I miss your hair," I play along. "And your fashion sense, and your good cooking, and your brilliant parenting. And those other parts I know you were really referring to that I'm not going to think about now." I change the subject. "So when will you be home? Wednesday, still?"

"Probably. Maybe Thursday. I wanna make sure we cover everything, so I won't have to come back."

A few air kisses later, we hang up. I turn to my computer, but before I plow into my work, I decide to get myself as present as possible. The Buddhist masters say engaging all the senses is a powerful way to do this.

I close my eyes and notice my feet planted on the floor, then move my attention to how my butt makes contact with the chair. I observe my erect spinal column, and the cold keyboard under my fingers. I inhale through my nose and smell the fragrant mangoes the company is offering in the break room a few doors from my office. I cock my ears and hear the background sound of ringing telephones.

Feeling, smelling, hearing. Check. What's left? *Taste*—those mangoes, of course, which I'll get later so as not to get up and distract myself. *Is that everything?*

I chuckle as I realize the sense I've overlooked: *sight.* The one we unintentionally allow to dominate most experiences. I soften my focus and lower my lids until they're slits, like that antique mail slot on my old neighbor's door growing up—the one they had to get rid of to keep people from peering into their home. *Lorna Crawford! Stop letting your mind run onto the spokes. Keep it firmly in the center of the wheel.*

The slits settle on a view outside my window: a park several blocks away. There's a huge banyan tree that provides shade for the entire half-acre. I breathe in the tree and the mangoes and the ringing phones and the smooth keyboard, and feel myself aligning with the here and now.

After a couple of minutes, I'm ready to work, knowing I'm going to be super productive.

3

When I finally get home, after what is indeed a successful work day, Lilah is mercifully calmer.

"She's been great," Erin reports—not just music to my
ears, but a whole friggin' symphony.

"Momma!" Lilah exclaims when I enter her playroom,
which I'm sure on the floor plan is a living room, but which
has been taken over by toys. She's building a city with
wooden blocks; everything else has been put away. Even the
throw on the couch is crisply folded. Lilah rushes into my
arms and I give her a squeeze.

"If you don't need anything else, I'll be on my way."
Erin picks up her purse and water bottle. "Regular time tomorrow?"

"Yeah. Thanks, Erin. You're a dream, as always." I nod
towards the pristine living room and adjacent kitchen, which
I can see also sparkles.

The door closes, and I release Lilah from my grasp.
"How's my beloved doing?" I believe it's important to use
loving words when referring to my daughter, no matter what
state she is—or I am—in. I hear other moms jokingly refer to
their "little monster" or their "holy terror." Since the

moment Lilah emerged from my womb, she's been nothing less than *my sweetheart, my darling, my angel, my love.* Even when she was too young to understand the words, I knew she could feel their lofty energy.

"Let's play, Momma!" Lilah enthuses, just as my phone sings its *crystals* ringtone, the setting for my sister. I let it go into voicemail. Angelica can wait. Mother-daughter bonding cannot.

"What do you want to do?" I ask Lilah, who is sitting on the floor, hands tapping from her head to her shoulders in a silent continuation of the song she undoubtedly sang with Erin.

"Play *Frozen*," she answers, reaching down to her knees.

I know she means her favorite game of acting out characters from the Disney movie, but I decide to let my playful side come through. I stop right where I am, arm scratching my shoulder, head askew, mouth forming a word that doesn't emerge.

"What'ya doing, Momma?" Lilah looks confused but intrigued as she halts her movement midway to her toes.

"I'm frozen," I reply without moving my mouth. "You said you wanted to play frozen."

She giggles, although I'm not sure she yet gets the joke. Sometimes it's hard to know what a two-year-old brain is capable of comprehending.

"That's not *Frozen*. *This* is." She picks up her stuffed Olaf. Okay, so she doesn't get it.

I remain still. "Doesn't frozen also mean when something gets stuck? Like the stuffed bear you left outside last winter that we couldn't scrape off the table."

I scan her face for a sign of recognition. It doesn't come. I explain how a word can mean more than one thing, and that while I knew she was talking about the movie, I was being silly and using the other meaning.

Finally, the bulb goes off. She smiles, then waves her arms like a madwoman before stopping in *her* own tracks. Her hands are upright, bolted to the upside-down stuffed toy that hangs over her face. She looks so cute I can't contain myself, so I start laughing.

"That's. Not. Frozen!" she screams, pointing to my shaking shoulders. "You're moving!"

I apologize, then suggest we play a game where we keep moving and freezing. She is all in. That's the thing with toddlers; they're able to embrace the moment, switching gears without getting worked up by what they had originally planned. This is a lesson I can learn from my daughter.

After we've frozen and defrosted ourselves dozens of times, we head for the kitchen. Dinner is grilled tofu, broccoli, and sweet potatoes. I'm fortunate that Lilah enjoys healthy, adult food. I hear so many stories of kids who will eat only crustless PB&J, or macaroni with that orange glow.

Afterwards, I take her upstairs and give her a bath, then read aloud a new children's book on mindfulness I picked up on sale. With its dense descriptions, it turns out to be too preachy for my liking, although Lilah doesn't seem to mind. I set it deep in her toy chest, doubtful I'll read it again. At eight o'clock, right on schedule, I bring her to her bed.

Lilah likes me to sit at the edge until she sleeps, and I'm happy to comply. It gives me a chance to return to the meditation that was interrupted this morning.

I used to think you could meditate only on a formal cushion near an altar—and don't get me wrong, I love doing that. But over time I have come to see that sujaling is about focus, not furniture. Realizing I can do it anywhere has liberated me.

Only one of the three sessions I aim to do daily—in the morning—is at my altar. The others occur in my car, my office, a stall in our company's bathroom, the waiting room at the pediatrician's or my accountant's office, or wherever someone is delaying me because they believe their time is more valuable than mine (what I truly think sometimes, even if that's not a very yogic thing to say).

For years I meditated for an hour each evening, but once Lilah came along and my exhaustion level hit the stratosphere, I constantly fell asleep (sitting up!) if I closed my eyes that long. My friend Sarah tried to convince me that sleep is the same as meditation, because in both you're communing with your higher self. But the whole purpose is to be aware of that link. If sleeping and sujaling were the same, we'd all know from birth that we're connected to the energy of the universe.

Actually, we do know it from birth, I correct myself. Watching Lilah as an infant—that contented smile, the dreamy look in her eyes—convinced me she stayed connected to the world our soul emerges from. But over time, we start forgetting—until you're a thirty-something woman like me, eagerly performing one practice after another to remember.

While Lilah shifts in her bed, I sit up straight and sujal for fifteen minutes. Once she's asleep, I enter my bedroom to listen to the phone message from my sister, who asks if I can pick up two dozen white balloons for her celebration. I think about texting *Sure* but decide to call. Speaking to someone as elevated as Angelica always lifts my mood.

My plan is to visualize an uplifting call before she answers, but Angelica picks up on the first ring. "Oh, man. Guess I should have done my visualizing *before* I dialed."

"If you want me to hang up, you can call when you actually want to talk," she laughs.

"Sorry. I didn't mean that. It's just that Janelle and I have been trying to do this thing of setting intentions for each part of the day, which we learned from one of the Esther Hicks books."

"I don't know why you can't call it the 'Abraham-Hicks' books, since that's what they're known by." Although her words could be taken as mocking, her tone, as always, reeks of Angelica love.

"Too weird. I know Esther says she gets her info from the nonphysical energy she has named Abraham. And I'm sure she does. But really, don't all great ideas come from there? I mean, Eckhart Tolle's work is genius, and he admits it enters his mind when he's tapped in to something beyond himself. But he doesn't flaunt the 'channeling' part by calling his work Abraham-Tolle, or Jesus-Tolle."

"True enough. Anyway, I'm familiar with 'intending.' I do it all the time—way before I heard Abraham . . . er, Esther Hicks talk about it. I discovered it years ago, when a monk got into a car after a lecture in Manhattan and told the driver to wait while he mentally envisioned his joy at his next activity."

"You make it sound easy."

"Simple, yes. But easy? No. I have no trouble remembering when I leave the house or get into my car. But catching a new segment when I haven't changed locations remains a challenge."

"Even for you?"

She chuckles. "Even for me. I wish you'd stop thinking this stuff comes naturally to me, Lorn. I was born into the same uptight household you were. They're called practices for a reason—you've got to keep doing them."

"I know. I was so dedicated for a while—a pretty long while, actually. Then I had Lilah." I realize how bad that sounds. "Not that I'd trade my cherub for—"

"Don't worry, I won't call the Mom Police on you. I know it's tough to find 'me-time' with a little one. Don't forget Radha is nearly fifteen. That's much easier."

I pull a pillow behind my back to get comfortable. "How *is* my splendid niece?" Talk about someone who hit the spiritual jackpot, being born into a family where both her parents are calm and present. The opposite of the mother who raised Angelica and me.

"She's terrific. Going with an interfaith mission to Haiti this summer. I'm thrilled for her, although it's making me a little crazy that she can't stop talking about it."

"Something makes you crazy?" I tug at the pillow to take more pressure off my back.

"Plenty of things make me crazy. In fact, I was sloughing off a difficult work day by walking my garden labyrinth when the phone rang."

"And you answered? I'm honored."

"I knew it was you. I gave you the *harp* ringtone—because of how angelic you are."

"You always know what to say."

We spend the next five minutes discussing the party her interfaith church is hosting to honor her appointment to a statewide commission. She needs me to do a few things in preparation. In typical Angelica form, she doesn't demand these favors or even strongly request them, leaving the door open for me to say no. Of course I don't.

"I'm happy to help," I reply genuinely. My sister is responsible for changing my life. She's the reason I got on, and for the most part stay on, my spiritual path.

We chat about my pregnancy and the idea of delivering outside of a hospital. She doesn't have an opinion, even though I'd kind of hoped she would make the decision for me, either by saying it's a remarkable idea or a ridiculous one, the two I vacillate between.

She suggests I sit with the prospect for a few weeks before committing, and stay open to the possibility that my knee-jerk resistance might spring from not knowing anyone who's done this.

We're nearly finished when Lilah yells. I hang up and rush to her room. She's standing on her bed, waiting to leap.

"It's okay, I'm here," I whisper, trying to lay her back in her bed while stroking her curls. "Momma will stay here with you. Let's go back to sleep."

"*Noooooooooo!*" she shrieks. "Momma and Daddy's bed!" I sense the futility, but I press on.

"But I'm in *this* bed. And it's so warm and cozy." I lie down and pull her into my arms. The time between her sobs opens, and for a hopeful moment I think I can lull her back to slumber. Then she springs up.

"Take me, Momma! Your bed!"

"All right, sweetheart." Lifting her silences her immediately. I guess that's an improvement over this morning, when she didn't settle until she was under my blanket. Still, I miss when she would slumber through the night. "Such a good baby," people would say, although I hated that expression. As if an uncomfortable child who wakes during the night—like my darling does now—is somehow not good.

Lilah falls asleep in my arms before I'm out of her room. I consider setting her back in her own bed; maybe if I'm careful, she'll sleep through touchdown. But when she whimpers at my hesitation—I haven't even pivoted yet—I decide not to chance it.

She snuggles deeply under the ridiculously beloved teal blanket, like a war bride breathing in the uniform of her deployed spouse. Within seconds she is asleep.

My stomach screams for food—because a full dinner somehow isn't enough for a creature the size of a banana. But I'd planned to do some yoga, and I can't with food in my stomach. I know from hard experience that if I stop to eat, the yoga will not happen.

I walk to the playroom and push away Lilah's doll stroller to make space. I grab my straps and blocks, which I didn't used to use. Now that I'm four months pregnant, my belly is altering my balance.

This also means I need to enter the poses slowly, which I have found to be a blessing. It's easy for me to forget, but yoga is about watching inside myself as the stretches make space in the body. Being forced to gingerly enter the *asanas* has been a good reminder. *Thanks, Deuxie,* I think as I rub my belly. Something else to be grateful for.

The last time I got to my yoga center, Om Sweet Om, my favorite teacher suggested I try a practice of standing poses. I decide to do that now.

Sun salutations are out because they require plank on the floor. Since I like to begin my session with a few of them, I mentally run through the twelve-pose series without moving. After four rounds, I surprisingly do feel calmer.

I do standing backward and forward bends (as far over as a pregnant woman can go), then move to the warrior pose series—my favorites, since they make me feel fierce and powerful. I finish my *asanas* with a standing spinal twist.

Starving but determined to end my practice properly, I head to the couch for a sitting deep relaxation. I do the quick version, wiggling my feet, bending my knees, squeezing my butt, puffing out my abdomen, raising my shoulders, and tightening my fists at the same time. After a moment, I release everything.

I move to my face, widening my eyes, positioning my mouth as if I'm about to eat a triple cheeseburger (*Lorna, stop thinking about food!*), and sticking out my tongue. Then I contract them—squeezing all the muscles towards the tip of my nose. It's a look Don teasingly calls my "fig face" when he spies me doing it. I end with a few-minute meditation.

As I rise from the couch, I take Angelica's advice and ponder the prospect of delivering Deuxie at home. Immediately, the hair on my arm rises. I'm not sure if that is *my* reaction to a home birth or to the idea of telling my judgmental mother.

Still, my bed does seem like a nice place to deliver. And there are the germs—or lack thereof. I read in one of Sally's pamphlets that even though we think hospitals are safest, the bacteria there could wipe out every living person in New Jersey. There are germs in my house too, but the pamphlet describes them as "friendly germs" my body is used to.

These are the positive reasons. The negative? Well, it's just plain weird.

Clearly I'm not going to decide today—and in any event, Don needs to be involved, although I'm pretty sure he'll say I should drop Deuxie anywhere I want to.

In the kitchen, I gather almond butter, carrots, and an apple while setting my intention for this segment: I want to provide good nutrition that satisfies my baby. I take a moment to send my appreciation to the farmers and truckers and grocers, along with my boss and Don for the money that buys our food.

Feeling energized in both body and mind, I pull open the fridge. I'm reaching for the milk when the appliance starts spinning. It's good I don't have the carton in hand, because the whole room joins the tornado.

A second later, I watch helplessly as I head towards our travertine floor.

4

Something is touching me.

I try to open my eyes to see what it is. I'm so woozy they don't respond.

"Momma?"

Lilah is leaning over, her face inches from my nose. "Why you on the floor? You frozen?"

I smile, pleased to observe my face muscles are returning, as, a moment later, do my eyelids.

"No sweetie, I'm not frozen. Mommy fell down. Sometimes having a baby inside your belly can make you do that."

I'm hoping this is correct, that fainting is just another unwanted symptom of pregnancy, like that wretched arrow-like line emerging between my navel and my vajayjay. As if somebody up there thought when the time comes, the midwife will need directions.

I push myself to sitting but keep my eyes trained on the floor, to prevent the room from spinning again. The stones have dark flecks I've never noticed.

Lilah sits next to me. When I feel strong enough, I stand her up and rise to my knees. I'm not sure I can walk, so I sashay on my knees towards the couch, dragging my feet behind.

"So funny, Momma!" Lilah can barely contain her laughter. *Another reminder to bring that childlike wonder into my own life more.* I pull myself onto the couch, staying motionless until I've shaken the woozies. Only when I feel steady do I notice through the open curtain that it's deep black outside.

"What are you doing up?" I ask.

"I missed you." I see that her eyes are aflame. She must have been seriously crying before she came downstairs.

I hug her. "I missed you too. And I miss Daddy."

Before I get worked up about Don not being here to reassure me that fainting is nothing serious, I suggest we both go to bed. I don't even try to put Lilah in her room; I settle her under my covers.

I scrutinize my face as I brush my teeth: no bruises from the fall. I consider calling Don, but what's the point, really? I don't want him staying up all night so he can't productively work tomorrow, or worse, hopping on the first plane out of Colorado.

It hits me that actually I don't want *me* doing that. Well, not hopping on a plane, obviously. But staying up all night fretting—I could easily fall prey. I'll call Sally in the morning.

When I exit the bathroom, Lilah is asleep, clasping the edge of our blanket. I get into bed and pull her towards me, happy to have a comforting presence by my side.

At exactly eight the next morning, I hit the "favorites" button on my phone and ring Sally. She truly is a favorite.

I was too anxious to meditate this morning, even though Angelica would say that's exactly the time you need to do it. My neck and shoulders are wound to my eyebrows.

Madison tells me Sally's out at a home birth, so I supply the details of what happened. There's not much to tell. I was feeling fine, if hungry, then I was on the floor. Madison reassures me that fainting does occur in the second trimester, although Sally will want to weigh in and possibly run tests.

"What tests?" I ask, suddenly alarmed.

"Nothing you need to worry about." Madison is trying to mollify me, although it's not working. "Let's see what Sally says."

Seven minutes later, when Sally calls, I hear a woman screeching in the background. "You torturing somebody?" I joke.

"Baby should be here momentarily. She's in the transition stage of labor, which can get loud." Sally pauses. "What's going on with you?"

I explain about the fainting. She asks how long I was out for, but I don't know. "Less than an hour. More than a few minutes," I guess.

"Any other symptoms? Headache? Blurred vision? Any bleeding?"

"No. Those sound terrible."

"Well they're not terrible. But they could indicate a problem with the placenta, or maybe anemia. Without those symptoms, I'm guessing you had a blood-sugar dip, or little Deuxie could have pressed on your vena cava."

I'm impressed she remembers what we call our offspring. My prior midwife could barely remember *my* name.

"What's a vena cava? Sounds like something you go spelunking in."

Sally chuckles. I wonder if the laboring woman appreciates the levity or is pissed that I'm entertaining her midwife at the apex of her delivery. "It's a large vein. It brings blood from your abdomen to your heart. Deuxie might have decided to take a stroll, cutting off the flow for a bit. Still, I want you to come in this week for a few tests."

"It's always tests with you people," I say lightly, recalling how much blood my prior midwife took over the nine months, even though I never fainted. "Fine. I'll call Madison and make an appointment."

Erin arrives a short while later and, after I call Don and tell him the news, emphasizing Sally's reassurance, I leave for work. Janelle texts while I'm in the car. I used to text her back right away, but when I saw a documentary about how dangerous it is, I became a staunch no-texting-while-driving gal. I don't even look at my phone until the red light.

Another day to enter the yoga mission field. Have you intended?

I'm impressed with her commitment to keep us on track. Now I'm sorry I skipped my morning sujal.

At the next stoplight, I do a mindfulness practice. I open my ears and hear the wind through the cracked-open window, so loud I'm amazed I didn't notice it before. I sniff the scent of cashew butter. (I gave up trying to keep Lilah's messy food out of the car long ago.) The steering wheel feels smooth under my fingers. I stare intently at the red in the light. It glows like fire.

Because I'm being present, my foot reacts immediately when the glow turns green; my car is halfway through the intersection before the car in the other lane starts moving. At the next red I text Janelle.

It's going to be a great day.

Because, really, why shouldn't it be? The spiritual teachings say that expecting it to be wonderful is what tilts the odds in my favor.

I recently learned that Esther Hicks's unusual teachings aren't even new. Ernest Holmes, the late founder of Science of Mind, wrote nearly a century ago that when you change your thinking, you literally change your life. It's so cool when various spiritual teachers line up.

Before exiting the car, I realize I'm about to start a new segment. Yay me—although with Janelle's text minutes earlier, it would have been pathetic if I hadn't remembered.

I pause, door open, and visualize my day at the office: the wonderful people I will rendezvous with; the productive work I will accomplish; the way I will maintain my desire to *experience,* not merely skate through, every moment of my life.

When I arrive at my desk, the first person who comes in is my absolute favorite coworker, our art director, Krista. I make a mental note that, once again, I have proof that this shit actually works.

"I want to show you my roughs for the public launch of S-Check, before I get too far in," she says, using the official name of the skin-cancer app. "I've taken your tagline to heart. It's so much more festive than the previous stuff we've done here."

"Well, coming from the world of ice cream, I'm into festive," I laugh. "But I do think since it's a consumer app, we can get a bit away from the 'medical' look this company favors."

"No argument here. I like the freer hand." Krista passes me her design for the logo, which will be displayed at the launch and featured in our brochure, press materials, and, this summer, on signs at our special events. Above my tag, "Surf your sun: the easy way to check for damage," she's drawn a cute cartoon guy on a board, surfing against the backdrop of a huge, bright sun.

"This is perfect. You're so talented," I say.

"You're not just saying that?"

"If I didn't like it, I'd be nice but you would know." I look closer. "There's not one thing I would improve."

I reach into my drawer and grab a small packet of high-end coffee, one of the little gifts I keep around so my colleagues know how much I treasure them. Krista thanks me profusely, more than a little java warrants.

Later that afternoon I oversee a discussion with a half dozen dermatologists in our conference room. These are the types of doctors we hope will recommend our app to patients. I present Krista's graphics. As I expected, they love it.

They also love the app—save one doctor. I'm having trouble telling whether this guy really has issues, or if he just likes being the center of attention. I keep picturing my mother here, saying everything she could to keep the spotlight trained on her.

Still, I want to take his objections seriously, in case he's seeing something we have missed. His main concern is legitimate: whether getting a negative result will lull someone into skipping their derm checkups, even though we carefully state in our materials that this preliminary screening tool does not replace a doctor's exam. I think it will actually be good for their business, since people paying closer attention to what's happening on their skin are more likely to bolt for their doctor.

Daniella tells the man she will work with coding to ensure our caution pops up several times during each session. This doesn't seem to placate the doctor. He keeps interrupting with new objections. *Yup, like my mother.* Unlike how I used to deal with Mom, though, Daniella and Jason handle this guy like an honored guest. I find myself growing increasingly annoyed—with him, and then with myself.

"Choose love, spread light, and know that the Universe has your back," one of my favorite spiritual authors, Gabby Bernstein, writes. I'm sure nobody in this room has read her book, but somehow my colleagues know her premise—that how we respond to people is a choice, and making the highest choice is good not only for them, but for us and for the planet.

After the focus group ends, I hang back to speak to the physician. I want to see if I can shift my thoughts about him.

"Thanks so much for coming today." I reach for a handshake. His grip is so firm it crushes my pinkie. I decide to ignore this, lest I become even more negatively predisposed. "I appreciate your willingness to be honest."

"That's why you asked us here. For our honesty." His tone is too opaque to read. I step forward to let other doctors pass behind me. Everyone but the man and I leave the room.

"I understand your concern as a doctor. We definitely don't want our app to cause anyone harm," I say.

"I bet. All you need is someone getting false reassurance and letting their melanoma progress to stage four and suing the pants off you." This isn't going as I hoped.

"Is your practice around here?" I ask, shifting the conversation to something neutral.

"Yeah. Near Sinatra Park."

"I love that park! Such views of the city. I take my daughter there all the time. Have you been there long?"

His edges soften. "Fifteen years. I've seen a lot of changes."

"Massive changes." Fifteen years ago, Hoboken was a town of worn-out apartment buildings and hard-partying bars. Now young couples who've escaped New York City, and the luxury developers who've followed them, have turned it into a family-friendly oasis.

"Too many," he says, pained.

"What do you mean?"

"Rents are out of sight. My office lease tripled the last time it was up. Now my landlord's doubling it again. I'll probably have to move my practice."

He shrugs his shoulders, then they sag. Yet again I see that when you scratch the surface of the gruffest person, there's often a hurting human below.

"That must be hard," I empathize.

"I'll deal." He toughens. "I've overcome worse."

I consider trying to shift him back to the openness we were on the cusp of. But I remember that my objective wasn't to change him; it was to change myself. I see this man in a different light: He's not a pompous ass. He's someone who's feeling powerless. It took me years to understand that's what prompts similar outbursts from my mother.

"Well, good luck with the lease negotiation. Maybe it will turn out well. In any event, we really appreciate your input." I shake his hand—this time his grip is looser—and show him the door.

Don returns home the following day, cutting short his trip as I feared he would. He decides to drive me to Sally's office.

When he turns on the car, the radio is tuned to news. A lot of women at my yoga center proudly proclaim they don't follow the news, but I'm a confessed news junkie who likes knowing what's going on. Anyway, isn't the real test not whether you can shield yourself from bad information, but whether you can know that stuff and remain centered? I met a swami from Miami who watches CNN every morning after meditating, and it doesn't ripple his peaceful state. I'm no-where near that, but he's my role model.

Don reaches out and switches the dial to a spiritual chant-ing channel. "I think we need calm, which we certainly won't get contemplating another mass shooting." The peaceful mu-sic does me good.

When we pull up to Sally's office, I ask Don to pause be-fore we get out of the car. This is one time I don't want to forget to set intentions. I typically say my wishes silently, but today I not only want to share them with Don, I'm hoping the universe will see I'm extra serious. "I expect Sally's tests will show everything's wonderful. And I know we will feel loved and cared for while we're here."

"Hear, hear," Don cheers. "I definitely feel cared for here, what with their aromatherapy and music, and those little salt diffusers that clear my sinuses when I didn't even know they were clogged."

"Good afternoon," the receptionist chirps. "Please take a seat, Lorna and Don. Someone will be right with you." I love how they include Don in everything. At my old midwife's, it was like they thought he was some stranger I'd hired to drive me—even during the delivery.

Don and I take a seat on the couch. Three other pregnant women are in the waiting room: a lesbian who sits with her partner; an older mom; and a teenage girl accompanied by a middle-aged woman, likely her mother.

I consider starting a conversation with the pregnant lesbian, who looks friendly in a Rachel McAdams, girl-next-door way. I like to chat people up when I come here—a great way to acquire the tricks for surviving a pregnancy. Last month a woman told me about the best maternity yoga brand. I went home and immediately purchased a bunch of their pants.

Before I open my mouth, I realize I'd rather be silent. This will help keep my mind in check, even though I'm not worried about what Sally might say. Well, not too much. I figure if it were serious, she would have ordered me to the hospital the morning I called, rather than asking me to swing by her office today. Plus I haven't fainted or been dizzy since. I am a little unsettled, though.

Naturally, as soon as I think about keeping quiet, Don starts blabbering. "I'm a nervous wreck. Do you think we're gonna have to wait long? I've never seen it this busy—have you?"

"It is busier. But remember we were squeezed in. We didn't have a regular appointment."

"You think the fainting was nothing, right?" The concern in his eyes makes me want to snatch him into my arms and soothe him. But I need soothing, too. I'm the one who watched the refrigerator do wheelies.

"Lorna," Madison calls from the partially cracked door to the exam rooms. "And Don," she adds after seeing he's here.

"I guess we're not going to wait long," I joke as we stand.

Inside the "Fuchsia" exam room, Madison takes my weight, blood pressure, and temperature. "Normal," she declares.

She sends me to the bathroom with a container, and when I return she inserts a test strip to check my pee. *I guess when they're worried about something, they don't ask you to do it yourself.* She asks a few basic questions, tells us Sally will be in momentarily, and exits the room.

Don and I look at one another. "She didn't seem concerned," I say. It comes out more like a question. When you're worried about your baby, you try to read the tea leaves everywhere.

"No. She seemed mellow. And your temperature, BP, and urine are fine, so that's good."

"Maybe we should take a few minutes to collect ourselves," I suggest. "To keep the wild dogs from running."

"Good idea."

We each straighten up in our chairs, uncross our arms and legs, and place our feet flat. Last week I found an online meditation by Buddhist teacher Tara Brach about filling the body with love. That seems especially relevant now. I can't remember the exact words Brach uses, but I have the gist: bring a smile through the entire body.

"Begin by feeling like there's a smile behind your eyes," I improvise, noticing the laugh lines increase around Don's gorgeous baby blues before we gently close our eyes. "Now feel the smile move down to your nose and sinuses, then to your mouth. You don't need to move your mouth into a smile, just visualize the openness and joy a smile brings." I pause to experience the sensation.

"The smile moves into your throat, opening it expansively," I continue, then pause again. "Now it moves to your heart. Feel the love as your open heart meets that wonderful smile."

"Hello both of—" Sally says as the door opens. She stops short when she sees how we're sitting. I open my eyes, although Don keeps his closed. "Did I interrupt something wonderful?" she says softly. "You're both iridescent."

"Lorna was leading a little *suj*—uh, meditation. To keep us from stressing," Don explains, eyes still shut.

"Don't worry about interrupting," I say to Sally. "We can finish later."

"What part were you up to?" Sally asks eagerly. "I'd love a little piece of that myself. It's been a frazzled day." I adore how open-minded Sally is.

"We were bringing a smile through our body," I reply. "I was about to move it into the abdomen."

"Will you continue?" Sally takes a seat on the exam table, since Don and I occupy the room's two chairs. She straightens her back and closes her thumb and forefinger into a *mudra*, or energy lock, like an old pro.

"I didn't know you meditate," I say, not really surprised.

"For years when I was younger. Although I confess I've gotten away from it. Clearly, I need to get back." She and I close our eyes; Don's never opened.

"Feel the energy of a smile filling your head and chest," I say, to get Sally up to speed, "then continue into your belly." Another pause until I'm one with this sensation, not merely uttering the words. "The smile brings a playfulness into the belly, and into the womb—if you have one," I nod in Sally's direction, even though she can't see, "and into the baby if one is in there." I silently chuckle, knowing there's only one of us who fits that bill.

"Now, the smile emanates from your body into the air around you, filling the room. Luxuriate in this joyful sensation." Pause. "Then feel it continuing outward into the office . . . the whole building . . . the whole town . . . the whole world."

For several seconds, no one moves. The silence—save for the ticking clock in the corner—soars. After a glorious minute I chant a single "Om."

Then I ask everyone to open their eyes, eager to know what Sally thinks about my health.

5

I am racing out of the tailor's on Saturday morning, seriously out of breath. Not just because I'm running late, but also because Deuxie has taken up the new position of sitting on my lungs.

My arm bears the bandage they put on at the lab a half-hour ago, taking blood per Sally's orders. I had made an appointment for the test so I wouldn't have to rush afterwards, but when I showed up they didn't seem to care. The receptionist waved me into the crowded room, where I waited nearly an hour.

I tried to feel accepting and peaceful, but each passing minute made me more pissed. I still have to pick up the two-dozen white balloons, go home to change and dress Lilah, and bring the decorations to Angelica's luncheon before everyone arrives.

In addition to bloodwork, Sally wants me to come in for an ultrasound next week. I already had my initial sonogram, plus a special one that checks for Down syndrome (which, thankfully, Deuxie doesn't have). But Sally wants to push up the mid-pregnancy ultrasound originally scheduled for my next regular appointment.

I would worry she's concerned about something specific, what with all this extra testing, but she seemed completely reassuring when we left our appointment. Or maybe she was feeling chill from our group sujal. That she is into meditation makes me appreciate her all the more.

In any event, I don't have time to fret about the baby right now.

I know I shouldn't worry later, either. Why project that bad things could happen, when good things are just as likely? Not even *good* but *excellent* things, since we're talking about a beautiful newborn.

I turn my attention to Angelica's event. I want it to be wonderful, since she's not acknowledged often enough for the amazing stuff she does in the world.

I hang my purple maternity dress on the hook in the backseat. I bought it the other day, inspired by Sally's exam room. I hadn't realized how much I like the hue, and how it complements my skin tone. The tailor gave it a hem so it sits just above my knees, rather than the dowdy length it had in the store. I don't know why manufacturers think pregnant women can't look sexy.

I still have to pick up the balloons. I pray they're waiting, filled with helium and tied with string. As it is, taking a shower is out of the question.

They *are* going to be ready, I decide as I pull into the store parking lot. "My balloons will be floating," I say, hoping the universe hears me.

Knowing what I know about this vibration stuff, of course, it's more about *me* hearing me. I'm the one who must get clear about what I'm wanting, because there's no God-in-the-sky prayer-granter bestowing wishes. It's about lining myself up with my desires.

The balloons are indeed inflated, and tied with attractive golden strings. I stuff them into the backseat alongside my dress and drive home.

Don is in his slacks and button-down when I get there, and I see that he's given Lilah a bath. She's running around naked with wet hair, which I find endearing but also distressing. That can only mean one thing: She wouldn't let Don put on her clothes.

"Sweetheart, where's your beautiful dress?" I coo, hoping to steer clear of this battle.

"I don't want to wear dress!" she yells. "Want to wear leopard costume!" I glance at Don, who gives me a knowing nod.

"Your leopard costume was for Halloween," I say, wondering if I should explain that she's grown so much it will never fit, then deciding logic is irrelevant. "The dress is for Auntie's party."

"The leopard's for party!" It's true; she wore it to Janelle's Halloween gathering. It's tough to argue with a two-year-old.

"This is a different kind of party. This is a dress party," I say, guessing what she's inevitably going to come back at me with.

"Daddy's not wearing a dress!" *Sigh.*

"Momma's wearing a dress." I hold up my lavender eyelet. "We can put on our dresses together!"

"Okay, Momma," she responds, deciding this is an excellent plan. Don exhales audibly. This must have been quite a fight.

We head to her bedroom, Lilah skipping all the way. Looking at her, you'd never know she was upset minutes ago. I'm sure my husband—like most adults—won't turn off his switch for hours.

Lilah lets me button her up in her green gingham dress and matching socks without a fuss. I comb out her hair and twirl it in a high pony at the top of her head—the way I used wear my own hair back when I was single. Then we go to my room, where I brush my hair, shimmy into my dress, and slip on easy-to-balance-in ballet flats. We're ready to go.

It's nearly one when we get to the Bimini restaurant. I'd hoped to be there by twelve thirty to set up the balloons.

Angelica doesn't seem fazed. "You're here!" she beams when I step into the sunlit party room, as if I were a long-lost friend spontaneously showing up on her doorstep, rather than the sister she phoned last night. "Oh my goodness, you are getting huge!"

"Finally made it," I say, ignoring the "huge" comment. I stifle my need to apologize for my tardiness; Angelica says that on the spiritual plane, everything is always perfect, so apologies are unwarranted. "Here with balloons. Where do you want them?"

I tug the blobs, one in each hand, under the doorjamb. I begin separating the tangled strings as Lilah races into the room, but Angelica says they look fine as two groupings. She places them on opposite ends of the room.

The space is cheerful, rows of massive windows lining three of the walls. Each of the twelve round tables is set with different colored tablecloths, all with a centerpiece of white carnations sprinkled with contrasting blue orchids. Leave it to Angelica to figure out how to convey purity without making it boring.

I suspect I'll be the only person here who knows those flowers aren't naturally blue. Hardly any species of flowering plants produce this color, I learned some years back when I included blue flora in an elegant Christmas promotion at my old job. The ones at the florist—and inevitably on these tables—are dyed by plant breeders.

Lorna, get out of your head! Who cares how they got to be blue? I catch myself in my biggest mindfulness trap: overwhelming my feelings with facts. I soften my eyes until the room blurs into a peace that washes over me. I inhale, watching this calm spread with each breath to every cell in my body. This takes less than one minute, but when I return my gaze to the larger room, I'm fully here.

As new guests arrive, Angelica runs to hug them, greeting each as if they are the most important people she knows. I love this about Angelica.

Of course, a number of truly special people are on the guest list. The governor created this interfaith commission to facilitate harmony among citizens, since a lot of religious tension has bubbled up lately. Angelica, a minister at an interfaith church, was selected to be the chair. Candace Silver, one of my favorite indie actresses, who's made religious tolerance a hallmark of her social-media platform, will be the guest of honor.

Candace retweeted my sister's post about the event last week. Angelica called me, practically hyperventilating, after she contacted Candace and she agreed to attend. Her appearance will raise the commission's profile immeasurably.

Also expected are the lieutenant governor, several bishops, heads of Jewish organizations, and other assorted religious royalty. And of course, there's my family, including my mother.

Remarkably, Mom is not here yet, I realize as I glance around. My mother—who believes being early gives you brownie points in heaven or some similar nonsense—is actually going to be late.

At twenty minutes after one, Mom finally blows in, on the heels of two bishops in black cassocks with red piping, her own red dress making them look like some sort of oddball singing group. She looks frazzled, spewing to the waiter handing her a flute of sparkling raspberry water—the virgin drinks a nod to some of the Christian traditions that don't condone alcohol—about how her car wouldn't start and she had to wait for the roadside service, who said they would come in ten minutes but took half an hour, and how she's so hot and sweaty she needs another shower. . . .

I walk away, eager to avoid getting hit by the rant. Although I'm feeling upbeat, my mother can easily puncture my mood. I spy Lilah entertaining two interfaith ministers from Angelica's church. She's dancing around an orchid one of them has placed on the ground. I know these guys well, so I trust Lilah is in good hands.

Don is at the back of the room, in deep conversation with a rabbi. They're discussing the prospect of getting local

Jewish organizations involved in environmental justice. The rabbi nods with interest, or maybe he's just being polite. I smile at my husband's persistence; he never misses an opportunity to save the planet.

I take this blissfully unencumbered moment to greet my niece and brother-in-law. I'm taken aback by the young woman in towering heels that my teenage niece has become.

"Radha, you look terrific," I say. As she beams, I silently contrast her reaction with mine at that age. Really, until a few years ago. I hated praise, even for things that might have objectively been true. In my heart I felt like a failure, so it made me feel like a fraud.

Radha has been raised by my sister and her enlightened husband, who have taught her since birth that she is part of the glorious universe. It's not that Radha thinks she's better than everyone else; it's that she knows we're all fantastic. Once when I took her shopping I heard a store clerk ask, "How are you?" and she replied, "I am wonderful and so are you." She told me she'd read that the late minister from a Center for Spiritual Living in Florida used to say that. I should co-opt this insightful line myself.

I hug Yonatan, who in recent years has felt more like a brother than an in-law. The two of us crow about Radha's upcoming mission to Haiti until someone announces the luncheon is starting.

Candace arrives as everyone takes their seats. Although her entrance generates murmurs and pointing, she looks decidedly low-key in a black dress and her own ballet flats. She's shown her place at the head table next to Angelica.

Candace isn't flaunting her wealth or fame, yet I'm still struck by a moment of jealousy. This ramps up another negative emotion, discontent, when my mother takes the seat next to mine. I knew she was at our table, but I'd hoped one of the priests my mother worships would have wedged himself between us. Don sits on my other side, with Lilah next to him.

"Look at that dress she's wearing," Mom says, leaning towards me and gawking at Candace. "Could be cashmere. Must have cost thousands. You'd think she'd be more sensitive about flashing wealth around these men of the cloth."

Mom's envy makes me realize how ridiculous mine is. "I think it's lovely," I say. "So is Angelica's." I glance at my radiant sister, whose white dress bears fashionable fringe.

The luncheon was initially planned by Angelica's colleagues as a small party to honor her. My sister insisted that all members of the commission be feted. Seeing her at the dais alongside an esteemed reverend, bishop, rabbi, swami, and representatives of religions I don't even recognize fills me with pride.

My big sister, who used to rescue bugs in our home before Mom could stomp on them. Who invited me to lie on the grass in our backyard for hours watching the handful of stars you can see in the suburbs. Who realized when she hit her late-twenties that something important was missing, and found it in interfaith spirituality. And who rescued me from my own malaise by opening me to my inner world.

Angelica has arranged for each of the commission members to say something about the person sitting next to them. Apparently, they had a meet-and-greet last month, so they know a little about one another. Each speaks about their fellow member's compassion or charity or sense of humor. Angelica talks about Candace. She praises her desire to use her fame for good.

"I read she gave a child up for adoption as a teen," my mother sniffs. I realized long ago that my mother thinks it's her job to rip the "false façades" off other people. Only in recent years did I understand this is because Mom clings to her own super-phony façade: an erudite image hiding a damaged little girl. I've had more empathy towards her since.

"Is that so," I respond, careful neither to attack her comments nor to side with them. This confuses her about what to say next, so she says nothing.

After the speeches, a reverend says grace and lunch is served. Lilah sits in her booster seat, taking everything in while she draws in her coloring book. Don and I use the moment to start the meal with a mindfulness exercise.

I lift my fork and stab one of the Kalamata olives in my salad. I examine its size and texture—larger and thicker than the ones I buy. My mind starts anticipating that it will taste moister, but I stop the thought so as to not leap ahead. After taking a sniff, I bite off half, letting it squish around my mouth.

It is indeed juicy. I observe how the texture and taste change with every chew. I don't yet swallow the tiny pieces; I propel them around my mouth with my tongue.

"Look at Angelica with all those lofty people," my mom interrupts, proud of her favorite daughter. I don't get upset that she's broken my concentration, since the goal of mindfulness is to stay centered no matter what is going on. I swallow the olive bits, paying close attention to the feel of them sliding down my throat. Then I turn to my mother with, if not quite unconditional love, some measure of tenderness.

"It is wonderful that people recognize how perfect Angelica is at bringing different faiths together."

"Momma, Auntie is up there," Lilah exclaims, joining the conversation.

"Yes. This whole party is for her. Because she's special."

"Everyone's special," Lilah replies, having been babysat by Radha.

"You certainly are," Don says, giving her a peck on the cheek.

The waitstaff serves the salmon entrée, followed by chocolate cake, which lights Lilah up.

"No thanks," I say, waving my own piece away. Not only am I trying to keep my weight in check, I'm wanting to eat more healthily now that I'm concerned about Deuxie. Of course, that thought causes my anxiety to surge.

Don raises an eyebrow. He has an uncanny ability to sense when I've thrown my balance off. I nod that I'm okay.

Lilah finishes her cake and leaps from the chair. I move to follow.

"This is your sister's day," Don says, nudging me back to my seat. "You sit and enjoy."

"What a marvelous husband you have," my mother says as Lilah takes off running, Don in pursuit.

"I certainly do." I gaze at him with love. I silently turn my attention to the alphabet game I had played about my mother, now thinking of descriptors for Don. The adjectives flow freely. Within seconds, I'm up to *S*, for *sincere*. One day I'll be able to conjure such a quick list about Mom. But for now, being able to do so for my *able-bodied, beautiful, charismatic, desirable, energetic, friendly* man is enough.

"What are you doing?" my mother's voice intrudes as I round on *W*, and realize my lips are moving. "Some of your spiritual nonsense?"

"Mom," I say, staring her square in the face. "How can you say that when everyone here is spiritual? It's what this lunch is about."

"Everyone here is *religious*," she corrects.

"No, Mom. A few may be religious but not spiritual, but most are both. And Angelica and her fellow reverends are not religious at all. As you well know."

It never ceases to amaze that my mother faults me for the things she praises in my sister. "I wasn't meditating," I continue, unsure why I care but noticing my voice rise in exasperation. "I was thinking about my terrific husband. But even if I'd been meditating, it's nothing Angelica doesn't do several times every day."

"You don't have to get so huffy."

I shouldn't let anything my mother says throw me. But even though I'm much better at ignoring her antics than I used to be, I can't help myself.

"Actually, Mother," I reply icily, "sometimes I do."

6

Monday morning comes faster than a meme flies around the internet. It's been a wonderful, jam-packed weekend. Angelica's luncheon was followed by a casual supper with several spiritual leaders in her home. Yesterday, Don, Lilah, and I spent the afternoon hiking in deep woods an hour's drive from our house. Lilah was mesmerized by the walk. She didn't ask to be carried until the very end.

The best part: I haven't thought about Sally or her tests.

That may change when I have lunch this afternoon with Don's sister. Daria will undoubtedly pepper me with questions, since I'm certain the reason for this get-together is that Don called her after I fainted. She never calls out of the blue to leave her busy pediatrics practice in the middle of the day.

I'm determined not to make the entire meal about the baby's health, so last night I peppered Don with queries about what I might not know about Daria that we could discuss. He didn't play along at first, but once I wore him down he told me a few things. Most intriguing is that, before I got together with Don, Daria went on a Tony Robbins retreat. I've never been, but several women at the yoga center are groupies—Janelle calls them the Robbinettes—and of course I've read most of his books. I'm curious to hear what the week was like and why she resisted becoming a Robbinette herself.

My morning at the office is incredibly productive. I send out invites for our skin-cancer launch later this month. We finish designing all the print materials. With so many competent people working in this department, I'm pleased to envision us arriving slowly and elegantly to the finish line, rather than scrambling in a mad dash.

I arrive before Daria at Janesberrys, an organic vegan restaurant halfway between her practice and my job. The walls are painted yellow and blue, as if we're outside on a sunny day. Daria picked this place because she hasn't touched a piece of meat in twenty years. I could never give up a good juicy burger, even as I'm eating more vegetables than ever.

Daria eats this way only partially for her health. She's told me many times that clearing forests for the world's billion-plus cows is partly to blame for climate change—along with the animals' methane-filled burps and farts. Plus, she has emphasized, we eaters consume small amounts of pesticides, but farmhands are exposed to gallons of the stuff. While in a rotation during medical school, Daria came across a pepper picker dying of cancer, and became a "conscious eater" on the spot.

I take a seat by the window and ask the waitress for a glass of water. She pours from a pitcher, making a big deal about the fact that their water is super-alkaline. I'll have to look up later why that's something to brag about.

I scan the menu, and it all looks so delicious I can't even decide which category to settle on—salads, entrées, flatbreads, or homemade soups. I settle on flatbreads just as a waiter places a large, colorful salad on the next table, which tosses me to the salad column. I'm admiring all the leafy options when Daria enters.

"So great to see you." I stand to hug.

"And *you!*" She steps back to take in my girth. "What a difference two months makes when you've got a bun in the oven—or as they say in Paris, a bacon in the drawer."

"What does that even mean? Don't they cook bacon in a frying pan?"

"No idea what it means." She settles into her seat and I retake mine. "Maybe it's not even a thing. I heard it when I did a college semester in France."

There's a pause in our conversation, so I steer it away from my fainting spell. "How come I never knew you went on a Tony Robbins retreat?"

"Don told you about that? It was ages ago." A bemused look crosses her face.

"I made him tell me. You know I'm into that kind of stuff. How come you never said?"

"I wasn't keeping it secret. It just didn't affect me the way it does others. I mean, finding my courage to walk across hot coals was valuable. But it wasn't orgasmic."

I chuckle, recalling how my friend Mandy *was* practically orgasmic describing her experience with this staple of Robbins's workshops.

"Maybe it's because I'm fine in the self-confidence department. As you can probably tell."

"'What we can or cannot do, what we consider possible or impossible, is rarely a function of our true capability. It is more likely a function of our beliefs about who we are,'" I recite.

"Is that from Tony Robbins?"

"*Awaken the Giant Within.* I love that quote so much I pasted it near my computer. I still sometimes believe in my limitations more than I'd like to."

"Maybe *you* could use a stroll over hot coals," she laughs.

The waitress arrives at our table and we each order the beet salad. The pause in our conversation as the woman walks away gives Daria the opening she wants.

"So tell me what exactly happened the other night." Her face becomes so serious, my once-formidable appetite disappears.

I gather my thoughts. "Not much to tell beyond what Don probably said. I fainted. For a few minutes, I'm guessing, although I'm not sure. My midwife ordered more tests. It doesn't seem serious." I pause. "Does it?"

"Probably not," she replies, and my hunger comes roaring back. "Pregnant women do faint. But it's good she's double-checking."

"What might she be looking for? Sally wouldn't speculate."

"And I won't either. That would be as bad as you Googling symptoms—which you better not do. Every parent who does that comes into my office convinced their kid has a brain tumor."

"Do you think I have a brain tumor?" I joke.

"No. And Deuxie doesn't, before you ask."

"I *have* refrained from Googling. But I can't promise I'll stay off without a tad more information. Maybe a hint of things it could be?"

"I'm sure your midwife told you it was probably nothing. A baby can sit on the part of the body that transports blood."

"Yes, she said. But if it was something worse?"

"Did you have any symptoms before you fainted? Headache? Blurry vision?"

"Nope."

"Any bleeding?"

"These are the questions Sally asked. You really do know your baby stuff."

"I'm sure Sally knows more than me. I deal with babies *after* they come out the oven door, not while they're baking."

The waitress sets our food before us. I don't want to treat her like an invisible servant, so I make meaningful eye contact. Angelica taught me to do this.

"The salad looks beautiful," I say to the waitress. She seems surprised I've addressed her.

"They use the best ingredients of anywhere I've ever worked," she responds after a beat.

"Have you worked here long?"

"Just a few months. I got laid off at my old job, which turned out to be a blessing," she says, more comfortable now. "I'm more aligned with clean, organic food than the processed stuff at the-place-that-shall-be-nameless."

"That's great that you can view being laid off in such a positive way," Daria says.

"It was scary when it happened. I have a two-year-old daughter to support."

"I have one too!" I exclaim.

"It's such a wonderful age," the waitress says. "People call it the terrible twos, but I say it's the *terrific* twos. She's so full of wonder."

"Definitely full of wonder," I reply. "But I can see where the moniker comes in. My daughter's sleep has become atrocious, which can make her surly—not to mention me."

"That's hard. Especially if you don't believe in Ferberization. Or Sleep Ladying." She pauses, taking me in. "Or maybe you do. I shouldn't presume we think alike just because you eat vegan organic."

"I could never Ferberize," I say, not letting on I'm sometimes a meat-and-potatoes gal. "It would break my heart to leave my child screaming in her bed. I'm not sure what Sleep Lady is, though." I glance at Daria. I figure she knows.

"The Sleep Lady Shuffle," Daria replies, as the waitress nods and walks away, alerted by the chef's bell that another customer's food is ready. "I have no idea why it's called that. You basically sit in a chair near your child and reassure her when she wakes up, but you try not to touch."

"Is that something you recommend?"

"I don't judge my families. People have to do what they need to get sleep. Humans aren't wired to function on a few hours a night, especially if they go to the office in the morning."

"Would you do it? When you have a child?" Daria's been single since Don and I started dating.

"Probably not. But then, I'm like you. A softie."

Daria and I tuck into our salads. During the meal, she asks a few more questions about my health, then lets it drop when it seems Don overreacted by calling her. I share some of the cute things Lilah has done lately. She entertains with stories about a wild weekend rock concert she attended. Oh, the freedom of not having a child—or a spouse.

We finish by sharing a vegan coconut pie. I'm surprised it's to die for. I would have thought dessert was one food requiring a juicy pat of butter.

Daria walks me to my car. "Try not to worry about the baby," she says, hugging me goodbye. "'Worry does not empty tomorrow of its sorrow, it empties today of its strength.'"

"The Dalai Lama?"

"Nope. Corrie ten Boom. One of my patient's mothers gave me her book."

"Is she a spiritual teacher? That's one spiritual author I seem to have missed."

"She wasn't spiritual on purpose. She was a regular Dutch Christian woman who rescued hundreds of Jews during World War II."

As we part, I make a mental note to swing by the library on the way home, one more book to add to my towering nightstand.

A few nights later, Don, Janelle, and I head for a *kirtan*, a chanting concert. Last year Janelle and I went to the king of *kirtan*, Krishna Das. My feet barely touched the ground for weeks afterwards. There's something about this repetitive Hindu music that lightens all your cells.

The couple leading this *kirtan* aren't so well known, but I'm equally excited.

We take our seats in the small auditorium, Janelle on one side and Don on the other. I lean over to her. "How did you know this was happening?"

"The same way everyone knows everything. It was on Instagram." *Must become less of a Luddite.*

I squirm left and right in my chair, trying to get comfortable. The person who designed auditorium seating never had a growing waistline.

Don leans over and kisses my forehead. I'm glad he could come. When I saw Krishna Das, he stayed home with Lilah. This time Erin is watching her.

The woman in front of me has turned around and is staring. "Do we know each other?" I finally ask.

"I'm not sure. You look familiar," she responds. "Sorry if I've been impolite."

"I have one of those generic faces. I remind everyone of their second cousin," I say. This is true, but it's also true that I appeared in the press with my prior job, so it's possible she caught me talking about ice cream on TV or in a magazine. That's not something I'm going to broadcast. Although the promotions I created were fun, since I left I've been a bit embarrassed about the role of our product in America's obesity epidemic.

"I'm sure it'll come to me—probably at three in the morning," the woman chuckles, turning back around as the couple leading the *kirtan* take the stage.

They introduce themselves as Jim and Cindy. It's odd to hear such mundane names. Most American *kirtan* singers take Sanskrit monikers: Douglas became Jai, Andy morphed to Miten, Jeffrey became Krishna Das.

I wonder if it will be the same hearing a Jim and a Cindy. *Way to be judgmental, Lorna!* I call up my "witnessing mind," as the yogis say, and push the thought aside.

"Welcome everyone," Cindy yells to the hundred people in the crowd. "This is a *kirtan*, not a performance. We expect you to sing along, especially with songs that are call-and-response. And if you brought a percussion instrument, join right in."

Suddenly everyone pulls out small drums and other instruments, from where I couldn't say. I'm wondering how they knew to bring these when Janelle lifts bean-filled wooden eggs from her purse and hands two each to Don and me.

Thanks, I mouth, savoring my appreciation of Janelle and deciding not to care that I wasn't in the know.

Cindy sits on the floor behind a *harmonium*, which is a cross between an accordion and a piano. One hand plays the melody on the little keyboard, the other pumps the connected bellows to push air through the reeds.

Jim picks up his guitar and the pair launch into the Hindu classic "Shiva Shiva Shiva Shambo," a tribute to the highest spiritual energy in each of us.

Practically at the first word, the audience sings and bangs their instruments. The three of us stand and shake our eggs. The evening moves seamlessly from one devotional to another.

Soon I'm falling into the timeless space that *kirtan* facilitates. Sound fills all my cells. It's hard to tell where my feet end and the floor begins, or my fingers end and the eggs begin. If I had worries about Deuxie when I entered this space (and I admit I did), they evaporate midway through the evening.

At one point, when Jim sings a sonorous note, I have the sensation of traveling on an undulating wave, ricocheting around the entire city as the note vibrates. It's a magical, mystical moment.

When the music ends and I check my watch, I'm stunned to see it's been three hours. After a long standing ovation, Jim and Cindy leave the stage. The three of us gather our things. The woman in front spins around again.

"I feel compelled to speak to you," she says. "I'm a psychic."

"Maybe we knew each other in another universe," I laugh.

She doesn't join me. "I'm not positive I know you. But during the *kirtan* I got a strong hit that I'm supposed to tell you something. I hope you don't mind."

"Do I have a choice? I have a feeling you'll follow me home to deliver this message if I say no."

"I just might. When the urge is this powerful I don't defy it."

"Okay, shoot."

I expect she's going to tell me that some long-dead relative wants to commune, which she can facilitate for a fee.

"You can handle anything," she pronounces. "That's what you're supposed to know. I'm not getting who wants me to tell you this, but it's important that you hear it."

During the drive home, Janelle and I sit in the back, because I'm desperate to talk to her about the woman's message. Don jokes about feeling like an Uber driver, but he understands.

"What did she mean by that?" I demand, as if Janelle can see into a stranger's mind. "Is something awful going to happen? Something with Deuxie? Something I need to 'handle'?"

Janelle rests a comforting hand on my shoulder. "It could mean anything. Or maybe it means nothing. Who knows if that woman really is able to tap into another dimension?"

"*I* know it," I reply. "The hair on my arms stood up when she said it. And *you* know it. You can sniff a fraud a mile away. Remember that supposed fortune teller in Atlantic City? The second she started talking, you got up and left the room."

"Okay, so she probably was sending a message. But 'you can handle anything'? That could be about your job, your friends, your house, your marriage . . . not necessarily your pregnancy."

"Hey!" Don pipes in from the front seat. "Why would she need to handle her marriage?"

"Sorry," Janelle giggles. "Maybe she meant your mother. You certainly *can* handle her better now than you used to."

"Come on," I say. "She wouldn't feel compelled to tell me I can handle my mother. Five years ago, maybe. But I know that now." I recall how annoyed I was with my mother at Angelica's luncheon. "Well, I mostly know it. This woman was telling me something I'm in the dark about."

We sit silently, the air thick and oppressive. Finally Don speaks. "I think it's time for some breathwork. *You* can worry that something's wrong with Deuxie. But *I'm* not going there. I'm taking my mind off this subject and putting it on my breath. You in?"

"Absolutely," Janelle says.

"You can't do deep breathing," I command to Don, since it can put you into a trance that isn't suited for driving.

"Fine," Don says. "You probably need it more than me right now. It's you who's getting all worked up."

Janelle leads me through a breathing practice she recently discovered called *sitkari*. It's a cooling breath like *sitali*, but instead of curling up your tongue, which Janelle knows I can't physically do, you draw in a quick breath, like when you're surprised.

She guides me to relax my jaw and set my teeth close together. The inhalation is a hiss into the small space between the teeth. You hold it a few counts before exhaling.

At first, I find the sound annoying, and the inhale stings my throat. But I know to give it time. The first few breaths are always warm-ups.

After two rounds I spy Don doing it. This pulls me out of the moment. After I harangue him, he promises to stop.

The next thing I know we're pulling into Janelle's driveway. "How did we get here already?" I wonder aloud.

"Nothing like the breath to get you out of your head, where time lives, and into spirit, where it does not," she says.

I give her a hug after we exit the car, her to go into the house and me to join Don in the front seat. He smiles as I tug the belt around my abdomen. "I missed you. The back seat felt like miles away," he says.

"Well, when we get home, assuming Lilah is asleep, maybe we can close the space between us further."

He doesn't need to say another word. The anticipation in his countenance speaks volumes.

7

The next day I have what I can charitably call a hiccup.

Despite all the techniques I supposedly know, I can't find one that mollifies me. While sitting at my work computer, I do all manner of breathwork, from my favorite alternate-nostril to basic abdominal breathing to that new *sitkari* breath. During lunch, I go for a walking meditation. All afternoon, I play spiritual music on my iPhone—*kirtan*, New Age, even gospel.

Yet nothing stops me from obsessing about the meaning of that woman's declaration.

This is the downside to being into a spiritual teaching that says we attract everything to us. It's hard to dismiss her message as meaningless crap.

When I get home, Don and Lilah are in the kitchen making supper. Lilah likes to "chop veggies," which involves making karate movements with a dull butter knife above a head of lettuce, before dropping the knife and tearing the leaves with her little hands. Don is sautéing mahi mahi with the fresh herbs Lilah picked from our small backyard garden, based on the way the leaves are raggedly torn.

"I have an idea," I tell them once I've put down my things. "Why don't the three of us do yoga together this evening?"

"Yay! Yay! Yah!" Lilah screams. "Lilah doing yoga with Momma—and Daddy!"

"But Daddy doesn't really do yoga," Don replies, raising his gaze to look straight at me. "I'm too stiff to get into the poses."

"Family yoga will be different," I say, acknowledging his difficulties at the weekend retreats we've attended. "You don't have to be flexible; it's for fun."

Lilah tunnels through her dinner in record time. "Time for yoga!" she announces as she drops her toddler fork.

"Not for a while yet, darling," I reply. "Daddy and I need to finish eating, and we all need to let our tummies get ready."

"My tummy's ready," she says, looking confused.

"I'm sure it is," Don says, but ours aren't yet. He and I finish our supper while Lilah stares like an eager puppy. Finally, Don scoops her into his arms. "Let Daddy wash you and put your PJs on you first. The one with the adorable lions."

"That will be perfect," I say, knowing there's a pose named after this animal.

The two of them head upstairs as I place the dirty plates in the sink. Don and I have an arrangement that whoever cooks doesn't clean. He's been the chef more often lately, something I am thrilled about.

I'm drying the last cup when Lilah careens down the stairs, hair damp but nicely combed. Her brown lion pajamas are hanging off since they're not fully zipped; Don lunges from behind to finish the job.

We head into the living room and roll out the two yoga mats I own, for Don and Lilah. I place a towel on the floor for me.

I haven't done an official practice with Lilah. Flexibility won't be an issue for her; I've seen her lie on her abdomen and touch her toes to the floor over her head—an actual yoga pose, I suspect, even if I don't know what it is called and will never be able to do it myself. The challenge will be keeping her interested.

Today at work, my productivity flagging, I noodled around researching yoga for kids. I never realized "Family Yoga" was an actual thing, but there are videos of suggested poses we can all do together.

"Since you're wearing the lion PJs, we'll start with lion pose," I say once everyone is seated. This is not one in my repertoire, but since it looked fun in the video, I may add it to my practice. *If I don't feel self-conscious*, I think, as I lead my husband and daughter through the steps: spreading knees apart, placing wide-fingered hands on our thighs, and opening our mouths. Then we roar.

Don booms like a supersonic jet. I had expected Lilah to be bold, but she holds back. So do I. I make a mental note to later explore my reservations.

"Let's try again," I say, turning to Lilah. "Let's you and I roar louder than Dad." This time—and the next—she and I let it rip.

A half hour later, we've run through a series of family-friendly poses, including a pack of flamingos, raising one leg behind and leaning forward like the pink birds; a knee-flapping butterfly family, sitting with soles together bobbing our bent "wing" knees up and down; and my new favorite, an island of volcanoes, where, standing with legs apart and, placing palms together at the chest, we "explode" our arms over our heads (to sound effects, which this time I perform with gusto first time out).

For our deep relaxation. I instruct Don and Lilah to lie on their backs while Lilah places her head on Don's stomach. I rest my head on Lilah's. She giggles, feeling Don's abdomen rise and, thanks to the weight of my bobbing head, her own.

While we lie still, I notice for the first time that Jim and Cindy's chanting tunes have been playing on Don's phone this whole time. *Guess I still have work to do to keep my senses focused.* I listen to the music, feel Lilah's moving stomach under my head, and smell the incense I lit earlier.

My heart is expanding beyond my body, encompassing my beautiful family. I feel so at peace.

Lila's outstretched finger pokes my shoulder. "Uh, Momma, could you get up. My tummy is getting rumbly."

"Of course, little angel." I gracefully roll off her and onto my side. I pull Lilah into an embrace.

Suddenly, there's a snort in the room. Lilah and I giggle as we turn towards Don. He has fallen into a deep sleep. Covering him with a blanket, I stand and lead Lilah upstairs, certain both of us are about to do the same.

Early the next week I'm racing to my office, late again. Lilah wanted to snuggle in our bed this morning, and I couldn't resist. What I planned to be a three-minute squeeze turned into a twenty-minute lovefest with the three of us. She kept saying, "More."

My boss is leading a focus group at nine for the atrial-fibrillation product we have in development. My car map tells me I will arrive two minutes after, which means I'm going to skulk in after a meeting has started yet again.

Sure enough, Jason is speaking when I open the door. I take an empty seat in back. He stops midsentence.

"Lorna, come up here," he says, causing everyone to turn and look at me.

I'm able to fend off any embarrassment with a joke. "Are you planning to use me as a stroke-victim dummy?" I ask, smiling.

"Actually, our new app might keep you from having that stroke," he says equally lightly, as I move foward.

Of all the innovative products this company has in the works, I feel especially excited about this one. My uncle died of AFib last year, which apparently occurs when the upper heart chamber quivers instead of beats.

Uncle Ned was standing at a meeting in a conference room—probably not so different than this one—when he collapsed. Someone jumped up to perform CPR, but by the time the ambulance arrived he was already gone. At least that's what my mother thinks, because his colleague told her he looked like the life shot out of his body the second he hit the floor.

Based on everything I've read since I began working here, my uncle was fortunate. I'd never use that word around my mother, who was so devastated by the death of her brother she didn't come out of her bedroom for weeks. But some people with AFib have a massive stroke. I know my proud, independent uncle would not have wanted to live that way.

"Doctors can detect AFib by running tests," Jason explains to the gathering of six men and six women who are here to ponder whether they might use this app, which will help us target our marketing messages when it is launched. "If it turns out you have AFib, there are things that can lower your risk, which could be as basic as having your doctor check your thyroid, or stopping your morning cup of coffee. Or it could require medication."

Several attendees squirm. I'm not sure if they're reacting to the idea of this condition or the thought of giving up coffee, something I agree is unnatural.

An Anna Paquin lookalike, with a similarly intriguing gap in her teeth, reaches for her heart, as if to reassure herself it's still beating. This is something I've observed since I began working here: When you mention something that could go wrong with the body, people worry it will happen to them.

Come to think of it, this is why they buy our products. This thought makes *me* squirm. I soothe myself with the notion that we're not selling the disease and—with the stuff I control, at least—we won't oversell the fear. What we sell is reassurance. And early intervention, which can be crucial.

Our app, dubbed AFab (to be changed to something more dignified before its launch) is a marvel. You simply place your phone camera near your face so it can detect the faint light and shadows. Through complex algorithms created by our team of geniuses in India, the app uses that light to calculate blood volume, which apparently is a marker for your heartbeat pattern. I'm not sure exactly how it does this, although I know machine learning is once again involved. *Note to self: Sit down with Daniella to gain a thorough understanding.*

Jason divides the participants into four groups of three, asking each to talk among themselves. This is a brilliant strategy he has honed for getting people to be honest about our products, because they're lulled into the illusion they're chatting with a couple of pals. Of course, Jason is listening intently, as are the recording devices sprinkled around the room.

We have been instructed by Jason to sit quietly during this part of the focus group, so as not to draw attention to ourselves and impede the conversations. Naturally, Deuxie decides this is the best time to deliver a swift and forceful kick.

"Oof!" I reflexively double over.

"Are you okay?" The Paquin woman jumps out of her seat and rushes towards me.

"I'm fine. Please ignore me."

"I know how uncomfortable pregnancy can be," she says, not only not ignoring me but moving closer and placing a hand on my back. "I delivered my fourth child a few months ago."

I eye her board-flat stomach and compare it to my Jupiter-sized gut. I can't believe this woman has any children, let alone four. My jealousy balloon starts inflating, but I'm determined to deprive it of air.

Deuxie's kick subsides and I straighten up. But before I can say anything, Deuxie kneecaps me again. "Yowza!" I yell as I bend.

"Let me take you somewhere you can lie down," the woman says, becoming my nursemaid. "You're such a beautiful pregnant woman," she adds, because somehow she knew I was demeaning myself.

I'm worried Jason will be furious with me—since I'm as inconspicuous as Mike Tyson's face tattoos. Everyone has stopped talking and is staring.

"Don't worry. We'll take care of her," Jason says, guiding the woman back to her chair and signaling to Krista to usher me out. I glance at Jason, attempting to read his facial expression, but I cannot.

Doing a sluggish shuffle, Krista and I arrive at my office. She lowers me into my seat, stacks a few books onto the floor, and lifts my feet on them. She rubs the small of my back until the kicking stops—or maybe that's the reason it stops. I picture Deuxie stretching himself out to enjoy the massage. A moment later, I order Krista back to the meeting, reassuring her I'll be fine.

Once she leaves, I realize how not fine I am. I know Jason is an ultra-caring boss, but my mind is slipping down its well-worn worry hole—that he is disappointed with me. Angry with me. Secretly sorry he hired me. Perhaps he's sitting in the focus-group room, silently reckoning all the wasted money because my outburst ruined the conversation. Maybe—oh, God—he'll want me fired.

My breath becomes so shallow I can't pull in air. My head spins. I drop towards my knees, but with my big belly I can't get down far enough to stop the sensation that I might faint.

Even in the midst of what I'm clear is a panic attack, I'm aware of how quickly my mind flipped from appreciating

Jason's sweetness to fearing his scorn. It's like I was enjoying the view from a plane when it suddenly lost an engine.

My logical brain knows my thoughts are ridiculous, but anxiety isn't driven by logic. My gasps continue. I'm too worked up to try any of the tools I know could soothe me.

Do some deep breathing, I finally command, the mere idea of which begins lifting me from my tailspin. I sit up and inhale into my abdomen, then into my ribcage, and finally my upper chest. But before I complete the first full exhalation, I feel dizzier. *Damn.*

Fearing I might spiral further downward, I call Janelle. She has a knack for helping me climb out of crazytown.

"Yoga mission field," she answers.

"Mission field my ass. That implies I'm elevating someone. I actually had a stranger literally try to lift me." As I remove my feet from the stacked books, my toe catches on one and accidentally knocks over the pile. "Damn it!" I yell, using all my willpower not to throw the books across the room.

"Oh wow. Tell me what's going on."

I walk her through the story: my interrupting the focus group, having difficulty breathing, and how I'm suddenly certain my boss hates me.

"I don't think this is about your boss," she replies evenly. "I think your worry about the pregnancy is spilling into other things." The second she says this, I know it's true. The wooziness subsides.

"I *have* been stressed about whether Deuxie is okay. And I know this adds to the stress chemicals I'm exposing him or her to. Which by itself is bad for Deuxie's health—"

"A train of thought that serves no one," she interrupts.

"How do I stop?"

"Tell me what you're most anxious about, in terms of Jason."

My brain cast about for something that doesn't paint me in too stupid a light. Then I realize this is my close pal. I can tell her the truth.

"That Jason's gonna come here after the meeting and look at me in a different way."

"You mean in a maternal way?"

"No. I mean in a 'you-suck' way."

"I've been reading this interesting psychology-slash-mindfulness book. You up for trying something new?"

"You know I'm always up for trying something you find. I went to that weird energy healer, remember?"

"And he helped you."

I can't argue with the truth.

Janelle has me close my office door so I won't be concerned about other people overhearing. This makes me nervous, but I remind myself to stay open-minded. Janelle has never led me down a faulty path.

"This one exercise intrigued me most when I flipped through the book."

"You haven't tried it yourself?"

"Nope. You're my guinea pig." She pauses, stifling a laugh. "Now don't judge this. What you're gonna do is sing what you're afraid of. Belt it out. Croon it loudly."

There's always a first time for that wrong path.

"You can't be serious," I say.

"Dead serious."

"Dead is what *you're* gonna be if you're pulling my leg."

I sip from the water bottle on my desk. It's too late to get out of this, so I might as well do it full-throttle.

"I'm waiting," she says.

"Okay." I clear my throat. "Jason's gonna burst through my door," I awkwardly start, loosely to the tune of Lady Gaga's "Til It Happens to You." "And he's gonna say, 'you suck, you suck, you suck.'"

"You're good. Keep going," Janelle coaxes.

"He's gonna be sorry he hired me. Because I suck, I suck, I suck." I stop, letting this settle in.

Eventually Janelle breaks the silence. "Repeat, please." I do. "Don't those thoughts seem silly when you sing them?" she asks when I've finished. "You know your boss loves you. And you know you're great at your job."

It's true. I am a good employee. And Jason's been nothing but supportive, even though I found out I was pregnant soon after he hired me.

If not quite breaking the irrational hold, this technique has dented it grips on me. My boss may be disappointed the focus group didn't go as planned, but he and I will get past it.

"Can I sing my Deuxie fears?" I ask, appreciating the power of this process.

"Of course you can. And you should. But you're gonna have to do that on your own: I have a meeting. Love you to pieces!"

"Love you too! And, as always, thanks," I say before she hangs up.

I decide to sing about my Deuxie anxiety later, so I can make progress on the skin-cancer events. If I can show Jason my competence, maybe it will ease today's sting.

I'm well into the event planning when Jason enters. Immediately, I taste bile. I try to counter my concern by silently humming, *He's gonna say, "you suck, you suck, you suck."*

"How are you doing?" he asks. "You seemed pretty miserable out there."

"I'm okay, I guess. But I feel terrible about ruining your focus group. I know how expensive they are."

"Ruin it? You made it a grand success. After your little escapade, everyone felt comfortable opening up about their own medical issues and health fears. We got so much data it will take eons to comb through it all. I may have you do that bit all the time."

"Even after I deliver?"

"I'll get you one of those fake pregnancy pillows." Jason turns toward the door. I watch as his bony frame turns a corner and disappears.

When am I going to learn that everything always turns out fine? Sometimes it takes a while to become fine—although here it was fine as soon as I left the meeting.

Taking the long, spiritual view, there's never anything to worry about. As I turn back to my computer, I recall the ancient proverb popularized by John Lennon: "Everything will be okay in the end. If it's not okay, it's not the end."

After Lilah falls asleep and while Don showers, I set a calming mood. I'm sure Don will see this as a romantic gesture, but that's not my prime intention. I light the candles on my altar, giving Kwan Yin a little nod as I do—as if to ask the Goddess of Mercy to keep sending more my way. I burn sandalwood incense, dim the lights, and set my iPad to stream chanting music.

I pull a small book from my nightstand stack before I settle in. I discovered it at a used-book store months ago, where I snagged it for a whopping fifty cents. The simplicity of the title, *Happiness,* leaped out, as did the fact it was written by a rabbi. Judaism seems much like the Catholicism in which I was raised. As the author Rabbi Zelig Pliskin says of his faith, it's easy to become separated from our natural state of happiness by shame and guilt.

Don will be out of the shower in a few minutes and will undoubtedly have other things on his mind, so I quickly set an intention as I flip through the pages: that my eyes will settle on the most important concepts.

Immediately I find practical tips: Have compassion for those who are unkind. Make music in your mind. (*I wonder if singing "you suck" counts? Probably not.*)

Then I spy his advice for when you find yourself in a hole, and read the passage aloud: "'No matter how masterful you become at accessing joy, it is almost inevitable that at some time you will fall. . . . Realize that you have the ability to bounce back quickly. Each moment you make a choice.'"

"So true," Don says, emerging with a towel around his waist.

"Right?" I agree. "Each moment you make a choice. Isn't that what Eckhart Tolle says?"

"And Esther Hicks."

"And Tony Robbins."

"And Wayne Dyer."

"And Angelica."

"And Lorna," he says.

"Well, I can recite the teaching. But it's time I start consistently living it again."

"Amen to that," Don says.

"What do you mean by that?" I spring up.

"Don't get me wrong. I just think you're off your game. Too worried about Deuxie. And that's throwing *me* off."

"*You're* responsible for your own BS, buster." My voice is rising, even though I'm usually conscious to keep quiet when Lilah is sleeping.

"True, but you're not making it easy. Look how you lost it at work today, with a boss who's been nothing but supportive."

Right now I'm sorry I told him about my day. This is the first time I've ever wished I'd kept something from Don.

"Are you saying *you'd* be more chill if it weren't for me?" He looks like he's about to say yes, but then he pauses.

"No, I wouldn't be," he says, his voice softening. "I didn't think I was worried, not after we saw Sally. I guess I am."

He doesn't apologize for his prior comment, but I forgive him all the same. The strain of anxiety is unraveling us both. What we cannot do is let it unravel our marriage.

Don obviously feels the same. Without saying another word, his towel is off and he leaps onto the bed. His mouth eagerly finds mine. I don't hesitate to respond in kind.

Afterwards, he spoons me, his hands around my protruding waistline. I envision him sending loving energy to Deuxie.

"We have to keep telling ourselves there's no point in worrying," I say, as much to myself as to him.

"Agreed. If it's bad news, we'll deal with it. And if it's not bad news, all that angst will be for nothing."

"You mean like Mark Twain said: 'I am an old man and have known a great many troubles, but most of them never happened'?"

"You know he didn't say that, right?" he says.

"No. Really?" I sit up.

"It's one of the million misquotes flying around the web."

I've been citing this for ages, so I have to find out if Don is right. I grab my phone and pull up one of those quote-investigator sites. Sure enough, this was attributed to Twain years after his death. Apparently, Thomas Jefferson said something similar, as did an old English poet and a Roman philosopher.

"Will wonders never cease," I say.

"Just goes to show."

"What does it show? That you can't trust what you read online?"

"That too. But I mean that you can't know what's going on in people's heads. That quote makes Twain sound like a worrier. Maybe he was a peaceful guy."

I snuggle back into his arms. "I do know Twain was an atheist. I read his autobiography in college. He thought God and religion were stupid. Used that exact word, if I'm remembering correctly."

"Lately I've been taking a more laissez-faire attitude towards religion," Don says earnestly. "I've decided if it works for someone—and by that I mean if it helps them connect to something bigger than themselves, and behave in a more kindhearted way—I'm no longer against it. I'm working with a lot of Catholics and fundamentalist Christians. Some great people."

I shift to face him. "How did we get on this topic? We were talking about Deuxie and now we're dissecting Mark Twain and the religions of your coworkers?"

"It's what makes life interesting." He wraps his arms tighter. "I'm going to work harder on not being concerned, to focus on how eager I am to meet our baby—to snuggle, read together, play peekaboo, toss around a baseball . . . "

"Does that hold if it's a girl? I don't see you playing catch with Lilah."

"I've tried!" he protests. "She hates wearing the mitt. I'm holding out hope she'll want to play ball when she's older. And I'll happily add watching ballet with our kid to my list, even if it turns out to be a boy."

"You hate ballet."

"Yes. But if our son wants me to watch, I'm in." After a moment's silence, he gives me a meaningful look. "We can't suppress our worry. It pops out whether we want it to or not."

"Like lava," I agree.

"We need to realize that the worst possibility isn't happening in this moment."

"So what you're saying is I need to re-read *The Power of Now*."

"I don't think so; I see a very dog-eared copy on your stack," he chuckles, pointing.

When the going gets rough, the most spiritual among us get inspired. That's what Janelle always says. Don is reminding me it's time to up my game.

8

My girlfriends and I are in the living room of Sarah's home. Her husband is out having drinks with a friend, so we have the place to ourselves.

Sarah has pushed her couch and chairs aside and has us sitting on cushions on her bamboo floor. I managed to get down with the help of the women sitting around me: Janelle and my old pal Gretta on the left; Sarah, Mallory, and Tina on my right.

The doorbell rings, and Sarah springs to answer it. Moments later, a statuesque Indian woman wearing a flowing printed skirt and huge Bollywood earrings steps into the room.

"Everybody, this is Pari, the woman I told you about," Sarah announces.

"I'm sorry I'm late. The traffic was worse than expected," Pari says, her voice as silky as her long black hair. She turns to our group, six women who make it a point to gather monthly despite jobs, boyfriends or spouses, and in a few cases, kids—or maybe because of all that. We do unique and joyous things together, everything from belly dancing and outdoor yoga to jewelry-making, rock-climbing, or an expert talk like we're having tonight.

Pari is a practitioner of Ayurveda, the ancient Indian "science of life." Since Sarah started on her own spiritual path, she's been open-minded about all these alternative forms of healing.

Sarah tells the group that Pari has been helping her treat a hormonal imbalance. Exactly what happens during these visits, Sarah doesn't say. What I know about Ayurveda is limited, so I picture her lying on an exam table while oil is drizzled onto her forehead, something I saw once in an ad. This is likely as ignorant as a Pacific Islander thinking all Americans drive Chevys.

When Sarah informed us Pari would be the guest speaker, it turned out I wasn't the only ignoramus. Mallory insisted she didn't want any part of Pari's medicines, since a study some years *baa-ack*, as Mallory sings her words, found Indian herbs may have toxic levels of mercury and lead.

Sarah reassured her that Pari won't prescribe anything. Apparently, the Ayurvedic system goes beyond medical treatments to every aspect of our being.

Pari begins by describing how this philosophy sorts our tendencies into categories, and how we can use this knowledge to improve our health. My skepticism antennae are extended, especially after Mallory's caution about the toxins.

"Have you ever wondered why someone else can easily eat a six-course meal, while you feel stuffed after salad?" Pari asks. "Why some people freeze in moderate temperatures while you're sweltering in the cold? Or why some are naturally calm while others are easily rattled?"

I would have answered *genetics* to the first two questions, but this last one has my attention. I wish I were naturally calm.

Pari explains how Ayurveda posits three types of energies, or *doshas*: *vata, kapha,* and *pitta.* Everyone has all of them to varying degrees, but we lean predominantly towards one.

When Pari describes the traits of a *vata*—wiry, thin, quick-witted, loves to travel, sometimes anxious and insecure—I realize this fits Mallory to a T. Apparently, Mallory recognizes herself, because she has leapt off her cushion and is waving her arms.

"*Pittas*, on the other hand, tend to have medium builds, are productive and hard-working, but can be irritable," Pari explains.

"Found myself," Gretta calls out.

"Me too," I say. "I mean I've found myself too. Not that I agree you are."

"But do you agree I am?" Gretta asks.

"Yeah. It's not surprising. We've always been peas in a pod."

"*Kaphas* can be loving and patient, forgiving, and grounded," Pari continues. "But they often feel stuck, and they can gain weight because of their urge to overeat."

"Don't I know it," Sarah says.

Pari has us take a quiz on our phones to confirm our primary type, even though most of us are certain. The questions are wide-ranging, from how quickly you process information to how fast you talk, to odd physical symptoms like how smelly your sweat is.

Gretta and I compare notes as we proceed, even though Pari urged everyone to work alone, "to avoid influencing one another." ("Of course we influence one another," Gretta whispered to me. "That's why we're friends.")

When we get our results, every woman who had previously guessed was correct. Gretta and I are indeed *pittas*.

Pari says she is an Ayurvedic physician who offers her patients a range of treatments based on their type—including dripping oil on a forehead, and I stifle a laugh. Tonight she will talk about diet—the good and problematic foods for each type.

"Do we get to eat?" Mallory trills. I'm hoping so, since Deuxie has me consuming enough for quadruplets.

Pari nods and calls Mallory and Sarah to the front of the room for an experiment. "If it involves food, I'm game," Mallory says, scrambling up. Before joining Mallory, Sarah heads for her kitchen and returns with a platter of cheese. I recognize cheddar and Swiss, as well as the softer havarti and brie.

"Will *we* get some?" Gretta asks resentfully. I used to be bothered by Gretta's lack of grace, but since my spiritual awakening I've come to accept her—even embrace her—as she is, although her ridiculous rivalry over my friendship with Janelle can get annoying.

"Soon. I promise," Pari replies.

Her beautiful clothing and exquisite looks intimated me when she first arrived, but now she feels like one of us. I listen intently. "Since Mallory is *vata*, her good, or 'pacifying,' foods include dairy products like cheese," she says. "As someone predominantly *kapha*, though, Sarah should stay away."

"But I love cheese," Sarah challenges. "I eat it all the time."

"And you can have some now." Pari holds up the plate and encourages the pair to eat whatever they want. Once they've finished gorging, she passes the platter to the rest of us. I sample the havarti and brie—two of my favorites.

Sarah and Mallory return to their seats as Pari continues describing ideal fare by *dosha*. When she gets to *pitta*, I take notes. Good to eat are a long list of vegetables, sweet fruits, and mellow spices, all of which I enjoy. Not good are fried and salty foods, which I rarely crave. When she says *pittas* are better suited for soft cheeses over hard, I think there may be something to this.

Still, Gretta and I roll our eyes when she suggests *pittas* should avoid alcohol. Neither of us drinks much anymore—I stopped entirely while pregnant and nursing Lilah, and again now—but we still view ourselves as drinking buddies. Who wants the image of teetotaling ladies?

"It's not that you can't eat foods that don't support you," Pari says, seeing our reaction. "But it's important that you make conscious decisions."

I want to pay attention to her description of *kapha*-friendly foods, because I think this may describe Don, but my mind flits back to her *pitta* list. Maybe I should try eating—and drinking—according to my type.

The others stand as soon as Pari finishes talking and makes a beeline for the bathroom. I lift my arms and Gretta realizes why. With pulling and shoving from my friends, I get to my feet.

"Isn't this stuff amazing?" Sarah says, more a statement than a question. Gretta and I agree to try the foods Pari recommends—although she says emphatically that she's not giving up booze.

"I'm dying to tell you all: I got a pro-mo-tion," Mallory announces, changing the subject.

"Wonderful!" Gretta says, even though she's been waiting for her own promotion for ages.

"I know you've wanted more challenges at work, Mallory," I say. "Congratulations on creating that."

"I did create it, didn't I?" Mallory beams. "I'm more skeptical than you are, Lorna, that we create what happens to us by knowing it will. But that's how it went down. I didn't even tell anyone at work yet. I just started thinking how great it would be to do a different job, and they gave one to me."

"I think that's how it happens," I say. "Although I also believe that 'There are more things in heaven and earth, Horatio, than are dreamt of in your philosophy'—from *Hamlet*, for those giving me a look. In other words, we can't understand everything."

"You mean like me not getting *my* promotion," Gretta says.

"No, we understand that," Tina laughs. "You've been annoyed about not getting the promotion, so you're not energetically open to it."

"I'll drink to that," Janelle says, lifting her Perrier in a toast. Janelle is also a *pitta*, and she rarely drinks.

"I admit that's true," Gretta says, ignoring Janelle as she often does.

Pari emerges and gathers us together before she leaves. She wants to know how Sarah and Mallory are feeling.

"To tell the truth," Sarah says, "I'm kinda tired. I'm not sure whether it's because I ate the cheese or because you planted the idea that I shouldn't."

"Fair enough," Pari says. "The mind is powerful. Why doesn't everyone eat foods for your energy type the next few weeks and text me if you notice anything."

"I'm feeling great," Mallory sings. "Of course, getting that promotion helps."

"Right. It isn't just food," Pari agrees. "What happens in our lives, and how we react to what happens, is also key. Take *pittas*, for instance." She turns towards Gretta and me. "They're usually happy. But when life gets challenging, they get angry fast. We have a saying in the Ayurvedic world: 'Imbalanced *pittas* don't go to hell; they create it wherever they go.'"

"I confess I do that. Especially if hell includes worrying," I say.

"It does," Pari confirms.

"True for me too," Gretta says. She turns to me, smiling. "But you have to admit we're both light-years ahead of where we once were."

9

It turns out yoga is good for *pittas,* especially the slow, mindful practice I prefer to do. I learned this from an Ayurveda book I bought online.

This has energized me to return to a steady practice. I've taken Sally's advice and subscribed to a streaming service, and I'm loving taking classes in my home. So far, I've done three. This morning was restorative yoga, using bolsters and blankets (in this case, my bed's pillows and comforter), which calmed my anxiety.

Last night, I let myself get wound tight about my ultrasound. I sang my worries like an opera diva, which helped, but when I woke up this morning, I needed to belt out a whole new round—plus do the yoga.

Now that I'm on my way to Sally's office for the test, the Zen all that brought me is dissipating. I'm not as crazed as earlier, but my nerves are crackling.

I pull my car into the lot and reach for a thought to settle me. I recall a story Eckhart Tolle once told: A guy is sitting on a bus, looking out the window and enjoying the expansive view. He doesn't let his mind wander to where the bus is taking him—to an appointment with his lawyer to file for bankruptcy.

Maybe I'm not as advanced as that guy on the bus.

Of course, I understand the importance of staying in the present moment. But the thought that maybe something isn't right with Deuxie has me projecting: Could I have a baby too sick even to hold in my arms? Ultrasound is a routine procedure, I try telling myself. So what if this one was pushed up a tad?

I'm on the bus, looking out at the view. Actually, I realize, I'm sitting in my car, which is nicer than a bus. Sally's parking lot may not face a gorgeous vista, but the curves of Spanish Revival architecture are pleasing enough.

I get out of my car and walk over to a fountain in the plaza's corner. Sally's office is the other direction, so I haven't looked at it closely before. I stand before the round, blue-tiled basin topped with a terra cotta urn, water rushing down its sides. The mist and gurgling settle me. I picture Deuxie enjoying this too.

There are still a few minutes before my appointment—enough time to set an intention: I intend for this test to go quickly, and for the results to be fine.

When I open the office door, Madison is in the waiting room, helping a very pregnant woman gather her things. I trace my hand over my abdomen, glad I still have months to go. I am not ready for the explosion a newborn brings to a family—what the parenting magazines dub "the baby bomb."

Madison smiles when she spies me. "Floise will be with you in a few minutes," she says. "Take a seat."

I'm lifting a copy of *Natural Awakenings* from the coffee table when my name is called. I drop the publication, push myself to standing, and follow the ultrasound tech to her room.

The last time I had my ultrasound, Floise was kind of a pill. I chalked it up to her having a bad day. But as she orders in clipped, distant tones for me to change into the gown, I suspect many of her days are bad ones.

"You're doing your scan early," she says flatly, while slathering cold gel on my abdomen. "Sally asked me to move you up."

"It's not much earlier," I say defensively. "Do you know what Sally might be checking for?" My concern begins rising. *I'm on the bus, looking out at the view.*

Ignoring my question, Floise methodically directs her wand, occasionally stopping to measure on the screen. *On the bus, on the bus*, I tell myself more frantically.

"What are you seeing?" I finally demand.

She sets the wand down and tosses me a towel. She prints a photo of my baby and mechanically hands it to me. "Sally will be in touch."

"Can you give me a hint? You must know how stressful this is." I look at the photo of my baby, hoping the grainy image will reveal something.

Radio silence.

"Will Sally talk to me today? Or not till my appointment?"

"Your next appointment. Unless she needs to call you sooner."

This woman has never had a baby, I think, as I wipe away the gel. My impulse is to grab the wand and throw it at her, but I resist. As Floise walks away, telling me over her shoulder that I can get dressed, I swiftly comply.

I can't get away from her fast enough.

At home, I struggle to make things seem normal. I tell a thrilled Lilah we will make her favorite personalized pizzas for supper. As we roll out the canned dough, Lilah happily pokes the blob and watches it spring back.

She tops her pie with the same broccoli, spinach, peppers, and portabello mushrooms Don and I favor—although she piles on three times as much cheese.

Once Don arrives, we sit at the dinner table, pizzas before us. As Lilah bites, she pulls the crust far from her face, creating long stringy threads. Normally, I would find her play infectious. But my nagging apprehension of what Floise has seen won't quit.

"Look—my slice has a face on it," Don says, showing a delighted Lilah that he rearranged his vegetables to make green pepper eyes, a mushroom nose, red pepper lips, and broccoli ears. I love this man. At least I'm on the bus *with him*.

"Mommy's pizza has a dog." Lilah points to a blob of mushrooms that don't form any canine I recognize.

"That's funny," I say anyway. "Is there anything on your pizza?"

"Yes!" She takes a bite and pulls, generating inches of string. "Cheese!"

There's no reason to try to make everything *seem* normal, I realize as I take my final bite, because everything *is* normal. My bus isn't going to the bankruptcy attorney. The only diagnosis I have ever gotten from Sally is that I am pregnant. I simply fainted one time.

It is easy to live in this moment because the moment is wonderful: a yummy dinner in the lively company of my daughter and my man, in my beautiful kitchen in my own home. Letting my mind create "what-if" stories is ridiculous.

I'm able to stay centered the remainder of the evening. Don and Lilah put on a performance rather than read a bed-time story, acting out scenes from one of her books about a young girl who gets her first ice skates.

Lilah assigns Don to be the mother. She places him in one corner of the living room when the mom is home, another when they're at the store buying skates, a third at the rink. With each change of scene, Don asks, "Is this right?" allowing her to adjust him. Some of her ideas make sense only in her little mind. When "Mom" brings the daughter to the skating shop, Lilah, the storekeeper, hands him diapers and milk, "because that's what you buy in a store," she explains. Throughout the show, she twirls herself around, relishing being a little skater.

Finally, after twirling so much she is visibly dizzy, Don tells her it's time for bed. We tuck her in together.

"Is Momma happier now?" she asks, gazing so compas-sionately into my eyes I hold back tears.

"Very happy," I reply.

She plants a string of kisses on my cheeks. "I like when Momma's happy."

10

I'm in my office when Sally calls.

"Hold on a sec." I rise from my desk to close my door and open a streaming music app on my computer, to cover any screams or cries that might result from our conversation. I lower myself into my chair and take the longest deep breath in history. "Okay. I'm ready."

"How are you doing? And how's your delicious daughter?"

"We're both fine. But I'm nervous as hell, so please be a doll and cut to the chase."

"The ultrasound was normal. Your blood work was normal too."

"Thank heaven." My shoulders descend inches, my chest softens. Until this minute, I hadn't realized how much tension I was holding in my body.

"You can be finished. Or, in the interest of full disclosure, there's one more blood test you can do."

"I thought you said everything's fine," I demand as my chest pinches ever so slightly.

"It is. But remember at our first appointment I mentioned the comprehensive genetic panel. That's still on the table."

"We already did genetic testing, didn't we?"

"Yes, but that was a guideline-based screening, which is the minimum I recommend. We didn't test for many conditions because you and Don aren't in any high-risk groups."

"Aside from my age, you mean. I'm at 'advanced maternal age,' if I remember the phrase precisely."

"That's a phrase that has *never* passed my lips," Sally asserts.

"True. I've read it in magazines. Those 'Moms over 35' articles."

"Well, the risk by age is mostly Down syndrome—which your baby tested negative for."

"So what would be the point of doing this panel?" I ask, even as I'm getting a strong gut feeling I should do it—and I try to never ignore my gut. "Is there something you're concerned he or she might have?"

She pauses, and I hear her smile through the phone. "Do you want to stop saying *he or she?*"

"What!?" I scream—so loudly I glance at my door in case someone comes to check on me. "You know the baby's sex?" I ask more softly. I was so focused on problems the scan might reveal, I forgot that a crucial body part may also be identifiable.

Don and I had agreed that since we don't have a preference, we would not find out in advance. We didn't learn Lilah's sex until she was born, which lent that old-fashioned "It's a girl!" thrill to an otherwise crappy birth. But if Sally is seeing it on a piece of paper, really, shouldn't I have her tell me? It *would* be easier not to keep saying "he or she." I'm not sure how Don will take this, but suddenly I'm flooded with a need to know.

"Let her rip." I take another breath.

"Actually, it's let *him* rip," she says, before I even finish my exhale. "It's a boy."

"A boy!" I'm over the moon. Not because it's a boy over a girl, which I truly don't care about. It's that hearing the sex makes the baby real. I'm not carrying a fetus. I'm not carrying an unborn baby. I'm not carrying Number Two. I'm carrying a boy!

The tension I've been collecting—in my shoulders and chest, which I was aware of, but also in my back and forehead, which I was not—immediately dissolves, replaced with an airy lightness I haven't felt in weeks.

Sally gives me a moment to frolic in the existence of my son. MY SON! I'm going to have a son! A girl and a boy. The perfect American sitcom family. All we'll need is a fluffy dog. Images of us romping outside a picket-fenced cottage flood my brain, even though this tableau looks nothing like my urban townhouse.

Her voice pulls me back from my television fantasy. "Congratulations! You're going to have a boy."

I suddenly remember she was talking about another test. "Tell me more about this genetic panel," I say.

She explains that Madison would draw blood from both Don and me, to be analyzed at a high-tech lab at the academic hospital. Apparently, a carrier screening sequences the DNA for hundreds of genetically-based diseases.

"Could one of those diseases have made me faint?" I ask.

"I think the fainting was a one-off. And I don't expect this test to uncover anything. But since we're being comprehensive, I wanted to remind you it is available. Of course you can say no."

"Of course I *can't* say no. I just don't love the idea of more testing. And more waiting. And more opportunity to lose my peace."

"There's no reason to lose your peace. Your test results have been wonderful." She tells us we can come by the office anytime, since Madison can squeeze us in between patients. "I'll see you at your next appointment. As always, if you need me before then, you have my cell." She hangs up.

I stare at my phone. Perhaps I'm hoping that the answer to what my intuition seems to be whispering might come through the line.

Later in the afternoon, Krista is sitting in my office going over her designs for our summer S-Check campaign. I'm trying to pay attention, both because we're making important decisions and because I know keeping my focus on work offers the best chance for reining in my mind. It keeps waffling between euphoria at knowing I'm having a boy—I picture him toddling off to preschool in a junior sailor suit—and panic about whether something still isn't right.

"So *do* you like my design for the S-Check stations?" Krista asks. It's clear from her tone that she's been waiting for my response.

"Sorry. Go over it again."

"I had a feeling you weren't seeing my drawing, even though your eyes are staring right at it."

"What does that comedian say? I was trying to daydream, but my mind kept wandering?"

"Cute. Never heard that."

"Sorry for spacing out. Show me again?"

"We can do this later if something's bothering you."

"No, everything is fine." I say this emphatically, as much to remind myself as to get on track.

Our plan is to set up free sunscreen stations this summer in large parks around the country. Krista has designed a colorful—and terrific—stand to hide the oversized tubs, so park visitors just see the sleekly designed pumps that dispense the lotion, plus a sign reminding them of the dangers of too much sun (and the benefits of our app).

"This is impressive. You're impressive," I say, now that I'm paying attention.

"Anything you'd change?"

This jolts me. Is there anything I'd change? *Yes, I want a pregnancy with no drama. And no more tests that rattle me.*

"Nope. I wouldn't change a thing," I say, to both of us.

The rest of the workday unfolds perfectly. We get approvals from two more cities for our stands, up to nineteen now—more than halfway to my goal of thirty. On kickoff day, we plan to have local celebrities stand near a cart and demonstrate how much sunscreen is needed—a full shot-glass worth when wearing shorts, even more with a bathing suit, and it needs to be slathered on repeatedly after sweating or swimming. When I learned this, I made a big note to do a better job protecting my family.

Before I leave my desk, I set my intention for a wonderful evening at home, but as I walk out of my office I realize I should also set one for the drive: My trip home will be enjoy-able. I will appreciate sitting in a comfortable car. The roads will be clear. And I'll get pleasure beaming love to other drivers, because I have discovered that sending out good feelings also floods them back to myself.

Don is waiting at the door when I pull my car in. Traffic was light the entire drive. Did I create that? I know the spiritual teachings say the universe responds to absolutely everything we ask for and expect, but sometimes I do have trouble believing it's that easy.

As I enter the house, I scan the room for Lilah, who usual-ly races to me, begging for hugs. If only I could bottle these moments for when she's an eye-rolling teenager. She's squealing upstairs in her bedroom, finishing a game with Erin.

"I had a brainstorm today," Don says, staring into my eyes. "Don't say anything until you hear me out."

"Why do I suspect I'm not going to think it's as great as you do?" I set down my purse. "Go on."

"So we were talking about taking a 'babymoon'—the two of us getting away before Deuxie comes . . . "

"You do know it would be the *three* of us getting away." I point to my bulge.

"But he's easy to take care of in there." Don pauses. "I still can't believe you let Sally tell you the sex—after we agreed she wouldn't."

I flash back to my phone call with Don earlier. Once the hot glow of learning it was a boy passed, I realized I had to tell him. As I dialed his cell, my stomach was knotted.

"I have exciting news about the baby, sweetheart. Actually two pieces of news," is how I started the call, praying he would think the ends excused the means.

"You got the ultrasound results?"

"Yes, and the baby looks perfect," I said.

"That's fantastic! I'm so happy! What's the second bit of news?"

"Sally knew the sex of the baby, and I couldn't resist having her tell me . . . Deuxie's a boy!"

The silence on his end seemed interminable. I wanted to jump in to defend myself, but first I needed to see how upset he was. Finally, he spoke.

"It wasn't right to do that without asking me." As the words emerged, I knew this was true. I should have gotten his agreement beforehand. There would be no defense.

Fortunately, I didn't need one. A moment later, his jubilance bubbled up. "I'm having a son!" I imagined his face illuminated, the way Lilah's was when she tasted her first birthday cake. "A boy, a boy, a boy!"

After a few rounds of this chant, I told him about the genetic panel. He saw it as just another test a pregnancy requires, which pacified me.

"So, what's your grand idea?" I say, bringing my thoughts back to this moment standing in the hallway. "You know I can only take a weekend. Work's too busy for more, especially before my maternity leave."

He clears his throat. Then clears it again. The juxtaposition between what should be a fun vacation and his hesitation telling me has me confused.

"There's a guy at my office who's been elated so much of the time. Today I asked what he's been smoking." His face turns serious. I'm still not grasping the disconnect. "He said he goes to a silent retreat not far from here, near the shore."

"That sounds great." I'm picturing our last yoga retreat at an ashram in the Berkshire Mountains, which Don loved even though he struggled through the poses. Still, there's Don's halting delivery. "As long as they have double rooms. I'm not going on a babymoon with you in the men's dorms, like at some of those yoga places."

"They have double rooms." He stops again. "There's one more thing."

"Spit it out." I fear a giant cloud is set to drown my lovely vision.

"It's not a yoga retreat. It's run by the church."

"A *Catholic* retreat!" I sputter, incredulous Don is suggesting this. "No way!" We grew up Catholic, and certainly my mother is still a believer—which is why we got married in the church. But between the horrid abuse scandals—two priests in my old diocese were implicated—and all the dogma, Don and I haven't attended since. Our choice not to baptize Lilah is still a source of friction between my mother and me.

"That's what I thought at first. But this guy went on about the beautiful property, the comfortable rooms, the tasty food, and . . . hear me out, Lorna," he says, noticing I'm barely paying attention. "There aren't sermons or lectures, really. We'd have most of the day for our own contemplation."

"And the rest of the day?" My arms are crossed. I don't even know when I did that.

"There's a brief talk by the priest each morning—a theme to ponder." When he pauses this time, I sense what's coming. "And one Mass a day—which is optional." He rushes this last part, like a drug commercial spewing the side effects.

"No! Way! No! Way!" I repeat emphatically.

"At least check out the website. It's on a lake. The reviews are all positive. It could be wonderful."

His doggedness alerts me this is not a battle I'm going to win right now. But I'm determined not to do this.

Thankfully, the discussion ends when Lilah flings herself down the stairs and into my arms.

11

A few nights later, I find myself arriving at a drum circle with my sister-in-law. With Erin babysitting, Don had planned to join us—in fact, it was his idea—but at the last minute a bigwig Seattle environmentalist came into town.

I've never attended a drum circle, something I attribute to the facts that one, I have no musical talent; and two, I don't own a drum. Don has promised neither is required.

This circle is held monthly in a city park, coinciding with the full moon. When we arrive, some fifty people are already here—several orders of magnitude more than I expected. I immediately sense that many are serious musicians, with how skillfully they are playing their elaborate—and, I'm guessing, expensive—African djembes.

Thankfully, some are clacking simple wooden sticks. With the tambourines I purchased at a toy store this afternoon, I'm praying Daria and I don't stand out. I know I shouldn't care what people think, but I confess I sometimes do. Being around experts when I am a newbie especially arouses my insecurities.

A dozen young women and a few men are dancing in the circle, to upbeat rhythms set by the leader. I watch one of the belly-dancers with a measure of envy, coin belt quivering over her low-slung skirt, hips defying gravity. Last year, my girlfriends and I had a lesson at one of our gatherings. I could barely get my hips to budge.

Outside the circle, people flip colorful hoops, perform acrobatic tricks, or balance on a slackline hung between two trees. I can't discern if this is a serious musical endeavor or a three-ring circus.

Eventually, I allow myself to ignore the group and melt into the rhythms. That's when I realize it is more than either: A drum circle is a meditation.

Thumpity, thump, thump, thumpity thump, thump. Thumpity, thump, thump, thumpity thump, thump, I shake my tambourine, and the soothing tempo enters me.

Daria is tapping timidly, yet she keeps a steady beat. I lean over and whisper into her ear. "You've got rhythm. Did you play an instrument as a kid?"

"No."

"I thought you might have. I know Don took guitar when he was younger."

"Yes he did." Her tone is sadness mingled with fury. "Actually, he smashed three of them on the living room couch before Mom made him give up the lessons."

These stories from Don's childhood, which I know are true because I witnessed them firsthand since our mothers were friends, nonetheless always catch me by surprise. It's like there are two completely different Dons: the one who lied, stole, and generally made an ass of himself until well into adulthood. And the caring, spiritually aware man I married.

Although I despised him when we were kids, I now understand he was acting out from his mother's medical battles, her cancer finally claiming her when he was a teen. Daria handled her overwhelming emotions by throwing herself into schoolwork, ultimately landing at an Ivy League college and medical school. Sometimes, her resentment leaches out about how Don misdirected his. But I'm in too good of a mood right now to go down the rabbit hole with her.

"So you didn't play anything?" I try again.

"I took piano in second grade. I ended up missing so many lessons with my mom being sick that I stopped."

"Sorry if you didn't want to talk about this." I return to my tapping tambourine, hoping she won't let my inadvertently insensitive questions ruin her evening.

THUMP, thump, thump, thump. THUMP, THUMP, THUMP. THUMP, thump, thump, thump. THUMP, THUMP, THUMP. I sway with the new rhythm.

Soon my body is moving of its own accord. I set my tambourine aside and stand, magnetically pulled to the growing throng of dancers.

I wave my arms and tap my feet. I'd forgotten how much I treasure dancing. Not the kind where Lilah and I prance around the living room (although that is fun too). The kind where innate movement propels mind and body beyond themselves.

I become one with the rhythm. Freed from disquieting thoughts, I watch as my latest angst about my son's well-being breaks loose from my body and floats away.

When the drummers take a much-needed rest, the silence startles me. Only then do I notice Daria is staring. This doesn't faze me. I'm not a dancer hired to entertain. I am a person allowing rhythms to speak to my soul.

The drummers begin another cadence. I sense my limbs start to undulate again.

Later that evening, Daria, Don, and I are having tea in a café. Don called as the circle was ending and met us here. Daria seems to have made peace with my exhibitionism. She's telling Don how inspired she is that I wasn't bound by what others thought.

"Hey, I wasn't *that* horrible," I interject.

"I didn't mean that," Daria says. "You moved pretty well—especially for a woman carting a junior watermelon. But *I* was worried people would watch me play the tambourine. *You* weren't afraid to wiggle in front of them. That's something I can learn from."

"It would be a good lesson," Don says, turning to Daria. "When we were kids you always shrank from the spotlight—although *I* admit I sought it in unhealthy ways. Isn't the ideal to do what you want and not worry about other people's judgments?"

"Again with the implication I was some sight to behold," I joke. "It's not like my water broke in the middle of everything."

"Thank heaven," Don says. He suddenly seems worried. "Dancing can't trigger early labor, can it?"

"Nah," Daria reassures. "Although some of your intense jumps did make me nervous, Lorna. I feared you might fall.

Fortunately, that was a small part of your choreography." She smiles, then takes a sip of her tea.

I sip my own, savoring the café's signature blend of peach, lemongrass, and spearmint herbs. When I return my cup to the saucer, I no longer feel the need to justify my dancing.

"Speaking of being nervous," Daria says. "I have to tell you both about a patient I had this week. You won't believe this story."

Don and I nurse our teas as she describes a ten-year-old boy who came to her office with a severely broken arm. Apparently the mother had waited a month after he'd injured it at baseball. She was convinced the Reiki energy healing she was doing would cure him. Daria feared she'd waited too long, and the surgeon she referred him to was livid when he saw the scans, because correctly setting the arm this late would be near-impossible.

"This boy spent two pre-op days in the hospital, where the mother and her friends feverishly did Reiki over him," Daria continues, her tale building like a detective novel. "At that point I encouraged her to do whatever she wanted, because he was scheduled for surgery, so what harm could it do? Plus, it would make the child feel cared for. The mother, though, kept saying the Reiki would fix the break."

She pauses to gulp her tea. I realize my cup is immobilized midair, so I set it down. My thoughts are scrambling. On the one hand, I've seen firsthand the power of energy healing. On the other, for a mother to put her child at risk is reckless beyond measure.

"The boy went into surgery yesterday," Daria continues. "And here's the kicker: When the surgeon opened his arm, the bone was already reset. Perfectly. Mind you, x-rays from a day prior showed the break."

"Wow. Wow. Wow," Don chants, his mind lurching, as mine is.

"What do you think?" I ask Daria. Now that I know she attended a Tony Robbins retreat, I don't fear she'll be dismissive. But like most physicians, I'm certain Daria didn't learn about energy healing at Yale.

"It has blown my brain to bits," she says, leaning forward. "Of course, I'm angry at the mom. I was even for calling Child Protection. With the infected tissue around that break, he could have lost his arm." She pauses to take a long breath—or as the yoga teacher from my last online class put it, she let a full breath come into her. "But then there's what I saw."

"I read a book last year about how before the American Medical Association ran everyone out of town, people went to herbalists, hands-on healers, and whatnot as often as to their medical doctor," I say.

"But is that a good thing?" Daria asks me. "Those methodologies have little research supporting their effectiveness."

"True." I notice Don settle back in his chair, slurping his hibiscus-chamomile. He knows this is a discussion I've been dying to have with a doctor. "But you have to admit there will never be money to fund big studies. Nobody stands to make billions off Reiki or acupuncture the way pharmaceutical companies do with drugs. Plus," I continue, on a roll, "not everything doctors do has good research supporting their effectiveness. Remember long-term hormone therapy? And cardiac stenting?"

Daria sighs, recalling the major studies that dealt knock-out blows to both these previously common medical treatments. It turned out the hormone therapy millions of menopausal women were prescribed to prevent heart disease actually increased their risk, with boosts in breast cancer and stroke thrown in for good measure. And stents, which were slithered into heart arteries in hundreds of thousands of patients each year, were ultimately found to do nothing.

"I never said medicine was perfect," Daria says.

"That's why they call it the 'practice of medicine,'" I reply, repeating a joke Janelle likes to tell; she's more hostile to Western medicine than I am. "But why must alternative methods that aren't dangerous be rigorously studied before they're recommended by doctors? People have been helped by them—cured, even—for centuries. You saw that yourself yesterday."

"Let me ask you this." She turns towards me. "If something serious happened to Lilah, wouldn't you want her to be seen by an MD?"

"Of course—but don't jinx her!" I gather my thoughts before continuing, trying to push out the image of Lilah lying in a gutter. "If anyone in my family developed something serious that could be cured with drugs or surgery, I'd want that. But there are many conditions doctors do so little for."

"Yes. Although a broken arm isn't one of them. Maybe a combo of Western and 'wacky' methods is best. I *have* been toying with finding an acupuncturist to refer the patients I really can't help. But I would never suggest that in place of drugs or surgeries that we have science for."

"I wouldn't either." I'm pleased my sister-in-law is open to what her fellow physicians would unquestionably consider the dark side, but which I'm convinced has a lot of light.

"Speaking of science," Don rejoins the conversation. "We're going to do more genetic testing."

"You're doing genetic testing this late?" Daria asks. "Typically it's done early. Before conception, even."

"We did do some earlier," I say, feeling the need to defend Sally. "But at our first visit our midwife also told us about this more comprehensive panel. Without known mutations in our families, we didn't think it was needed then."

"So why do it now?" she asks.

"I don't know. Guess I was spooked by that fainting episode. I want to be confident Deuxie is okay," I reply.

"Are these tests even accurate?" Don asks his sister.

"Yes—and getting more so each year. Especially for single-gene diseases."

Don goes where I'm afraid to. "Like which? The single-gene diseases, I mean."

Daria shakes her head. "I'm not giving you a laundry list of medical conditions. And don't go searching online yourself. You told me Lorna's latest bloodwork and ultrasound were perfect. Deuxie is going to be a healthy baby boy."

Hearing this reassurance from a trained physician—yes, the kind I just sort of disparaged—doesn't completely extinguish the underlying concern I've carted around for weeks. But it's enough to tamp down the embers as we rise from the table and head out the door.

12

I look around at the panel of white coats we've assembled, feeling an odd mixture of respect that these people regularly save lives, and annoyance that at least this bunch so arrogantly knows they do. My conversation with Daria a week ago ricochets in my brain. I comfort myself with the thought that at least some physicians are open to the possibility of healing occurring in any number of ways.

This group of doctors assisting with our official S-Check launch do not share this belief. They are bigwigs in academic dermatology with teaching positions at top medical schools in New Jersey and New York. I need them here because, for some reason, the media are more inclined to quote a "professor of dermatology at La De Da School of Medicine" than a dermatologist in private practice, even though the latter is plenty prestigious.

Having these docs speak about the importance of early skin-cancer detection—even if none mention our app by name, which they have pointedly told me they will not—will be catnip for the media.

A few weeks ago, one of these dermatologists spent half an hour on the phone with me spouting off the number of Porsches he currently owns (two, plus one for his wife), all the awards he's been given during his career (seventy-four and counting), and how long the wait is for new patients to see him (I have no idea, having spaced out well before he got to the answer). When I finally was able to get in a word and tell him what I needed for my event, he told me he was out of time and I should call the "girl" in his office.

What makes me crazier than a guy who doesn't have a minute to hear what he's being compensated very generously to do, is a guy who refers to a grown working woman as "girl." But I knew not to rock the boat. Plus, I'm trying not to let stupid things set me off.

Last night and again this morning, I spent more than an hour visualizing in detail how I want this event to unfold: what the conference room in this hotel will look like (easy to do, since I set it up yesterday), how my panel of experts will perform, the throng of media who will write about our app, and the smile on the face of my boss for a job well done. I even marinated in the sensation of Jason telling me he's so impressed he is giving me a bonus.

The audience has started trickling in. Along with the health reporters, I've invited leaders of medical and patient-advocacy groups.

We finished hanging our last decorations, a row of special bright lights that mimic the sun, just minutes ago. I couldn't decide where to display them. I tried near the entrance, then spaced out around the room, but neither placement looked right.

At the last moment, I instructed the staff to arrange them in a single line over the speakers's platform. Brightly lighting the panel of docs will convey how intense (read, dangerous) sunlight can be. I wasn't positive these broad-spectrum orbs would be right when I ordered them, but now that they're properly hung, they're perfect.

I mosey over to check the food table. In addition to our sun-themed snacks, Krista suggested yesterday that we add orange-colored champagne punch, set in a large bowl with fluted glasses to form "rays" around the circle. I didn't expect anyone to drink alcohol so early on a work day, but several glasses are already gone. I rearrange the remaining ones to keep the "sun" intact.

"How's it going, sis?" a familiar voice asks, and I spin around.

"Angelica—what the heck are you doing here? Is everything all right?" I am momentarily alarmed that perhaps she's here to deliver bad news about a family member. Like maybe Mom. Before she answers, I mentally check my reaction; I'm relieved to see I would be sad.

"I've come to support you, silly," she replies. "You've been talking about this event for weeks. I know it's important to you."

I chide myself for having unmindfully conjured up a future tragedy. Obviously my spiritual practice has a ways to go.

"I'm so glad you're here." I glance behind my sister, picking through the crowd. "You came alone? Without Mom?"

Angelica chuckles. She knows I've been trying to get back to that place my mother and I inhabited for a brief spell, when I actually enjoyed her company. But those buttons my mother presses run the depth of the Mariana Trench. "Yes, I'm here without Mom. She doesn't know I came."

I usher Angelica to a seat in front. I don't care if taking this valuable real estate means some hotshot reporter gets bumped to the second row; my sister deserves the best. Plus, having my unconditionally loving sibling nearby will calm me.

Indeed, it does. I breezily give my welcome to the audience, then introduce the panel. Each doctor discusses the importance of early skin-cancer detection. This goes so well, I feel relaxed enough to take a seat next to Angelica. Daniella masterfully describes machine learning in a way that is so direct, Lilah could understand. Jason follows with information about our summertime sunscreen-in-the-parks promotion.

As our stiff CEO, Michael Mills, takes the stage, I hold my breath. But his description of our app, and how the company came to develop it, goes as planned.

I had to beg him for weeks to mention his niece Kalia, whose bout with melanoma at the age of twenty-six was his inspiration. It took more badgering for him to allow Kalia to participate today. Michael was hesitant to "exploit" his family, but I knew she would provide powerful drama. It turns out Kalia was thrilled to lend her voice so others could avoid a similar trauma.

Now, at the podium, Kalia is sharing her heartfelt tale. "It was a shock learning the mole I had assumed was nothing was a deadly melanoma," she says. "I was just a few years out of college. And the worst thing was that my doctor said if I'd had it checked earlier, it would have been easy to remove. Instead, I could have died."

A burly health writer from an online publication wipes his eyes—an excellent sign. I begin to mentally formulate my lead-in to the Q&A that closes our program.

Suddenly, there's a bang. The room lets out a collective gasp. My first thought is that one of our dais physicians has pulled out a gun. (I've definitely got to improve my opinion of these doctors!) I glance at the podium and see the doctors staring at the orbs above their heads. I follow their gaze.

One of the glowing balls has fallen from its wire attachment and crashed to the floor. Kalia is rubbing her foot, a sinking indication she's been hit by flying glass.

I try to stifle my rising panic. I know if I let fear untie my brain, I won't be able to knit together a coherent response. Jason, who has been sitting in the back of the room to survey the crowd, is racing forward.

I must beat him to the stage. I'm the one in charge here; the mistake is mine.

I leap up the three steps leading to the platform, impressed how fast I move in my condition. I scan the remaining lights to make sure no others have loosened.

"Is everyone okay?" I wait for the nods, including Kalia's, despite a narrow stream of blood trickling down her leg. I motion to Krista to usher Kalia off the stage and tend to her. I take a slow, spacious breath. Angelica nods her encouragement.

"Well, we said the sun was dangerous, didn't we?" I joke, and ripples of laughter shift the mood. Jason pulls up short of the stage, allowing I've got this. "We know the sun can injure and kill. We just didn't expect it to threaten all of you today."

I apologize for the mishap, then forgo a formal Q&A, telling everyone to congregate near the food table in back (far from the threatening orbs), where they can buttonhole the presenters.

My plan to take full responsibility does its job. Everyone seems sympathetic as they empty their seats. Once Krista tells me glass merely nicked Kalia's skin, I sigh with relief. Massive misfortune averted.

A half hour later, when the guests have exited, Angelica sidles up to me. In my concern about the incident, I'd forgotten she was here.

"You handled that superbly," she says. "I noticed you take that big breath. I'm sure it helped."

"I could use another. My knees are still shaking."

Angelica wraps her arm around my shoulder and guides me to the back corner, passing staffers scurrying around.

"I don't get why this happened," I say. "I spent so much time visualizing this day going flawlessly. Does the notion that our thoughts create reality maybe have some kinks?"

"Maybe your thoughts had some kinks. Were you feeling good about the event?" I nod. "Did you like those suns?"

I admit I didn't at first. "But once they were hung in front, I loved them."

"Maybe that's why more didn't fall, or nobody got hurt. But you're saying your energy about the lights was not purely positive. The law of attraction could have been acting on that."

"Maybe. I don't know."

Angelica instructs me to close my eyes, and despite colleagues milling about, I comply. She guides my awareness inside my feet. I'm to feel the energy of life dancing inside, while at the same time experience their grounding. Within minutes, I'm a new gal.

Jason strides over as I open my eyes. I introduce him to my sister, who after brief pleasantries gives us privacy. Fortunately, Angelica's exercise has created space between my anxious thoughts about how Jason might judge me and my ability to see that everything turned out fine today.

"Great save," he says, reaching out to pat my shoulder. "You even got to the stage before I could—even though I was moving fast."

"It was my event. And my error. I knew I should own it."

"The apology was better coming from you. It seemed heartfelt."

"It *was* heartfelt."

"I don't get the sense it will affect our media coverage at all."

"The speakers did well. They are the big unknown, but everyone was great, including Michael and Daniella. And of course, you." I say this sincerely.

"I knew from your prior job you're a real pro when it comes to events," Jason says. "But you're even more impressive up close."

I try to contain the blush rising up my cheeks. But another thing I've been working on is my ability to receive praise. There's no reason to diminish myself, I've learned. Plus, people feel happy when you let them honor you.

"I know you're saving your vacation days for after the baby's born," he says, looking at my waistline. "But Michael and I want to give you a few days off in the next few weeks. A bonus for a job well done."

I thank him profusely. This wasn't exactly the bonus I had envisioned last night. But it's wonderful just the same.

13

"Hallowed be Thy name." *Maybe it doesn't have to mean worshipping a God in the sky, or getting upset with yourself if you say "Goddamnit," a phrase that sends my mother into convulsions. Maybe it can mean adoring anything. After all, the alphabet appreciation exercise I did about my mother opened my heart towards her.*

"Thy kingdom come, thy will be done." Rather than an order to obey some thousands-year-old rules, perhaps there's a more meaningful way of seeing this. Like when we do "God's will"— i.e., loving others—our lives are happier.

I put down my pen and consider my words. They do resonate, even though part of me is horrified that I'm even thinking about the Our Father, a prayer drilled into my brain before I had my first Holy Communion, but that never spiritually clicked. Catholic teachings just don't uplift me the way New Thought ideas do.

I can't believe Don wrangled me into coming here. Taking full advantage after Jason said I had extra days off, Don pressed me about this long-weekend retreat, in a convent housing a small community of sisters. I don't know why I relented. My saying *yes*—after a dozen *no*s—likely had to do with the moment Don begged loudest, after a rare evening of uninterrupted (by Lilah) sex. I couldn't find it in me to turn him down, especially when Angelica said she could watch Lilah.

I have no idea why Don is drawn to this. He doesn't subscribe to a traditional view of God. We married in a church only because my mother would have had a heart attack if we didn't—on the morning of the event to make her point, I've no doubt.

I pleaded to go to a yoga or meditation weekend, or even a hotel in Manhattan, but he stubbornly clung to this.

So here we are.

Don sits on a sunny bench opposite mine. Early this morning at the group gathering, the priest recited this psalm and asked us to deeply ponder its meaning. I watch as Don flips his page over to continue writing. I return to my own paper.

"Give us this day our daily bread." It means Holy Communion, of course. And nourishment for the body and soul. But why "bread"? Maybe it's a plea for living simply. I prefer that way of seeing this phrase, but it's still not in line with my belief that there's nothing wrong with prosperity. The law of attraction brings abundance to anyone who aligns with it. Still, not overdoing what I eat keeps my body contented, and when my body is happy, it's easier to stay mentally relaxed.

"Forgive us our trespasses as we forgive those who trespass against us." This one's a no-brainer to get behind, since I believe

in the power of forgiveness. It can be tough to do, however, as I've long experienced with Mom.

I set my pen down again, before I have to grapple with "deliver us from evil." I stopped believing in the devil eons ago. Still . . . evil could be a word for behaving in an unloving manner, which we all do when we disconnect our lower self from our higher one. With this thought, my pen almost magnetically presses itself to the page.

Nearly 20 years ago, Pope John Paul II delivered the catechesis that gave my mother such concern. Heaven isn't a physical place, but a state of being that results from connecting with God, he stated. And hell isn't a doomsday location, but a state of disconnection. I think Mom was miffed that all the people she felt had wronged her in life—my late father who left the family years ago being at the top of the list—might not get their comeuppance. But as long as I can remember, even when I still called myself a Catholic, I doubted heaven was a reward for the few, rather than a joy available to everyone. Now that I meditate, I enter that heavenly state more of the time.

I pause to contemplate this. Maybe meditation is the way I am delivered from evil.

The bells chime for lunch. I'm glad for the excuse to stop this exercise, although I admit it passes my longstanding test for any spiritual activity: Do I feel more elevated having done it? I actually do.

The two-dozen attendees—all ages, races, and life stages, I'm pleased to see—file towards the retreat house, where a buffet lunch will be served. My stomach rumbles loudly, bringing knowing chuckles from two women passing by. I guess they're familiar with a fetus who is never sated.

After another minute, Don sets down his pen. Words swim across both sides of three pages. I'm trying not to compare, but three pages? Really?

Don eyes his feet as he walks towards me. During the orientation session last night, the retreat leaders suggested everyone avoid making eye contact, to help us stay in our zone. I'm finding it beneficial not to try to read the smoke signals in people's eyes.

Don extends an arm, which I use to lift myself. We mindfully stroll past the stained glass doors into the dining hall. At yoga retreats, I typically pile my plate with a wide assortment of vegetables. Now that I've learned certain foods are better for my *pitta* constitution, I pick around the buffet carefully, placing cooked carrots, squash, and mushrooms, along with white-meat chicken, on my plate. *Give us this day our daily bread*, I think, smiling.

Later in the afternoon, it's time for chapel. I'm trying to keep an open mind, but Mass is unquestionably the most challenging part of being here.

When Don reminded me of the Mass as we were packing to come here, I actually screamed at him. Literally screamed. Not very spiritual, I concede. After I calmed down, he challenged me, and himself, to find our own meanings in the readings and rituals.

Father Paul is talking about sin. Before coming to Mass, I spent time envisioning how the homily would inspire me. So far, it is not. I don't believe in sin, nor do I think confessing to a priest absolves me of anything.

I glance at the rosaries in the priest's hands and recall that the Hindus use beads too. I've never minded seeing the *malas* in a swami's hand. Maybe Don is right; maybe I am lugging extra baggage here.

"How can you say to your brother, 'Let me take the speck out of your eye,' when all the time there is a plank in your own eye?" Father Paul recites.

Matthew 7:4, I think, shocked that the memory of the citation is still in my head, courtesy of Mom being a Bible fanatic. But did I ever grasp what this means?

"The language is old-fashioned, so we may not get the relevance of this," Father Paul continues. "It's saying if you come across someone with a minor imperfection, a tiny speck of wood, how can you point out their flaw when your own mistakes are bigger—when you have the whole beam?"

What crosses my mind is how quickly my mother whips out her condemnation—gossiping about a neighbor, faulting my parenting skills, even critiquing my wonderful daughter. Then it dawns on me that *I'm* judging my mother for judging me. Maybe her beam *is* bigger, but clearly I've got some in my eye too.

People start lining up for Holy Communion. I haven't taken it in years and feel conflicted about it now. Of course, I haven't killed anyone, cheated on Don, or otherwise committed a mortal sin; I'm not excommunicated; and, despite always being hungry with Deuxie onboard, I haven't eaten in the last hour. But I know I'm supposed to believe in the doctrine of transubstantiation, that this bread has actually become the body of Christ.

Clearly, I do not.

Don and others in my row bend onto the kneelers, so I follow. As I descend, I recall how the late astronomer Carl

Sagan used to say that our bodies are made of "star-stuff," writing that the iron in our blood and the carbon in our genes were produced billions of years ago inside a red giant star. When my professor recited those words at Swarthmore, they set my intellect on fire. We are part of the stars!

Now I see it in a spiritual vein: Christ is part of the stars. His body was made from the stuff of the universe. So are the wafers.

Our row moves to the front. I feel peaceful about the experience as I head towards the altar. I clear my mind of all the times I've tasted the Eucharist, the cynical thoughts I've had. I come to this moment new. The priest puts the wafer in my hand and I deposit it into my mouth.

I taste the wonder of the stars. Of the universe. Of the people at the retreat, of my husband and children, and even of my mother. In a sense, of Christ.

Don places his wafer on his tongue as a sense of tranquility also passes over him. This experience too has met my spiritual-activity threshold: I absolutely feel more elevated than before.

A few hours later, I decide to take a walking meditation around the lake. Moving meditations are a staple of yoga retreats, where we amble along as a group, a centipede to an unsung aria. Today I'm going alone. I tried signaling Don to join me, but he was so engrossed in his book he never glanced up.

I stroll passed a neatly trimmed flower garden and direct my full attention to the sensations inside my body. Once on the nature path, I feel the tickle of soft grass pushing into my sandals. I notice my arms gently swinging by my side. I sense my thighs in motion.

A moment later, my mind is pulled to a flapping-bird feeling in my gut.

Are you okay in there? I inquire, my worry about that genetic test Don and I took and the results we have yet to receive suddenly spiking. *I mean really okay?* Deuxie flits again. Is he trying to answer?

I cock my head, thinking about the blood test. Then I catch myself. I have wandered from *experience* into the land of *thought*. Not even a thought about the present, but anxiety about what might come. *Stay in the moment*, I remind myself.

Step. Step. Step. Step. I continue scanning my body one section at a time. After I reach my head, I turn my focus to my surroundings, to the bright, cloudless sky; the flitting blue jays; the statues of Mary Immaculate and Archangel Michael. I ponder Michael's fanciful wings, recalling that he's the patron saint of warriors. I round the bend, spying Saint Therese. As I pass her holding her delicate flower, I struggle to remember what she is the patron saint of. Thankfully, my impulse to call up this fact doesn't last.

Soon I'm wandering around the large, shimmering lake. With each step, I connect myself to its liquid essence, willing it to swallow me. It's not drowning I desire, but to be embraced like a long-lost love.

Like I felt during communion.

Step. Step. Step. Step.

My peace in each moment alters my sense of time. Bells chime. Could it be suppertime? The sun's perch over the lake tells me it must be.

Don will worry if I'm not back for grace. I pick up my pace and enter the dining room after everyone has started. I pile my plate with cottage cheese and sweet fruits—other good choices for *pitta*—skipping the heavier fare my body doesn't want right now. I take a seat next to Don and am happy to sit silently rather than make conversation, although I sense he is relieved to see me.

After an evening spent reading, Don and I go to our bedroom. We sit on the small double bed that fills most of the room. I gaze into Don's eyes, ignoring Father Paul's advice. I grasp his hands, creating what Angelica calls an energy circuit. Don stares back, in a Tantric soul-gazing exercise we enjoy.

It's wonderful how Don is so open to spiritual experiences. The women in my yoga classes are always complaining that their husbands are skeptics. One woman told me she asked hers to join her morning meditation, but he laughed her off, saying—

Lorna, I chide myself. It's not enough that my eyes are seeing Don; my heart must too. This activity often leads to sex, but tonight we rise, change into night clothes, and fall into bed.

I glance at the crucifix on the wall. Maybe we should not feel guilty about getting physical here. The Christ I believe in cherishes the love Don and I have.

On the final day of the retreat—after two more days of dissecting psalms; drawing and painting exercises done without self-judgment for my lack of artistic talent; daily Mass; and even some fooling around this morning after I shared my observation with Don—I realize I'm going to miss being here.

The priest is reading a closing prayer: "Do not work for food that perishes, but for the food that endures for eternal life, which the Son of Man will give you." Eternal salvation comes when you believe in Christ, the source of all our food, the priest explains. His words strike me metaphorically, rather than in the literal way he means since the passage follows Jesus feeding the loaves: When we grasp that everything has a spiritual essence, we are always content.

Deuxie takes this moment to scoot around my womb. *The food that endures for eternal life . . .* that food is love, soul, connection. I get it, Deuxie. There's no need to worry about you, because you are spirit. I squeeze Don's hand, clear (for now at least) that Deuxie is fine.

A sister passes around an evaluation form. I answer questions about the location, building, food, leaders, grounds, and room, rating each the highest number.

The final query: What was most meaningful to you during the program? *Was it reexamining traditional prayers?* I wonder. *My serene walking sujal? Eating in silence? The ability to disconnect from work obligations, and yes, even my daughter, to rejoin my always-present core? The meaningful Holy Communion?*

In large capital letters, I surprise myself by writing "EVERYTHING."

14

"Mommmaaaaaa!"

Lilah flings herself at me the second Don and I step over Angelica's threshold. I know Lilah loves Don equally, but she always begins her interactions with me. I lift Lilah, then stretch one of her arms around so Don is part of a three-way hug.

"Daddy!" she shrieks, nestling her little head on his chest, which brings a smile to his face—and mine.

"Welcome home, kids." Angelica walks into the foyer toting Lilah's small suitcase. I know there's a bigger bag somewhere, filled with clothing and diapers and other essentials. She's holding the bag Lilah insisted she pack herself, stuffed with her Magic Cabin baby doll, felt blocks, and other favorite toys.

"Ackolick!" Lilah shouts as I unwrap her arms and return her to the floor.

"She's been saying that word for days," Angelica says to me. "She's so frustrated that I don't know what she means."

"Catholic," I explain. "She overheard Don and me talking—well, arguing—about whether I could go through with a Catholic retreat, and she started using that word."

"Ackolick," Lilah says firmly to Angelica, as if showing my sister how stupid she has been.

"Don't feel bad," I soothe. "This is the age when kids need a parent-translator on speed dial."

"You mean like *dee*," Angelica says.

"It means *fan*." I point to the ceiling fan the same moment Lilah does.

"How is that possible?"

"You had your own two-year-old once," I reply, as if that should explain.

"Radha's words were close to the real ones. She'd say *diker bag* or *vimatin*." I know my sister isn't intentionally saying her child was more advanced; Angelica doesn't have a mean bone in her body. Still, it's hard for me not to hear it that way.

"You mean like *Ackolick*, which sounds like *Catholic*," I say defensively.

"Did you guys have fun?" Don asks, changing the subject before my mood sours.

"FUN!" Lilah replies. "Went to park and Chuck E."

"Chuck E?" I can't picture my holistic sister taking her niece to a pizza arcade.

"She was homesick the first night, so we had an outing there," Angelica explains. "I'm not opposed to the rides and games. I just don't buy their food."

"Pizza!" Lilah exclaims, giving away my less-than-perfect parenting.

Don constantly cautions me to stop comparing myself to other mothers, especially my sister. He gives me a look to remember that as he takes Lilah's hand and walks her to the living room, where a large Lego castle sits halfway completed. Angelica and I follow.

"We so appreciate your watching her," Don says to Angelica as he wedges a turret onto the castle's corner.

"I agree. You're a total doll for taking her," I say.

"You're very welcome," Angelica replies, accepting the compliment graciously. "I forgot how much I can learn from a toddler. Her level of presence is amazing."

As if on cue, Lilah absorbs herself in laying blue pieces to create a moat.

"True, although it's also amazing how well toddlers can multitask. She's just as completely focused on us. Like if right now I were to say, *chocolate* . . ."

"Chocolate!" Lilah screams without taking her eyes from the piece she is snapping in. We adults laugh.

"What's funny? Chocolate?"

"Chocolate isn't funny. It's delicious," Angelica says, walking towards her kitchen. Before I can express my shock that my sister has such contraband—as I always have in my own house—she returns holding a bag of carob chips.

Lilah digs in, seeming not to notice the difference. I make a mental note for when I'm at the store, since carob doesn't have the caffeine I'm trying to avoid.

"So tell me about the *Ackolick*." Angelica settles into her couch. I follow, happy to be off my swelling feet.

My sister and I discussed the religious aspect of the retreat from the moment Don brought it up. And when I panicked about going as we dropped Lilah off, Angelica parroted Don's remarks: There are ways to reframe Catholic doctrine so it better speaks to me.

"It was surprisingly terrific." I dip into the carob bag.

"Sorry, I should have offered you food," my sister says, horrified. "Give me a minute and I'll whip up something for you guys."

"Don't be nuts. You've done so much already." As I say these words, love pours from my heart, obliterating my prior jealousy. I return to discussing the retreat. "I got a lot out of it." Don smirks, waiting for me to say the words. "Yes, even the Catholic stuff. Maybe *especially* the Catholic stuff."

"She even has good things to say about the Mass," Don says.

"So do *you*," I counter.

"But I never thought it would be painful. You feared the Yoga Police might arrest you, or something."

"There are no Yoga Police," I say, even as I know he's right. I generally tell my girlfriends every spiritual thing I do, but I haven't breathed one word about this retreat to any of them.

Later that night, after Don gives Lilah a bath and settles her in her bed, he comes into the bedroom. I'm wearing my comfy maternity pajamas and reading.

"May I join you?" He pulls a book from the suitcase, which we decided to unpack in the morning. He strips off his jeans, leaving on his underwear and tee, then lies next to me.

"When the heck did you get that?" I ask, eyeing a biography of Catholic saints.

"At their bookstore."

"Are you thinking of returning to Catholicism?" I'm unsure how I'll feel if he says *yes*. I can't see myself becoming a
Sunday regular again.

"Not especially. But I loved filling my mind with the
saints at the retreat." A perfect answer.

I reach out and run my fingers under his shirt.

"Are you propositioning me?" He sets his book unopened
onto his nightstand. "I won't say no."

"I am. And I was hoping you won't say no."

After kisses and caresses and the offing of clothes, Don
tries to get on top. Despite squirming and repositioning, he
can't make this work. "Why don't we change places?"

I try to move but my sense of gravity is thrown. I'm
feeling like an ungainly rhino as I try to twist myself off my
back. It takes an actual heave before I get onto all fours.

Instead of shifting on top of my husband, I lumber off the
bed and burst into tears. "I'm such a mess. You can't possibly
want to have sex with me!"

"Of course I want to have sex with you. Do you see me
saying otherwise?"

"It didn't come out your mouth, but you're thinking it."

"How can you know what I'm thinking?" Don slides off
the bed—more gracefully than I had managed—and cups my
tear-streaked face in his hands. "You're a gorgeous, glowing
pregnant woman."

"I. Look. *Terrible*."

He shifts his hands to my abdomen. "You haven't even
put on weight anywhere but here. Remember my friend Lucy
during her pregnancy—she gained over sixty pounds."

"She looked like Texas!" I stammer. "And I do too." More tears pool, but I'm determined to hold them back. I don't want blotchy cheeks to go with my bulging body.

"We don't have to have sex. Let's just sit together," Don says. I walk to my closet and pull on a robe. I will not be naked when I'm feeling so vulnerable.

Don ushers me to the edge of the bed and sits beside me. He begins a round of *"Hari Om"* chanting like they do at my yoga center—the first two times regular pitch, the next two higher, the last two low. I ignore him the first time around, then repeat each line as I am supposed to. My voice has less enthusiasm than his, but I know even a middling effort will lift my spirits.

"Ha-ri Om, Ha-ri-Om, Ha-ri Ha-ri Ha-ri Om," he sings. His final refrain is mellow. After I repeat it, we sit in silence. I sense myself returning to an even keel.

"I didn't let the glow from that retreat linger long, did I?" I say. "Not even half a day out and I'm already losing my peace over nonsense."

"I'm glad you're able to see it's nonsense." Don reaches for my hand.

"After yoga retreats I always felt like I was floating for weeks. How is it possible I'm already into self-judgment?"

"I don't know." Don pauses. "Could it have anything to do with the Catholic—sorry, *Ackolick*—aspect? Maybe it triggered something."

I wonder if this could be true. I do associate Catholicism with judgment—perhaps unfairly. "It *is* ironic that the thing I'm judging myself on is my appearance. How much less spiritual can you get?"

"Now don't go judging yourself for judging yourself," Don admonishes. He suggests we find a timing app we can set for every half hour from morning till evening, like the church bells we used to center ourselves at the retreat. Each chime will cue us to notice if we're judging.

Several years back I had set my sports-watch alarm to similarly remind me to be present. I can't for the life of me recall why I stopped. As with many spiritual exercises, I got busy and forgot.

We noodle around the app store until we find the perfect one that chimes on the hour during the day.

"You are a powerful creator," I say as I tap "install."

"As you are, madam."

"I love you, you know." I rise and pull him into an embrace.

"Enough to realize I don't care if you've gained a tiny bit of weight while you're baking our bundle?" He gently tugs at the sash of my robe.

"Enough to realize that," I reply, happy the chanting has settled me.

I yank off my robe, push him back on the bed, and climb aboard.

15

We lie on our parallel mats on the studio floor at Om Sweet Om. My monthly gatherings with my girlfriends are typically held on Wednesday nights, but when Janelle discovered Om was having this "sound alchemy meditation" tonight, she begged us to switch.

I thought Don might not agree, since Friday evenings are our family "Trio nights"—so named before we realized we would someday have another child. I dread telling Lilah when we rename it "Quad." Sweetheart that he is, Don urged me to go. He's taking Lilah to a pizzeria. When I left the house, she was running around shrieking about getting slices with "*ushruins.*"

The program hasn't yet begun, but rather than chat with my girlfriends, I want to use this time to commune with Deuxie. Yesterday I realized the main message I have been sending him is concern. I don't want him thinking I'm agitated about his coming; actually, I can't wait.

Three cushions prop up my head to keep Deuxie off my lungs. Lying comfortably, I place my hands on my abdomen and send a mental loop of love from my heart down to my uterus, up to my head, then back to my chest. I visualize Deuxie basking in my swell of affection.

A few blissful minutes later, a moan pulls me from my cocoon. I open my eyes to find a man blowing a six-foot long wooden tube—a didgeridoo, an ancient Australian aboriginal instrument.

"Take a slow, complete breath, feeling the waves of this resonant sound fill your cells," a woman who introduces herself as Nina coos as the moans continue, deep and haunting. I return my attention to my boy, encouraging him to absorb this powerful energy.

"Gina here is going to add flute sounds," Nina continues. *Nina and Gina. I wonder if they're sisters,* I think, before realizing my curiosity is not worth losing my focus. The melodious flute deliciously combines with the didgeridoo.

Nina starts playing crystal singing bowls. I am familiar with these bowls, since my favorite yoga teacher, Consuela, occasionally adds them to our deep relaxation. When a mallet is rolled against the rim, the tones of the quartz-and-sand bowls are said to align the body's chakras.

I settle into the melody—from the bowls, the flute, the wooden pipe—and am transported to an ethereal space. I'm not at a beach or a lake, as I typically am during a deep relaxation; I'm inside a swirl of green and yellow and blue, a sea of fluffy, colorful clouds.

Ding. Nina taps the edge of a bowl, and an eddy of pink joins in. *Dong.* The clouds expand. I've heard the expression "being on cloud nine," and now that my body shifts from one cloudlike substance to another, I sense getting to nine will be spectacular.

I am light. I am sound. I am energy. I am spirit. It strikes me that the answer to the question, Are we body or soul?, is an unqualified "both."

After a who-knows (and who-cares) period of time, the instruments cease. We lie in blissful silence until Nina directs us to our root chakra as she taps the bowl corresponding to that energy center. She goes up the line, to the sacral chakra around the uterus—where I feel profound love, knowing my Deuxie is there—then the solar plexus, heart, throat, "third eye," and crown. Each is accompanied by a tone and color.

My crown is encased in violet. I unite from this energy center with my friends, who until now I'd almost forgotten were with me. Light exits the top of my head, traveling with adoration to each woman going through this journey of life with me.

The other instruments rejoin the bowls, and my overwhelming reverence directs itself to my child. I sense Deuxie is trying to tell me something. I strain to listen.

I love you so much, Momma, he says, something I experience less as a series of words than as a penetrating vibration. My breath, which had been deep and slow, catches in my throat.

I love you so much, baby.

Without needing to verbalize my next thought, *Is everything good? Are you perfect?* I get the answer. It comes with such a knowing, my breath starts flowing naturally again.

In this world, where body and spirit are one, how can any of us be anything but?

Nina closes the program by having us sway our limbs and bring energy back to our bodies. I've taken hundreds of classes in this room, so I am intimate with every cranny, but when I open my eyes as Nina instructs, something has changed. Nothing has physically shifted. But I feel transformed.

Before I get my bearings, Mallory is hovering over me, reaching out a hand.

"Do you need help getting up?" she lilts. I realize everyone is standing, rolling up their mats, and hugging one another.

"Yes, please." My voice comes out as delicate as I feel. I stretch my arm and she takes hold. Two tugs later, I'm still on the floor.

"Gretta, give me a hand," Mallory says. The pair pull on my arms. Finally, Tina joins in, and on the fourth yank, I am standing.

"Thanks." I finger brush my hair, which is flying everywhere.

"You look different." Sarah steps back and takes stock of me.

"I *feel* different. That was incredible." I'm not sure how far to go. I've encouraged most of these women to believe we are more than our bodies and our minds. But still I worry they will not understand.

"I myself feel connected to all of you," Gretta says dreamily.

"I feel that too," Janelle says. She stares straight at me. "But you look like something else is going on." That's the thing about Janelle. She doesn't let anyone hold back, but she challenges you so gently you can't resist.

"D-D-Deuxie talked to me," I barely squeak out. "Well, not *talked* exactly—"

The women form a circle, locking me in their embrace. I absorb their affection.

"So? Did he say something good?" Sarah finally breaks the silence, bringing a laugh to everyone.

"Yes," I reply. "He let me know everything's wonderful."

Tina suggests we keep the evening alive by going to a diner. Once the waitress takes our order—my fellow *pitta* Gretta noticeably passing on the wine she typically drinks here—we break into animated conversation.

Gretta discusses her promotion, which she finally got last week. Tina and Mallory share their successes eating according to their Ayurvedic types.

Distracted as I am by what Deuxie has told me, I barely register their words. It's more than his reassurance that he's fine, although that relieves me. It's the way I *sensed* his communication, through my cells. I have believed since I began my spiritual journey that we can all converse with the spirit world. But to have experienced it so viscerally . . .

"What are you thinking?" Tina asks me pointedly.

I pick up a packet of sugar to have something to do with my hands. "I don't know how to explain it," I start. "It's like the crystal bowls and other instruments took me beyond my mind, out to that field the poet Rumi talks about. And I met my baby there." I realize how ridiculous this sounds, even to me. "Or something like that."

"'With no effort the soul drinks directly from God,'" Janelle says. Everyone turns to look at her.

"Huh?" Sarah says.

"Yes!" I let the sugar drop. "That's it! I released *effort* and *thinking* and, most importantly, *worry*, and 'God' talked to me through my son."

"Where is that saying from?" Mallory asks.

"Teresa of Avila. Lorna's Catholic retreat piqued my curiosity. I checked *Interior Castle* out of the library yesterday."

I had told Janelle about the retreat the night we returned, and my other friends via group chat last night. Thank goodness I did, since Gretta would be furious if Janelle was in on something she was not.

"You're not even Catholic," I say to Janelle.

"But you are . . . well, nominally anyway," she adds, before I can push back. "When I mentioned your retreat to a woman at work, she told me about the Catholic mystics. I hadn't known there was such a thing. I mean, I've heard the names Teresa of Avila and John of the Cross, but I had no idea they were meditators. And in the Middle Ages!"

"They were?" Tina inquires. "I thought Catholics pray and Buddhists meditate."

"Catholicism has actually had a mystical side for centuries," Janelle says.

"I want to get back to what you said." Gretta pivots to me. "Did you really *feel* God talking to you?"

"Kind of." I'm grasping for the right words. "I mean, it was Deuxie, but it was way more powerful than a single person—let alone a baby. And the words flowed from the inside out, rather than the outside in."

The waitress returns with a fully stacked tray and starts auctioning off the food. Normally, this irritates me. "Who has the scrambled eggs?" shouldn't be something a person who just took our order in a clockwise direction should have to ask. But I'm in an expansive mood, feeling affection for everyone. "They're mine. Thanks so much," I say, smiling as I take the plate. She returns the grin before auctioning Mallory's grilled cheese.

When she walks away, Sarah jumps back into the conversation. "Why did you go on a Catholic retreat anyway? I get a yoga retreat. Even a Buddhist one. But I thought you abandoned Catholicism."

"I have. It was Don's idea. He promised it would mostly be a regular silent retreat, which it largely was."

"Don't downplay the Catholic part. It moved you," Janelle says, throwing my words from the other night back at me.

"It's true," I admit. "I was able to see its spiritual underpinnings."

"Like meditation?" Mallory asks.

"Yes. But more than that. Some of the rituals felt inspired."

"Which is why I checked out St. Teresa's book," Janelle says. "She describes the soul as a castle, filled with mansions populated with rooms. Enlightenment involves moving from one mansion to the next."

"But . . . ?" I prompt. I know Janelle well enough to sense she's hedging.

"She does talk a lot about sin, which doesn't resonate with me."

"Or me," I say as Gretta and Mallory, also lapsed Catholics, nod in agreement.

"But we can view sin differently than the way traditional Catholics describe it," I say, recalling my thoughts during the retreat. "Maybe sin is us getting away from our connection to our highest self."

"I'd use a word other than *sin*," Gretta says.

"As would I. I'm simply saying if you go deeply enough, we can reframe and embrace many Catholic teachings."

By the time I get home, Don is asleep in our bed. Lilah is lying next to him, snuggled under the teal blanket. Her hand lies on his back as they breathe in unison. I'm not surprised to find her here; Don is a sucker for Lilah's requests.

The light from the bathroom illuminates the room. I stand and admire my two loves. Then I remember I have three—four, if I count myself.

I place one hand on my abdomen and the other on Lilah's curls. Because she's holding Don, an energy loop unites us. I sense it flow from me to each of them.

You're right, Deuxie, I think, smiling. *In this world, where body and spirit are one, how can we be anything but perfect?*

16

Lilah is "reading" a book at our kitchen table when I finally get the call I've been dreading the entire two weeks since we gave that blood.

"And then the man drinks his coffee, and then he walks out the door to go to work, and his baby waves bye," Lilah says mimicking a reading cadence, describing what she sees in the picture.

"Is this Lorna?" the woman asks the second I answer the phone.

"It is. Madison?" My caller ID shows it's my midwife's office but she doesn't sound like Sally.

"Yup." I shift in my chair, steadying myself to absorb what's coming. "Sally wants you to see the genetic counselor. It's a woman named Mai Eng. She set up a tentative appointment for you and Don for Friday at five. Does that work?"

I shift again. Obviously, there is no getting steady. "You know, you have this terrible tendency to leave me hanging. I'm not going to be able to keep my blood pressure down if you don't tell me more than that she wants me to see this woman."

"I don't know more than that. Honest. I got a note from Sally to call you with the referral."

"Does she do that on purpose?" I demand, only partially kidding. "To give you plausible deniability?"

Madison chuckles, and the lighter moment downshifts my anxiety one gear. After what seems like an interminable silence, she responds. "Don't sweat it until you hear if there is something to sweat. Actually, if I'm remembering correctly," she adds, "*you* would say don't sweat it even if you do hear that."

She has me there. I'm the one who preaches keeping your inner peace; living in the moment; not worrying about things you can't control; yada yada yada. Another opportunity to enter the yoga mission field.

But when I hang up the phone, I burst into tears.

"What's wrong, Momma?" Lilah asks, setting down her book and hugging me.

I'm not sure what to say. Don and I made a commitment never to lie to our child, especially about our emotions. We each grew up in households where our mothers told us everything was fine even when it wasn't. His mother was literally dying the last time she said this. Yet I can't tell Lilah I'm concerned about the baby, since she's so enamored of the idea of him.

"Momma's not feeling well. I just got a little news that upset me." I'm happy with this remark, and it will hold as long as she doesn't ask me what the news is. Fortunately, she hones in on the "feeling well."

"Momma want to lie in bed? To feel better?" Exactly what I asked her when she had a tummy ache last week.

"That's a wonderful idea, Lilah. Want to join me?"

"Yes. I help you feel better." As we walk up the stairs, hand in hand, I realize she already is.

Later that evening, after Lilah is asleep, I break down in Don's arms. "Something's wrong with Deuxie," I burst out. Before he can tell me I'm fearing nothing, I tell him about Madison's phone call.

"Are you sure she didn't say why?" he asks, after I relay the conversation verbatim.

"Believe me, I asked." I get hold of myself so I can speak. "We're supposed to wait till Friday afternoon for news. I'll be a wreck by then—and that's before we even hear what this counselor has to say."

"You'll be fine." He soothingly strokes my hair. "You know how to stay present when you need to."

"No, I don't," I snap, convinced it's true in this moment.

"Then how about reminding yourself by asking those Byron Katie questions? They're perfect for a time like this."

"You're right—and amazing." I walk over to our bedroom bookshelf. After scanning the shelves twice, I spy Katie's classic, *Loving What Is*.

I grab the book and plop onto the meditation cushion by the altar, eyeing my statue of Lakshmi. *Please send us good fortune*, I silently implore her.

"Okay, let's work through her process." I flip it open. We start with her first query, challenging the truth of our thought that something's wrong with Deuxie.

"We don't know for sure there's a problem with our son," Don admits.

"Yes, but we wouldn't be seeing a genetic counselor if the results were squeaky clean. They'd tell us over the phone."

"You don't actually know that. So the answer to whether we know that something's wrong with him is *no*."

I concede his point. We move on to another question, how we react when we believe the thought.

"It feels horrible that something could be wrong with our baby," Don says soberly. "If I'm remembering right, we're supposed to go deep inside with this one."

I light an incense stick on the altar. Red rose, my new favorite. I breathe in the calming scent and drop into my body.

"When I believe something might be wrong with Deuxie, my heart pounds hard," I say. "My mouth gets dry. My uterus weighs a million pounds. And my brain tells me I'm a failure as a parent—that I can't even make a healthy human being."

"What she said," Don replies. "Absent the million-pound uterus."

We observe these sensations for several silent minutes. Then Don moves on to the final question. "And if we didn't believe our terrible thought?"

"No idea, since this thought is consuming me. What's your answer?"

"I'd be the calm, easygoing person I'd like to be."

"Yes, that's it."

"I'd also be a parent eager to hold our wonderful newborn in my arms."

"So let's be that," I say with sudden clarity. "Let's aim to be that."

"Isn't that another step mentioned in the book?"

I flip through the pages. "Good memory. *The turnaround.*"

"That phrase reminds me of a jazz album from the sixties. I love that old stuff."

"Isn't it also the name of a movie?"

"Is it?" Don whips out his cell phone, because since the invention of the smartphone, no uncertainty can ever remain. After flipping through some websites, he confirms my assessment. "Something about a young guy who loses his parents and starts seeking God."

"Sounds interesting. We should stream it."

"We're getting off point," he smiles.

"Very." I grasp for an expansive thought. "Here's a possible turnaround: Nothing's wrong with Deuxie. Or even, something's wrong with me for thinking that."

"Or," he pauses, aiming for precise language, "nothing can ever be wrong with Deuxie, because he's eternal."

"Remember what I told you about my experience during the sound meditation? That I heard Deuxie tell me—well, kind of tell me—that everything's perfect at the level of spirit?"

"Yes. I love that idea," Don says. "That's what I'm going to hold onto. That no matter what we learn Friday, everything is ultimately perfect."

"I like that too." I nod to Lakshmi and wonder if it's a belief this goddess will help me hold.

In the days until Friday, I'm pulling out all the stops —an expression I learned refers to a pipe organ, because when the player yanks the knobs, called "stops," you hear all the tones simultaneously. I'm trying to hear so many tones that the beautiful melody drowns out my fears.

I've been meditating, deeply breathing, visualizing every new segment, practicing prenatal yoga, pondering spiritual teachings, and trying to hold onto my "turnaround" resolution again and again.

Still, I'm a wreck.

By Thursday, I have to do something different. I decide to take my lunch break at my favorite independent bookstore. I like to walk slowly, passing shelves and noticing the books that jump out at me. Typically, most are in the New Age section. Today, though, I'm drawn to the back of the store.

The first book that calls me, in the philosophy section, is the *Tao Te Ching*. I'm familiar with this ancient treatise by Chinese philosopher Lao-Tzu, although I've never read it.

"Let this be what to rely on: Behave simply and hold on to purity. Lessen selfishness and restrain desires. Abandon knowledge and your worries are over," I read. *Isn't that the truth?* If I could release the facts I'm holding about how genes work, I'd feel so much better.

I snap a cell-phone photo of this page. I plan to enlarge this last line and post it on my office computer. Actually, I'll make copies for my home bathroom mirror and fridge. And maybe one for my car dashboard.

I amuse myself with a vision of me wearing hundreds of Post-it notes bearing this message—probably what it will take to keep recalling it.

I skim further. The wisdom is deep—"The sage knows without traveling . . . Meet the big while it is small"—but I crave a message that directly addresses my situation. I give the book my ritual air kiss and slide it back on the shelf.

I amble from the philosophy department, sensing where my body wants to go next. *To the bathroom,* I realize. A pregnant woman can't last fifteen minutes without peeing.

After that's taken care of, I saunter again. Now I'm being pulled to the psychology section.

I move past Freud and Jung and the classic cognitive-behavior books. My hand reaches for a title that makes me chuckle: *Get Out of Your Mind and Into Your Life.*

Ain't that the truth, I think. Being in my mind—in the knowledge that's bringing me worry, as Lao-Tzu puts it—is gutting me.

As is my habit, I let it fall open where it wants. I believe that when we do this, we call a message to ourselves. As I silently read the words, my brain scrambles to make sense of them. "The problem with identifying with any particular aspect of who you are is that once you become attached to that particular aspect of your identity, you set yourself up to distort the world in order to maintain this vision of yourself."

"Psychobabble," I pronounce loudly, earning a stern look from the frizzy brunette perusing other books in this category. A shrink or a psychology grad student, I surmise. Anyone else would have agreed with me about the BS.

I move to return the book, but it's glued to my hand. Taking that as a sign, I flip to a different section.

"'*Defusion* techniques are not methods for eliminating or managing pain,'" I read out loud—because now I'm kind of enjoying annoying this woman. "'They are methods for learning how to be present in the here and now in a broader and more flexible way. . . . When you think a thought, it structures your world. When you see a thought you can still see how it structures your world (you understand what it means), but you also see that you are doing the structuring. That awareness gives you a little more room for flexibility.'"

This sounds enticingly Buddhist. Intrigued, I leaf further. The book is about something called "acceptance and commitment therapy"—apparently a type of cognitive behavioral therapy. There are myriad exercises for what the author calls *"defusing"*—as in un-fusing yourself from unhelpful thoughts. One of the exercises is to sing your fear. This must be the book Janelle was reading when she had me do that! I love the way the universe orchestrates "coincidences"—which I am slowly accepting perhaps never are.

Another exercise is to repeat a tormenting thought rapid fire. When you say the word *milk* over and over, the book explains, it becomes a sound, uncoupled from the white stuff.

The woman is gone, so I try this now. What word best reflects my worry? *Birth defect.* But as I say it, it occurs to me that not only is this two words, it's not the crux.

Genes. My dread is my genes. That I've passed a horrible, defective one to my baby, which is going to make him sick.

"Genes. Genes. Genes. Genes. Genes. Genes. Genes. Genes. Genes," I repeat quickly, like the instructions say.

When I pause to inhale, I notice that two preteen girls are gawking at me. As soon as I smile at them, they run away. *They could use this exercise,* I think, because as they enter puberty they will inevitably infuse every thought passing through their brain with overblown emotion.

"Genes. Genes. Genes. Genes. Genes. Genes. Genes. Genes. Genes."

As with the singing I did with Janelle, this does lessen my angst. I pull out my phone and press her number.

"Yoga mission field," she announces. "And boy am I in it. I just dealt with the rudest client, and kept my peace. You?"

"I'm at the bookstore." I explain how the book I discovered was the one she read, and about the method I just tried.

"It's amazing how you found the same one," she says. "I've been doing the singing thing myself; it's helping loads."

"I should do that one again."

"The book has dozens of exercises. Pick a few you like and stick with them. Another I find intriguing is the 'buying the thought' thing."

"I like that too," I say, after she explains it means asking yourself whether you consciously want to take ownership of a thought or whether you're just mindlessly adopting it. "No wonder we're friends."

"Well, *this* friend has to get going. Another client. I'm praying this one's lovely."

"Enjoy." I notice as I hang up that I'm a bit jealous Janelle is having an easier time staying centered.

"Jealous. Jealous. Jealous. Jealous. Jealous. Jealous. Jealous," I say under my breath as I tuck the book under my arm, grab my purse, and head for the register.

Friday afternoon finally arrives. The night before was the longest of my life, and that includes the time I was in labor with Lilah. I kept tossing and turning, trying to mimic my sleeping husband rather than allow myself to get annoyed by his slumber.

This morning I interrupted my work several times for the "genes" drill. Once, I turned it into a song. My boss walked in mid-croon. Fortunately, Jason thought I was mangling Michael Jackson's "Billie Jean," and I played along.

I haven't mentioned the genetic-counselor appointment to anyone. I fear if I say it out loud, the precarious balance in which I'm holding my nerves will collapse in a sinkhole.

Finally, just one hour to go. This is when Krista bursts into my office shouting about an emergency. It seems one of our cities is putting all kinds of limitations on the signs for the skin-protection kiosks, to the point where nobody will see them. Krista just got off the phone with the events coordinator for their parks department, which didn't go well. She is hyperventilating from stress.

Part of me wants to instruct her to sing her worries, but the other part—the one that aims to keep my office reputation as a normal woman intact, especially since I don't know her beliefs—wins out. I tell her to take a few slow breaths (advice even staid physicians recommend) before describing the details. Apparently, the man who granted our preliminary approval didn't know their official signage regulations. They're insisting ours must be smaller than we need.

I'm not concerned. My years of doing special events have taught me that the hard exterior of city bureaucracies is always worse than their softer inside.

"We'll find a way to work around the rules," I tell Krista, but she remains alarmed. "Listen: There's no point worrying about something you fear might happen in the future." I smile as these words emerge from my lips.

"Are you making fun of me?" she asks.

"Absolutely not. I'm laughing because I've spent all week worrying about something *I* fear might happen in the future."

Krista immediately goes into helper mode. "Is there anything I can do—about whatever you're concerned about?"

"You already did. You got me to tell you what *I* needed to hear."

"Is it something about work? What you're worried about, I mean. You're not thinking you're going to get fired or something?"

"Is the 'or something' that I'll have to fire you?" It's fascinating to watch someone else's delirious mind in action.

"Will you?" she asks, horrified.

"Your job is safe. And as far as I know, mine is too. I'll say it again: There's no point worrying about something you fear might happen. As I've been telling myself: If something happens, you deal with it then. I'm going to call the people I know in that department to see if we can't resolve this."

"But you put me in charge. I'd hate for you to think I'm dumping it back on you."

"Relax," I reassure her. "There's no dumping. I'm volunteering. Why don't you take a break from this project and move on to something else?"

Krista leaves my office, and I laugh out loud. The universe has such a funny sense of humor.

This encounter elevates me to the point where I actually get work done before it's time to leave for my appointment. (I save dealing with the cantankerous parks department for another day; I'm not *that* enlightened.) On my way out of the office, I text Janelle. I finally spill about the genetic counselor and that I need emotional fortification.

Her return text is a quote from Esther Hicks. *"You can choose the thought that makes you worry or the thought that makes you happy; the things that thrill you, or the things that worry you. You have the choice in every moment."*

Thanks! I text back.

If you need me after, I'm here.

XOXO. I shove my phone into my purse and race out the door so I won't be late.

I pull into the genetic counselor's parking lot and turn off the engine, but I remain seated. If there's any part of any day I want to set my intention for, it is right now.

I envision the genetic counselor as a middle-aged Asian woman with short black hair. She's sitting behind her desk, smiling broadly. Everything's fine, she reassures Don and me, save for some teeny little thing that caused Sally to refer us, but that actually is nothing. I bathe in the relief.

When I exit the car, Don is standing outside Mai's office. "How are you doing?" He pulls me into his embrace.

"Surprisingly well," I say after hugging him back. It is true, in this moment at least. "I've had my ups and downs, but right now I'm up, so that's what I'm going to focus on. Everything's gonna be fine."

"I wish I thought that. I've been a mess all day," Don confesses. I step back and scan his face, observing the worry lines on his forehead and around his eyes that appear whenever Don's out of sorts.

"I wasn't sure how you'd be today. It's why I didn't call you. My hopeful state is pretty fragile."

"It's why I didn't call *you*. I figured the odds of my bringing you down were higher than the odds of you lifting me up."

I share my tale about helping Krista out of her funk. An easier prospect than lifting Don, however, because he and I are fretting about the same thing. I pull out my phone and read Janelle's text aloud.

"I love that Esther Hicks," he says. "I'm gonna choose a thought that makes me happy." He glances left and right and points to a small bronze sculpture of a young girl on a bench, positioned so she's standing on the armrest. "That's charming," he says, his lines lessening slightly.

"She looks powerful," I say.

"Because she knows she has the power of spirit at her disposal. And so do we."

"We have it? Or we know we have it?"

"Right now we have it. That's got to be enough until this appointment is over."

Don opens the door and holds it for me. I take a step forward, ready to face whatever Mai Eng has to say.

17

The receptionist ushers us into the counselor's office as soon as we arrive, handing us four forms and telling us Mai will be with us momentarily. Don and I flip through the papers—standard cover-your-ass stuff about how genetic testing isn't foolproof, along with a million questions about our family ancestors and their history of various diseases.

"This is going to take a while," Don says, filling in the cancers his mother and great-grandfather had, although none were the genetic kind. He's scribbling on the second page when I finish all four, my family history mercifully clean, although I don't know all of my father's relatives. Don puts down his pen just as the office door opens.

Instead of an older Chinese woman, a young, model-tall blonde sashays in. "Hello, I'm Mai," she says, extending a hand. "Yes, I know, you were expecting someone who looks different." She is obviously accustomed to our stunned expressions. Don and I each shake her hand.

"Nice to meet you. I confess I did think you'd be Asian," I say, wondering if that's insensitive.

"You and the rest of the world," she jokes. "My parents were diplomats in China when they had me. They loved China so much, they shortened their last name from Englander to Eng. Mai means 'elegance,' so at least I hope they got that right."

"Do you look like them?" I ask, envisioning this tall Scandinavian couple working among the Chinese people.

"Actually, they were short and dark-haired. They definitely fit in better," she says. "We moved back to the US when I started school, or I would have been teased mercilessly. Even so, I remember a lot of staring."

"So you're a walking example of the hidden genes that can affect us," Don says, eager to steer the conversation to why we're here. I myself like the distraction.

"Well, obviously, there were tall relatives in my ancestry. My parents were the shortest of their respective siblings. I've been told my great-grandmother was a giant."

I can't picture a woman taller than Mai—she must hover near six feet—but I don't say anything for fear of putting my foot in my mouth again.

Don's had enough small talk. "Sally sent us to talk to you, apparently based on the results of our tests."

"Yes. May I see the forms you each filled out?" She takes the papers from our hands and skims them for a silent, eternal minute. "So the only disease you know in your family history is cancer?" She sounds surprised in a way that immediately revs me up. My mouth is suddenly dry, so I pull out my water bottle and take a sip.

"Please cut to the chase," Don says. "The suspense is killing us."

"How far along are you?" she asks me, even as she flips to see where I wrote my conception date on the form. "Nearly six months," she answers, before I can make enough saliva to say a word.

Don fidgets in his seat. "Relax, darling," I say, now that the water has done its job. I clasp his hand. "You're making me nervous. We'll find out soon enough."

"I'm not hiding anything," Mai says. "Just trying to get a full picture."

"*OF WHAT?*" Don bellows, unable to contain himself any longer.

"This is a test that helps us get more information about risks for the pregnancy." Mai stops to take her own sip of water. "As you know, nothing in your history flags you as a candidate for genetic problems. And, from what I see, your first child is fine."

"She's perfect," I reply, my mouth overrunning with grit.

"My forms ask for more details than Sally's forms, and about more relatives." She gestures towards our papers. "So I expected to see something." She waves a hand at Don to cut him off before he can say a word. "Your tests show that both of you are carriers of Tay-Sachs disease."

The phrase lands like a grenade. My brain is exploding. I nearly fall off the chair.

"Isn't . . . isn't that a Jewish disease?" Don asks, his eyes intense on Mai.

"Jewish . . . or Irish, French-Canadian, or Louisiana Cajun, although most of those other groups don't realize they're high risk," Mai responds unemotionally. "But it can also occur in any population."

"Even in two people with no relative with that disease?" I demand. I can't believe she is saying this, so I've decided she must be wrong. "Maybe you're confusing our tests with some other unlucky couple's. Or maybe the test is mistaken."

"I can assure you these tests are accurate," Mai replies. "Years ago we used to look for the enzyme involved in Tay-Sachs. Later we did genetic screening only for certain mutations. But our lab sequences the entire gene involved. It's bulletproof."

A bullet is exactly what she's sending my way.

"Is Tay-Sachs serious?" Don asks.

"It is indeed," Mai says, her voice becoming robotic, as if she's not aiming her bullet right at my womb. "Babies born with Tay-Sachs lack a vital enzyme called Hex-A that is crucial for the nervous system. Life expectancy is poor, only a couple of years. That's why I asked how far along you were. Some people choose to abort—"

"We're. Not. Aborting!" Don says sternly.

"Let her finish, Don," I say, both of their words swimming inside my gray matter, as if I'm under water.

"At six months, you're outside the option to abort," Mai says evenly.

"But we have no one in the family with this." I insist again, as if my arguments can alter the results.

"Well, it definitely is much less common for two people outside the risk populations to each be carriers. But I assure you it does happen. You probably had relatives with the disease far back in your tree so you don't know of them."

Mai calmly explains how if only one parent is a carrier of the Tay-Sachs gene, the child will not develop the disease. That's why it can skip so many generations.

"So our baby has Tay-Sachs?" Don asks, eyes widening like a trapped animal.

"Not necessarily," Mai replies. "When both parents are carriers, as we have in this case, there's a one-in-four chance the child will have the disease."

"Only twenty-five percent. That's good." I feel my emotional roller coaster sliding onto the relief track.

"To find out for sure, you would have an amniocentesis. It's optional, of course. Unfortunately, it takes several weeks to get results. After that we can talk again."

"That's it?" Don shouts at her. "You drop this missile in our laps and we're supposed to go on with our lives for the next few weeks."

"I know this is hard, that this information is devastating and unexpected," Mai says, finally exhibiting a modicum of compassion. I guess maintaining emotional distance is crucial for doing this job without burning out. "It's normal to feel confused and upset. But look at it this way: at least you're getting advanced warning that this is a possibility. Before genetic sequencing, we only looked for the Jewish mutations. People who had other mutations found out their baby had Tay-Sachs when they started developing symptoms at six-months old."

The word "symptoms" gets caught in the viscous ooze that has slid from my brain into my entire body. I can't move. The planning part of me wants to ask what kinds of symptoms, but the heartbroken mother side can't hear that right now. I take a breath. *Sick. Sick. Sick. Sick. Sick. Sick. Sick. Sick,* I repeat silently, hoping to take the sting from the word. Instead, it cements itself like a belt around my belly, enveloping my formerly flawless baby.

Mai stands and walks to her filing cabinet. "I have a handout on Tay-Sachs. And another on some breathing and mindfulness practices to help when you get overwhelmed. Of course, I'm here for you if questions come up."

"We're familiar with mindfulness practices," Don says, his voice softer and more compassionate now. I'm glad he's getting hold of his emotions. I can't say the same for me.

It's not just sadness—I'm feeling rage. If Mai comes closer, I might punch her in the face for delivering this horrible verdict, and in such a horrible way. *And after I envisioned such a different scenario,* I think—wondering if my intending didn't work because I had pegged Mai's looks all wrong, even as I know that's nonsense.

After a few minutes' stewing, I stand to leave. Mai extends her hand, but this time I don't shake it. Don hesitates, then rises and reaches his arm out. I notice he isn't giving her the full embrace he usually does when he says good-bye.

We walk out of the office in stunned silence, my legs weaker with every step. By the time we've reached the sidewalk, they can't support me. I drop to the ground, inelegantly enough that I skin both knees.

Don joins me on the cement. I want him to hold on to me and tell me everything will be all right. But I also know that if he does that, I will feel as enraged towards him as I do towards Mai. He can't save Deuxie, so he can't save me.

Anyway, it's not fair to ask him to be the strong one; he's obviously reeling too.

Don takes a few abdominal breaths. Then he turns to me and asks softly, "Do you want to breathe together?"

I don't even know if I can. Still, I answer *yes*.

Neither of us has the ability to do anything elaborate, so there's no Darth Vader *ujjayi* sounds or *kapalabhati* bellows. We just take in air, slowly and deeply.

My mind jumps wildly as we begin, but eventually I'm able to put some attention on my breath, and it calms me. As soon as I notice that, however, I'm pulled out of the inward focus, and fury rushes into the space.

Determined to get a hold of myself, I visualize the anger as a red, ragged oval. I watch it trudge upward from my abdomen to my throat. I see it continue through my head and out the crown chakra.

Fear comes up afterwards. I color it green and view it as an acute-angled triangle. It too makes its way up and out. I go back to the breathing. After a while, I think maybe I can stand.

Don must sense this. He rises and grips his arms around my back, pulling me up. We walk to our cars, not saying a word that might fracture our fragile peace.

18

Sally is calling my cell. I recognize the name popping up on the screen, but my mind can't seem to settle on who she is or what she might want. I toss the phone, unanswered, back on my nightstand. It feels like the middle of the night, since I'm lying in bed, but I'm in my day clothes. Anyway, it's light outside . . . ?

The phone rings again. The sound is bringing my thoughts into focus. We returned from seeing Mai. Don relieved Erin from watching Lilah; I came straight up and crashed on the bed.

I look at the time: seven thirty. The facts become clearer, and suddenly I understand who Sally is and why she is calling. She obviously spoke to Mai.

I swipe to answer seconds before the call goes into voicemail. "Hello?" I croak.

"Lorna. It's Sally. Are you and Don all right?"

"Not really." My voice sounds distant even to me.

"I just spoke to Mai and heard how it went. I knew the results when they came in, of course, but I thought she was better positioned to explain. I'm sure the news is a shock. But remember that even with both of you as carriers, the risk for the baby having Tay-Sachs is only twenty-five percent."

"Tay-Sachs," I repeat, realizing this is the first time the name is passing my lips. "We're not even Jewish."

"Doctors talk about diseases belonging to certain groups to raise awareness among the people most at risk. But I think they do a disservice in making others think they can't get them. White people get sickle cell, for instance, and people who aren't Jewish can carry Tay-Sachs."

"But we have nobody in our families with this," I insist, as I did with Mai.

"You have people in your families who have carried one of the mutated genes. They have just never been in the unfortunate position of marrying someone else with it."

The unfortunate position. Is that what my marriage to Don has become? Before today, I would have said it was a miracle.

Sally realizes her error. "I didn't mean you aren't fortunate to have found Don. He's an amazing man. What I meant was—"

"I know what you meant," I say without rancor, realizing I don't want to be rude to this woman I adore. "I'll keep trying to remind myself there's only a small chance the baby has this disease." I notice this is the first time I didn't call him Deuxie. Am I already distancing myself from my boy?

"We'll get you in for the amnio this week. I use Dr. Barnes—he's very experienced, so the risks are tiny."

"Risks? There are more risks?"

"Every test carries risks. There is a risk of miscarriage after an amnio. But it's extremely small and, as I said,

Dr. Barnes is excellent, so his rates are really low. His office will explain the procedure, but if you need to talk to me about it, of course you can call."

"Yes. Thank you," I say, pleased my manners are holding. Sally tells me Madison will set up the amnio and get back to me with the time.

She ends the call with a little cheerleading. "Lorna, Be brave, be bold." I notice she leaves off "be authentic," the other phrase on that sign in her office. I suppose she realizes if I let myself be authentic, I'd scream for hours.

More waiting. More waiting to take the test. Waiting for the results. How is a person expected to do that?

Solace has always come to me through reading, so I sit up and grab the e-reader next to my stack of books. I recently discovered that our public library lets you check out e-books. As soon as I learned this, I downloaded a bunch.

I click on *Prayers of Teresa of Avila* and read her wisdom: "Let nothing disturb you. Let nothing frighten you. Everything passes away except God." I recall the retreat—the reason I got interested in Teresa. The peace of mind I cultivated there seems light-years away.

But if I can hold onto this notion that all the things I worry about—indeed, all things, period—are fleeting, a belief put forth by Lao-Tzu, Esther Hicks, and most spiritual teachers, I might just be able to get through the waiting intact.

The following day, Don, Lilah, and I are in the car, on the way to New Hope. I waffled this morning about whether a last-minute day trip to this cute Pennsylvania town on the Delaware River is a good idea, since Don and I remain in a massive funk. Driving in our mental state might be difficult, and once we get there we may not enjoy ourselves. On the other hand, we both agreed, sitting and stewing is pointless.

Lilah has packed an overnight bag, even though I explained that we're coming home after dinner. "Trip! Trip!" she shouted all morning, which made me smile.

The two-hour drive is uneventful. When you've had the week we've had, this is a much appreciated thing.

Don and I had visited this charming tourist town back when we were dating. This time, with a two-year-old in tow, we won't be seeing the art and antique shops, wine bars, and theater that New Hope is known for.

Instead, the three of us head for a park, where we play with the balls and sand toys I brought. This makes us hungry, so we amble down the main street searching for a lunchtime restaurant that looks safe for kids—no easy feat with the fragile antique housewares that give many of these eateries their historic feel.

Lilah spies a restaurant with a cartoon elk mascot painted in the window. She escapes Don's hand and slips through the open door before Don and I even notice the place. The hostess smiles as Lilah fawns over a life-size version of the quirky elk. I take this as a sign our daughter will be welcome.

The hostess leads us to a large booth, near two others with toddlers underfoot—literally in one case, as a boy has positioned himself beneath the table, cooing as we walk by. I swap my concern of Lilah being spurned with worry she'll join these boys and become an ear-piercing posse.

At one moment during our meal, Lilah and the boys do woo one another by laughing hard, but this passes swiftly. All in all, the lunch is superb. Lilah and Don enjoy their burgers (decked high with grilled veggies and gourmet cheddar for him; plain without even a bun for her). My kale-and-spinach salad topped with white-meat chicken (all good for my Ayurvedic type, I now know) is delicious.

Lilah finishes early and sits so quietly as Don and I eat, I keep looking to see what she's up to. Eventually I realize she's simply intently watching me chew. I'm not sure there's such a thing as mindful eating when someone else is doing the eating, but if so, she's mastering it.

The waiter asks if we want dessert. "Es-sert!" Lilah yells at the mention of the word. We splurge on their signature s'more—chocolate frozen yogurt served with graham crackers and a hanging skewer of already-roasted marshmallows (my *pitta* aim to avoid white sugar be damned).

After lunch we head to the family-owned toy store next door. Lilah rushes from one end to the other with the thrill of a teenage girl discovering the makeup counter. She plays with stuffed animals and a wooden train. Fortunately, she doesn't ask to bring anything home.

Don whispers that maybe we should check out the real train, a vintage railroad that runs a bucolic, forty-five minute trip from town—one thing we did not do last time because the line for tickets wrapped twice around the station. I'm in no mood for a long wait, but Lilah has developed bionic hearing, so the word *train* sets her into another fit of jubilation.

"Choooo-chooooooooo! Choooo-chooooooooo!" She runs in circles while pulling an imaginary whistle cord. Watching my girl's glee when I agree to go almost makes me forget my anxiety. Almost.

"Gene. Gene. Gene. Gene. Gene. Gene. Gene. Gene. Gene."

"What you say, Momma?"

"Nothing important, sweetie. Momma's excited we're going to the choo-choo."

Surprisingly, I am. It's odd how I can feel both happy and sad. Delighted and doleful. Eager and anxious. I know that being around Lilah is a prime reason for the *happy, delighted, eager* side. Kids so easily find things to feel good about.

This time the quaint train station is not crowded. The woman at the ticket window tells us the next train leaves in fifteen minutes, pulled by an authentic 1925 steam locomotive that Don is especially excited about. Little boys never outgrow their train obsessions, I think, smiling.

She doesn't have to repeat her parting words, "there are no bathrooms on the train." The only way this pregnant gal is going to survive the ride is to go just before the train pulls away. We walk with Lilah around the station, Don describing the history behind the artifacts, as if she might understand.

We are called to board a few minutes later. Don leads us from one car to another before he chooses the one he likes. Its rows of high-back, bench-style seats are out of an old Western. Although each seat is meant for two, they are small. Don glances at my abdomen and announces to Lilah that "Momma will get her own seat."

"No. I sit with Momma," she demands.

"Lilah, it's easier for Momma if you sit with me."

"No! Sit with Momma."

"Well, Momma has to go to the bathroom, so now that I know what car you are in, you sit with Daddy until I come back," I say.

"No!" She pushes Don to one seat and takes her place across the aisle. "I wait."

An independent thinker, I tell myself. Someday I will be pleased she exhibits this trait, even if it can be a challenge now. As I rush to the bathroom, I picture Lilah standing atop a table, leading some important social movement. That image immediately dissolves into one of the same table, empty. *Will my son be healthy enough—and live long enough—to do that?* Before I go down the path of answering, I push open the bathroom door.

The engine is burping steam when I return. I climb the stairs with the aid of the conductor and make my way to our seats. I find Lilah perched next to Don. I don't know how he did that—really, I don't want to know. I like believing in his magical abilities. Maybe he'll have them with Deuxie too. I smile internally, happy I'm able to use our baby's nickname again.

"They're pulling out in a minute. I was afraid you'd miss it," Don says.

"Did you really envision me not making it?" I ask, reminding him of the importance of visualizing what we *are* wanting, which I only sporadically remember myself.

"A little," he confesses.

The engine whistles. I can't tell whether Don or Lilah is more excited. I settle into my seat as the train lurches forward. An older man begins to narrate, pointing out the grand homes and gorgeous country vistas.

I mostly tune him out, preferring to wordlessly absorb the breathtaking scenery of forests, creeks, lakes, and the occasional bird and deer. Lilah clutches Don's hand. Looking at them, and at this wonderful world, expands my heart.

Eventually the train turns around and makes its return voyage, lurching to its final stop. "Let's do again!" Lilah shouts. This gets a round of applause from the passengers.

"We will come back, but another time," I say.

"This run is especially striking in fall," the woman behind me leans in to tell us. She looks about sixty but has a youthful vibe. "I highly recommend returning in October."

"Not likely." I point to my belly, which the tall bench has obscured. "He'll be born by then."

"A boy! Congratulations! I have four of them," she says.

"Any girls?"

"One girl. The youngest. People always thought I kept going to get the girl. But I treasure my sons. They are amazing people. And they were certainly easier to raise than my daughter was."

I want to confide in this grandmother type that *my* daughter may well be easier, because my son might turn out to be sick. But I hold my tongue. This is neither the time nor place, and if I open that door even a smidgen, I'll go to pieces.

Gene. Gene. Gene. Gene. Gene. Gene. Gene. Gene. Gene.

"That was incredible," Don says, once we're standing on the platform. "A real old-fashioned steam train."

"Steam train!" Lilah yells, although I'm sure she doesn't know what that means.

"Such a stunning countryside," I say, easily reaching for a thought that feels good. "The world is such a beautiful place."

"It certainly is," Don says. "The whole day was beautiful. Let's run through all the things we've loved."

He's luring me into an appreciation exercise, and I'm happy to oblige. My list includes the fun park, charming town, lovely restaurant, s'more desert (which I mouth so Lilah won't get any ideas), old-fashioned shops, relaxing train, and, of course, spending time with my family. Don adds Lilah's holding his hand throughout the ride.

By the end of this recitation, I'm feeling so good, anxiety cannot penetrate.

"And Deuxie is experiencing our first day trip," I add.

"Deuxie!" Lilah exclaims, hugging my belly.

Don pulls all three of us into a tight embrace. After soaking in the love, we walk to our car. I don't even mind that we have a long drive home.

19

Janelle is sitting on my living room floor, legs crossed behind her head. She has finally mastered *dwi pada sirsasana*, the aptly named two-legs-behind-the-head pose.

"Your body doesn't feel like it's cracking?" I demand.

"Actually, it's surprisingly calming to sit like this." She brings her hands together in prayer position for emphasis. "Ommmm."

"I wouldn't call that sitting," I say, even though her butt is solidly on the floor. It's everything below it that's unnaturally perched behind her body.

Two days ago I finally had the amnio. I've invited Janelle over because it's been a challenge maintaining my inner peace as we wait for the results. Don and his work friend took Lilah out for Chinese food to give Janelle and me quiet time together.

Janelle initially suggested going to a juice bar that has live music at night, but I'm not up for going out. That's when she proposed coming over for yoga. We're supposed to both be doing poses, but so far I haven't been in the mood to move.

I'm sprawled on the couch, while she's taken the opportunity to break out her highlights reel—first scorpion and now this.

"How do your hips flex like that?" I ask. "Even if I weren't pregnant I could never get mine to open that far."

"Actually, I've heard hips get *more* flexible during pregnancy. Something about hormones loosening the ligaments, I think."

"That's probably true. Hormones are loosening the ligaments in my feet. They've grown to boat oars." I point, and Janelle looks like she's about to comment. "Don't you dare say they're cute, like all my pregnant parts," I cut her off.

"No. I was going to agree they're monsters," she laughs.

"Nice. How long can you stay in that position?"

"I'm glad you asked." She immediately lowers one leg and then the other back to terra firma. "My hips were officially spent, but I've been waiting till you invited me to exit."

"You needed an invitation to take your feet off your neck?" I chuckle.

"I didn't want you to think I can't hold the pose."

Janelle rises and pulls me off the couch. She walks us to the spot we've set up for chair yoga, which I'm supposed to do while she does comparable standing poses. I stare at the seat without lowering myself.

"Not doing so great, huh?" she asks.

"I hate to admit it. But no." Tears well behind my eyes. I squeeze my lids to keep them from flowing.

"Don't 'hate to admit it,'" Janelle says softly. "It's understandable you're emotionally fragile."

I step back to face her. "I should be doing better. I know how to stay in the moment and not project into the future.

And anyway, there's seventy-five percent odds he's fine. More than that, even, if I believe I create my own reality, which I sort of do. Why am I letting my panic get ahead of the facts?"

"Because you're human. Because it's your baby you're talking about. You've done a great job not being a hysterical, hovering mom to Lilah. But concern is baked into the motherhood creed. You know: 'Mothers don't sleep, they just worry with their eyes closed.'"

"I've heard that expression. And I swore I would never be that kind of mother."

"And your spiritual practice tells you never to say *never*. Life throws curveballs. You react as best you can. And as authentically as you can, which right now means owning up to being afraid. You may create your reality, but Deuxie creates his too. So you can't know for certain what's in store."

My tears gush forth. Janelle reaches over and hands me a box of tissues.

"Okay, I'm ready to do the yoga," I say after wiping away the stream. We probably have only forty-five minutes before my family returns. If Don tries to keep Lilah out past her bedtime, her meltdown will be unbearable.

I plop onto the folding chair. Janelle takes her place on the mat nearby.

"You lead," I command. "After all, you're a certified yoga teacher now." While I was busy getting married and having babies, Janelle took the year-long certification program at our yoga center.

"Certified or not, you know as much as I do." She locks her fingers together and reaches her arms overhead.

"So not true. But whatever, I'm in the mood to follow." I mimic her movement. The stretch feels delicious.

"Let's start our *asanas* with downward-facing dog."

"You're nuts." I point to my abdomen. There's no way I can get my hands on the floor.

"With the chair, silly. Face it and plant your hands on the sides of the seat. Then step back with your feet apart and raise your butt."

"I can handle that." I follow her directions, while she goes down in the standard variety. With my butt raised and my back flat, it almost feels like I'm in the true pose.

We hold this for several minutes. Our yoga center emphasizes that the magic of yoga comes from breathing into a pose and maintaining it for a while.

Janelle breaks the peaceful silence. "Next is plank."

I try to envision dropping my hands to the floor from this position. "No way."

"On the chair," she says sweetly.

"How?" I begin to step my legs back farther, but Janelle stops me.

"Leave your legs there. Just straighten your body line." I press my butt down and, miraculously, I am sort of in plank. We hold and breathe.

"You're good at this," I say when I eventually stand, wrists crying out from the pressure. "Did you learn these modifications in teacher training?"

"Sort of. It wasn't part of the official curriculum, but there was a woman in my class with a physical disability. She did modifications for herself. I was an astute observer."

"What's next?"

We move to crescent lunge, where I face the chair and place one foot on the seat before stretching forward; and triangle pose, where I bend with my hand resting on the seat. Then Janelle has me sit for a spinal twist (as much as a person with a rock-solid gut can rotate) and neck rolls.

The final pose before our meditation is my beloved warrior. I like the power I feel as I stretch upward or forward—power I hope to bring to the yoga mission field, and to my amnio results. Still, I'm unsure about keeping steady now.

"Push the chair under your front leg," Janelle instructs, sensing my anxiety. "When you bend far enough, rest your thigh on it. Also, keep your hands on your hips as you get into position. For support."

"These are great ideas. I'm accepting that it's fine to have support." Janelle smiles, understanding I mean both physical and emotional support, and about more than yoga.

I step one foot back and bend my front leg, squaring my hips. Janelle does the same. Once I'm stable, I lift my arms overhead, palms close together, and arch my back a tad in warrior one. Energy flows through my arms and space opens in my chest. After we switch legs, we do warrior two, one arm thrust forward, the other stretching back. Warrior three is out, since there's no way I can balance on one leg.

I'm a resilient fighter, I tell myself through the series. *I have more strength than I know.*

I move to the couch and lean against its cushions, to be comfortable during our meditation. Janelle sits erect on her mat. She directs us to close our eyes.

For years I have focused on counting the breath as it goes in and out my nose. Recently, though, a teacher in an online yoga class had us focus on the sensation of the breath in the chest, silently repeating the words *rising, falling.* There's something about bringing my awareness deep into my body and focusing on a feeling rather than a count, I discovered, that quickly pulls me into my soul space.

The rising and falling envelop me in stunning peace—the calm oasis far below any crashing waves. Eventually, Janelle softly rings the Tibetan bowl she had grabbed from my bedroom altar.

"Bliss," I say, my voice floating out of me.

"Bliss," she echoes. She is quiet for a moment, as am I. Then she proclaims, as if inspired, "If you're faithful to your practice, your practice will be faithful to you."

"I love that!" I say, opening my eyes. "Where did you get that from?" Janelle's an even bigger spiritual book reader than I am. I get many suggestions of what to tackle from her explorations.

"James Finley. He studied with Thomas Merton, both Catholic monks. They've each written some great books."

"I've heard of Merton," I reply. "One of the Catholic authors I've been thinking of reading."

"The church is calling you back," Janelle teases.

"No way. But the spiritual Catholics have piqued my interest. I always thought those words were an oxymoron. I just started *Dark Night of the Soul.*"

"Still feeling like *you're* in a dark night?"

"That's what drew me to it." I rise from the couch and walk to the kitchen, grab the book from the table where I'd left it this morning, and return to Janelle. "But actually, it turns out St. John of the Cross didn't mean 'dark night' the way I thought. He means the emptiness of our soul that we should fill up with God."

I open to the verse I read this morning. "'Trust in God, who does not abandon those who seek him with a simple and righteous heart. He will not neglect to give you what you need for your path until he delivers you into that clear, pure light of love,'" I read aloud.

"Sounds hopeful," Janelle says. "I confess I didn't expect that in a 'dark night' book."

"To be honest, a lot of the book *is* dour. He disparages seekers who want God to make them feel good."

"God shouldn't make us feel good?"

"*I* believe that God—or, really, my higher self—absolutely should. Maybe I didn't read him right. The text is kind of confusing."

"I like what you just read. Repeat that last sentence, about how God won't neglect to give you what you need?"

Before I have a chance, the front door swings open. I hadn't heard the car pulling up or Don putting the key in the door.

"Mommaaaaaaaa!" Lilah yells, running to me and planting kisses over my entire arm.

I turn to face Janelle. Nothing more need be said.

Lilah is so wound up about Auntie Janelle being here that even though it's past her bedtime, Don can't peel her away to go upstairs. Janelle sits on the floor with Lilah as they spread their legs wide and roll a ball back and forth. Don and I take this opportunity to sneak into the kitchen for a few minutes of hugs.

"How are *you* doing?" I ask. "I know I've been wrapped up in myself, but I recognize this is hard on you too."

"Hanging in there." He pauses. "Actually, not completely. I made the mistake of going online today and reading about Tay-Sachs. What an awful disease." He steps back from our embrace. "Do you know that Tay-Sachs babies are perfectly fine for the first six months? That's almost more cruel, because you see how magnificent things could be. Then they start going downhill."

"Don't go there, Don." I lean in and encircle him in my arms again. "We're trying to stay in the moment. And in this moment, our precious baby is happily swimming around in here." I place his hand on my abdomen, watching him light up as Deuxie shifts. I allow his joy to lift myself up even more. It's striking how helping someone find their peace always benefits the person doing the helping.

Don tells me about his evening with Lilah. Tonight she discovered chow fun noodles, which she practically inhaled. And when her favorite *Frozen* song played over the sound system, she squealed with glee. After dinner, they stopped by Don's friend's house to walk his three-legged dog. Lilah kept asking how she could make the dog feel better.

"She'll be a loving big sister," I say, allowing myself the hopeful vignette of a regular family.

A loud crash pulls me into reality.

"We're fine in here," Janelle yells as Don and I race in. The ball hit the fake hibiscus tree in our living room, which has fallen inches from Lilah's extended leg. She is laughing uproariously.

"Knocked over!" Lilah says between cackles.

"I guess we got a bit carried away," Janelle responds sheepishly.

"No worries," I reassure her. "As long as no bones are broken."

"Broken bones," Lilah chants, as I realize I ignored the cardinal parenthood rule: Don't say words you don't want your child repeating. "Broken bones. Broken bones."

"I think it's time I put you to bed," I tell her.

"I'll do it," Janelle offers. "You two don't get enough time together."

"You sure? She's overtired. It's not going to be easy."

"Want Auntie Janelle to read you a story in bed?" Janelle asks Lilah.

"YES!" Lilah replies.

Janelle scoops her up and heads upstairs. I open my phone and turn to the streaming service to hear my new beloved *kirtan* performer, the Sikh singer-songwriter Snatam Kaur. They're playing my favorite, "By Thy Grace."

I take in the spiritual words before turning to Don. "Want to do that conscious heart touching practice from that workshop last year?"

He's totally in. He pulls over the folding chair so it faces the couch. He guides me onto the sofa and lowers himself on the chair. Lilah is banging around her toy box, no doubt pulling out the big-sister book that is her new everynight read. I tune the noise out by bringing awareness to how much I love my husband.

"I forgot how to start," I say.

"By synchronizing our breath, to tune in to one another." Don is breathing more quickly than I am, so I let him slow to my rhythm. I watch his chest until it mimics my measured pace. "Now, tune in to your thoughts," he instructs. "Don't change them. Simply become aware of what they are. Watch as if they're clouds floating gently past you in the sky."

My first thought is how delightful it is that Don is starting to sound like a professional yoga teacher. But I know even that thought, positive as it is, is judging, which means I'm not being mindful. I return to watching my thoughts. Over the next few minutes, ideas about whether Janelle needs help, why I'm right now having baby heartburn, and the pile of work on my office desk slide into my mind, but I successfully keep from entangling with them.

"Now become aware of your heart," Don says softly. "How it's beating inside your chest. Sending healthy, oxygenated blood to your body. Know this is where love begins. The love you give to yourself, and the love you share with the whole world."

"And with you," I smile.

"And with me," he beams. He pauses to take this in, his grin widening. "Now place your right palm on *my* heart." I do as he says, as he does the same on mine. "With this 'giving' hand, feel yourself passing love to me, as you are aware that I am sharing my love with you."

Don is looking intensely into my eyes. It feels awkward, but I remember this is part of the exercise. Something about the eyes being energetically connected to the heart. "Now place your left hand over my right hand, as I do the same to yours. Feel the hand rise and fall with the breath, with the outpouring of love."

A Deuxie-induced burp churns into my throat, but I'm able to watch it dispassionately. I focus on Don's hand on my heart, mine on his, and the energy I sense flowing between us. Before I tell him how much I love him, I remind myself I'm to keep that energy from dissolving into dialogue. Instead, I amp up my adoration through my fingers.

Feel his heartfelt love, I tell myself, understanding that receiving is as important as giving. *Know that he shares it honestly and graciously.* I suddenly notice what has always been true: Don treasures me unconditionally. Even if I can't completely keep my peace while waiting for the amnio results. Even if I might pass defective genes to our baby.

Life is a path he chooses to walk with me.

I marinate in this complete acceptance until I notice Janelle is standing at the bottom of the stairs. Self-conscious, I move to drop my right hand. But she shakes her head, places her finger over her lips to silence me, and blows a good-bye kiss.

She opens the front door and slips out into the darkness, leaving me to bask a little longer in Don's affection.

20

Two weeks later—and three long days before my amnio results will be in—I'm in the car with Janelle and Daria. It's a beautiful Saturday afternoon, and we're driving to Gretta's house for the baby shower-ish ceremony my friends have insisted they throw.

It's called a Blessingway, which Janelle discovered a couple of weeks after she and Gretta hosted my baby shower for Lilah. She's been kicking herself since—even though I've told her a thousand times it was a terrific shower. She so much wanted to host a Blessingway she offered to hold a second event before Lilah's birth. I told her that was ridiculous.

If Janelle were beaming any brighter now, we'd need eclipse glasses. She's excited to get her chance to shower me in this different way. The women had planned to wait until my eighth month, but they moved up the event to before I get my amnio results. They felt this celebration would be just the thing to raise my tottering mood. I'm grateful, because my mental state can use all the help it can get.

"What's a Blessingway again?" Daria asks from the back seat. I chuckle at the question, which Daria has asked me twice this past week. Apparently, my convoluted explanations haven't sufficed, probably because I barely know the answer.

"Conventional showers are about gifts for the baby," Janelle responds from the driver's seat. "A Blessingway is about spiritually honoring the mom and her birth. It's modeled on a Native American ceremony."

"How did you hear of this?" Daria asks. "I've been to dozens of showers and nobody's ever done a Blessingway."

"I read it in a book," Janelle replies, smiling at me.

I'd heard that Gretta and Janelle had a tussle over who would host this event at their home. Eventually Janelle took the high road and let it go. Another reason I love her.

During the twenty-minute drive, we all chat about the weather, new movies, and things that happened at each of our workplaces. I'm happy to be discussing these light topics.

I've hardly slept the past two weeks, waiting for the test results. At this point I'm eager just to know, even if the news is terrible. Well, maybe not, but this in-between space is destroying me, despite Janelle's constant reminders that Esther Hicks says nearly all of life is lived in in-between spaces.

We pull up to Gretta's apartment building and the valet guy takes the car. After getting through the front-desk security, we ride the elevator to her fourteenth-floor flat. From the hallway I hear the distinctive voices of Mallory, Sarah, Tina, and Mandy.

When the door opens, I'm happy to see Angelica is also here, along with two of our spiritual cousins. Thankfully, my friends have not invited my mother. She would hate that it's not a traditional shower.

As soon as we close the door behind us and move towards the main room, the door reopens, revealing Krista and Daniella from work. I'm momentarily stunned that these women are spiritually open enough to be here. I've been so busy hiding my own woo-woo side at the office, it never occurred to me that other people might be keeping theirs buried too.

"Wow. I didn't expect you two at this party," I say, unfiltered.

"We can leave if you prefer," Daniella jokes.

"You know I didn't mean that." I give each woman a hug as she passes in the narrow hallway. "I didn't know my friends invited anyone from the office."

"Just the nicest ones," Krista smiles. "Janelle and I have gotten to know one another when she's come around to meet you for lunch. We've been talking spiritual stuff. She called to invite me and asked if anyone else from work would be into this. I said Daniella."

"I would have said Jason if men were invited," I interject. "I don't know if he's into this, but I'm the luckiest woman in the world to have him as my boss."

"*I'm* the luckiest woman—to have you as mine," Krista says.

"Okay, okay, hold those compliments for later," Sarah pushes in, ushering everyone past the Buddha in the foyer and into Gretta's living room.

When Don and I moved into our home, Gretta bought a three-bedroom with a humongous living room, fifteen-foot-high ceilings, and windows overlooking the river in this luxury apartment complex. She lives here alone, unless you count her Maltese, Legend, so I never understood why she needs so much space. Janelle says Gretta moved here to keep up with the Lornas. I'm not sure if that's true—Janelle has her own baggage when it comes to Gretta—but she did get Legend the day after I had Lilah, so who knows.

Throw pillows have been arranged in a circle on the floor, with one throne chair decked out in colorful silks and flowers, presumably for me. My favorite dark chocolate bars beckon from a corner table. Snatam Kaur's "RaMaDaSa" rings through the speakers, a song honoring sun, moon, earth, and infinity. I'm touched they have incorporated these details.

"Since everybody's heeeere, let's get started," Mallory trills. "The chair is for Lorna, but if anyone else needs one we can get it." Nobody takes her offer.

I excuse myself and race off to the bathroom. Then I settle myself into the chair, which thankfully is positioned as part of the circle. I'd hate being the grand marshal at the head of the parade.

Sarah emerges from a bedroom carrying a stack of floral crowns. She passes one to each woman, saving the most elaborate for me.

"These are gorgeous." Mandy places hers atop her relaxed black hair; she looks like Cleopatra. "Did you make them, Sarah?"

"It was nothing," Sarah blushes.

"It certainly *is* something," I say. "I'm touched you spent so much time creating these gorgeous things. It means a lot." My eyes threaten to mist, primarily from gratitude, but worry is never far behind any of my tears these days. I sniff the delicious flowers before placing them on my head, determined to stay present.

Gretta heads for the kitchen and returns with a large bowl filled with steaming water. She places it at my feet. "This is the first of many ways we will pamper and honor you today," she says to me, grabbing a bottle of essential oils off an end table and sprinkling in a drop. She invites the other women to take a different oil and join her. I slip off my sandals and dip my feet into the fragrant water. All tension in my toes melts away.

"Everyone, close your eyes and take long, slow inhalations, including Lorna," Janelle says. I didn't expect my feet could relax any further, but they do as we sit for several minutes, breathing deeply. Gretta pulls out a towel, seemingly from nowhere, and slowly begins to dry me.

"Next we're going to take turns massaging Lorna's arms, legs, neck, back, feet, and her bulging belly," Mallory sings.

"One person at a time," Sarah clarifies. "Otherwise we might knock her over."

Each woman comes forward, spending a few minutes rubbing a different body part. This surpasses every massage I've ever experienced, since each stroke is offered with love. Recalling the joy of receiving, I allow myself to accept this completely.

Gretta is last, and she rubs my belly. She moves her hands in a circular, clockwise motion that is said to clear energy in this "sacral" chakra, while quietly humming "vam," the mantra associated with this section. At this moment it's hard to believe Gretta once made fun of my spiritual interests. She ends by placing her hands flat against my bump. "This boy is so lucky, since you're going to be the best mother to him. And I can tell that he knows it."

"Amen," Daria replies, kicking off a round of amens from all the women, including Daniella and Krista, who clearly are not wigged out at all.

"I know you're smart, multitasking women, so next we're going to do a few things simultaneously," Janelle says to everyone. Out comes out a large roll of yellow ribbon. Mallory grasps the loose end and begins unspooling it around the circle until each woman holds some.

"Everyone has a small scissor next to you, to use in a few minutes," Janelle says. (I hadn't noticed this. So much for mindfulness.) We're instructed to hang onto the ribbon as one woman at a time lets go of her end and stands in the center, saying something they appreciate about me. I redouble my determination to receive these compliments graciously.

Angelica begins, stepping before me. "Lorna is such a loving mother to her beautiful daughter. And she will be equally loving to two—or more than two."

"More than two?" I ask, as titters erupt. "You know something I don't, Sis? I am not having twins."

"Certainly not. I meant down the road. I picture you with a whole brood."

"It's a good thing I started too late to have said brood," I say. "We have no plans to go beyond this one."

"Let's not break the focus," Mandy interjects. "Keep your comments serious so Lorna can soak them in."

The compliments that follow, about my kindness, friendship, work talents, generosity, and even my looks, overwhelm me. After each woman speaks, she snips off a section of the ribbon. I notice that the ribbon is falling to pieces, which I have been trying hard to keep myself from doing.

When the last woman has sung her praise, Janelle asks everyone to cut more of the ribbon until each holds an eight-inch section. "Now we tie the ribbons onto our wrist," she says. "Feel free to get help from your neighbor, because like birth and motherhood, some things are best not done alone."

"As you slip on your ribbon, say aloud, *I love you, Lorna*," Gretta adds, "followed by, *This will remind me of our bond*." The women comply.

Once everyone except me has done this, Angelica reaches over to tie mine. "I love you, Lorna. And this will remind me of our bond," she says as she makes the knot around my arm. My heart feels so full with joy there is no place for any other emotion.

"Later, we're going to light a candle," Janelle continues. "At that time we'll tell you what you can do with the ribbons when Lorna goes into labor."

Gretta invites everyone into the dining room, where a large table is decorated in gold. There are finger sandwiches, little bowls of spinach-and-lentil salad, tiny quiches, scones, pastries, and homemade cookies—the latter apparently made by several of the women, who gathered at Mandy's home last night.

"What a glorious high tea," I say, taking a cucumber-and-goat cheese sandwich. And there is tea galore, carried in pretty mugs from the kitchen by Sarah and Tina. There are eight different flavors of loose leaves, served with colorful animal-shaped infusers that Gretta says are party favors.

Mine is a bear, which reminds me of Lilah's new favorite teddy. I smile to think of my girl.

After the feast—and another run to the bathroom—I am ushered back to the living room. Gifts are as integral a part of a Blessingway as they are in a baby shower, Tina tells me. But these gifts are to pamper me, not to clothe or feed my future child.

Mallory and Sarah pull over a table piled with festively wrapped presents. I am eager to unwrap everything.

First up, from Krista, is a box of organic essential-oil bath bombs. She's heard me talk about appreciating the buoyancy I feel in our home's large tub. Next is an herbal tea sampler from Mandy, which elicits a groan from Mallory. She hands me her gift—same company, nearly identical tea selection. "Great minds think alike, I guess," Mandy shrugs.

"One can never have too much tea," I say.

Angelica bought a gift certificate for a salt therapy center. Apparently, you sit in a cave-like room with salt strewn around the walls and floor. My sister admits it sounds odd (quite an admission, coming from her) but says it helps open her sinuses and feels relaxing.

Daniella brought a package of stretchmark oil and "bottom" balm. Leave it to the engineer to think about the mechanics of birth. A box of artisan Swiss dark chocolate is from Gretta, who knows my indulgences even if sugar isn't on our *pitta* plan. Janelle gifts a long body pillow; the store clerk told her it's the best thing for helping a pregnant woman sleep.

When all the items have been opened, I walk around the circle hugging each of the women. I take a moment to send her my appreciation and love. Who else could make me feel this good when I'm on the cusp of potential disaster? It's a testament to all of them that I've hardly thought about the amnio at all.

"Gifts aren't finished," Gretta says, urging me back into the chair.

"I've gotten something from everyone," I protest, scanning the room.

"One more. From all of us." Sarah lifts a small envelope from her purse.

It's a gift certificate for a two-hour couple's massage and mud bath at a local day spa. Don and I are to use it after the baby is born. It comes with a handmade coupon promising one of them will watch Lilah and the baby when we go.

"You guys—" I start to say, but my voice catches in my throat. I need not say more. These are the women who complete my life. Who are there when I need them. And who will shore me up if the amnio results are bad.

As I stand and others rise from their floor cushions, Mandy stops us. "One more thing," she says. Everyone returns to their places. Mandy holds a bag from which she removes a white soy candle in a glass container. She hands the candle to me, then takes out a dozen smaller white candles and passes them to each of the women.

Mandy lights my candle, then has me pass it to Angelica, who is instructed to light her candle with mine. Angelica passes mine to the next woman, until the candle of everyone is lit. With the circle radiant, my candle returns to me.

"Everyone close your eyes and set the vision for a beautiful, easy birth for our Lorna," Mandy instructs. "You can make that wish too," she says to me. "I'm sure you want that more than we do." I picture Deuxie sliding out more peacefully than Lilah did.

"Ladies, open your eyes and blow out your candles." She pauses as we do. "When Lorna lets someone know she has gone into labor, she'll tell the rest of us, and we light our own candle. To be in solidarity. And so the wishes we just made will float their way back to her."

"Also," Gretta adds, as if she's just remembered, "when you hear that Lorna is in labor, cut off your yellow ribbon and place it around the base of your candle."

"Just make sure it doesn't catch fire," Daniella says.

I'm touched by this ritual, knowing that these women will energetically be with me as I give birth. "I love that you'll be there, even though you won't physically be there," I say.

"That's the idea," Mandy says, "although if you *want* us physically there as you deliver, we'd be thrilled."

"Not all of us would be thrilled," Tina says. "Blood makes me queasy."

"Ditto," Mallory says. "Although for my Lorna, I'd do it."

"You're all off the hook. Don wants it to be intimate between us."

"You mean the intimate group of the two of you, the midwife, the nurse . . . " Gretta jokes.

"Have you decided where you're giving birth?" Mallory asks. I had talked to them weeks ago about my struggle with this decision.

"I still don't know. Probably a hospital. But maybe a birthing center, since it seems like a compromise between a hospital, which I didn't love with Lilah, and my home, which seems scary."

"She'll decide for sure when her water breaks," Sarah laughs.

"Hopefully before then," I say. "You're all welcome to come meet Deuxie wherever we are the day after he's born."

"We're holding you to that," Gretta says, as we all start hugging in anticipation of leaving.

I glance at the ribbons around their wrists and the waiting candles in their hands. Suddenly, I feel like the luckiest woman alive.

21

My ringing cell phone makes me jump. Today's the day I'm expecting my amnio results. I close my office door, take a deep breath, and realize it is Don.

He claims he's checking to see how I'm doing. Really, I surmise, he's reaching out to shore up his own wobbly state. We talk for a minute, spend another air kissing, then say goodbye.

I've been surprised I'm getting work done today. I thought the entire day might be lost, but the support from my Blessingway is carrying me through. I've even kept up my appetite enough to have lunch—a chicken-and-broccoli salad Krista and Daniella bought me. They've been periodically walking by my office to keep a watchful eye.

I can't believe someone set up a system where they give you potentially life-altering news over the phone. The nurse said they do it because the results don't always come in exactly when expected. If they schedule an appointment, the news might sit on their desk for several days. Alternatively, couples might trek over when the report has not yet arrived.

Still, it seems heartless to hear this from a disembodied voice over the ether.

At two o'clock, the phone rings with the number I recognize as the gynecologist's office. All my sujaling by my altar this morning—an extra half hour—is suddenly for naught; my chest tightens like a tourniquet. I can hardly get air in as I click on the phone.

"He-e-e-llo," I croak, slipping the earpiece into my ears so no one walking by can overhear.

"Is this Lorna Crawford?" the crisp man's voice asks.

"Ye-es," I manage.

"This is Dr. Barnes." The longest pause in history. The truss cinches. "I'm afraid I have bad news. The amnio came back positive for Tay-Sachs."

The tightness has moved to my ears, which are pressing hard against my head. I'm waiting for him to say not to worry, that my child has the curable kind, or maybe that there's a treatment Deuxie can get while he's still inside me or right after he emerges that will make him whole.

He doesn't.

"I'm sending this report back to Ms. Eng and your midwife, who can help you prepare. I see you're six months along, so termination is not an option. I'm really sorry, Ms. Crawford."

He hangs up the phone. *How can he hang up the phone?* He first has to tell me there's been an error, that Deuxie's enzymes are fine, that they're going to work perfectly for the eighty or hundred years of his life. Instead he has basically condemned my boy to not seeing his fifth birthday.

I rip the buds out of my ears, hoping that's been the cause of the squeezing, but taking them out doesn't stop the pressure. My eyes are falling out of their sockets. My tongue feels so loose it's about to be swallowed. My chest is no longer constricted, but that's because it's dropped out the window and to the ground below. I'm aware of every pore in my skin, burning, burning, burning.

Tears have apparently been flowing since the end of the call, but I'm only now conscious of the river on my shirt. I have no throat, no voice, no ability to utter a sound.

I feel a boiling urgency to call Don and let him know, but I cannot do it. That will shatter my heart into more pieces than could ever be put back together.

I grab my purse and race out the door, not stopping for anyone—including Krista, whom I hazily hear calling my name. When I slam my car door behind me, I have a moment of lucidity, so I text Erin to please stay with Lilah. I know Don is not going to be able to tend to her after he gets word.

I want to gently and lovingly tell him—the opposite of the cold cruelty delivered by the physician—but my fingers won't dial his number. Instead, I watch dispassionately as they type out the text *It's Tay-Sachs* and hit send.

I drive, and drive, and drive. I must get away from this news, from my life. I'm not heading somewhere, because anywhere I go will have me and my swollen baby belly in it. I'm simply moving to keep the world from catching up. I vaguely hear my phone ring, the same way I vaguely hear traffic on the road as I roar ahead. But I don't, I can't, answer it. It will be Don. Talking to him about the results will make it real. The phone rings several more times until eventually I stop paying attention.

I cross out of New Jersey into Delaware. I haven't been to this state since Gretta and I vacationed at the shore when we graduated from college, a wonderful week spent exploring wildlife refuges and partying in the towns. How different my life was then. How innocent it was of the most horrible heartbreak that could ever strike a human being.

I'm nearly out of gas when I reach Rehoboth Beach. I pull into a parking lot near the ocean, and have the longest, hardest cry of my life. Yelps punctuate every sob until, spent, I can weep no more.

I open the car door, grab my purse, and walk onto the sand. I plop myself down by the ocean, not caring that I may not be able to get myself up.

I look at my phone. Don has sent fifteen increasingly frantic text messages. I know how unfair I'm being—making him worry about my safety on top of his own grief. I compose a text. *I'm okay. Just need some time.*

He responds immediately. *Please call soon. We're in this together.*

Are we? I know he's hurting. But did he get the literal kick in the womb I just did? He hasn't been carrying Deuxie inside his body, giving him life with every breath, swallow, and heartbeat. He won't pass this baby into the world from his uterus, or nurse him with his breasts.

Don is a fantastic father to Lilah, I know that. But, at least for the first year of a child's life, there is a difference. There's an energetic umbilical cord attaching Lilah to me. It has lessened as she has grown, but I still sense it. Over time, I know parents can be equals—I see that with Angelica and Yonatan—but early on, the mother gives more. And early on may be all the time we have with Deuxie.

Dusk has fallen. The indigo hour. I look around, my eyes seeing for the first time since I arrived. This has always been my favorite time of day, but now the brilliant sky brings forth no emotion.

My clothes are covered in dampened sand. Normally, the mess would bother me, but today it matches the untidiness that has become my life. A mosquito is biting my ankles, but I can't work up the energy to swat it, never mind to scratch the itching.

After a while, thanks to the crisp ocean air, my head and body begin returning to their natural places. I sense the bone and muscle inside my feet. I feel my fingers, which had so violently disconnected themselves from my hands, I can't fathom how I drove these past hours. I listen to the crashing waves and command myself to become conscious of the moving liquid inside me.

Let nothing disturb you. Let nothing frighten you. Everything passes away except God. This phrase from the *Prayers of Teresa of Avila* rings in my head. Her notion that nothing—and she meant *nothing*—should scare me begins to open my heart.

I gulp ocean air, then turn to my womb. It's painful to picture Deuxie swimming in there. It's as if I've dropped cyanide into his pool. He kicks me hard. In anger that my mutated gene has poisoned him? Or a message to stop seeing myself as his murderer?

I flash back to that moment at the yoga center sound-healing event, when Deuxie "responded" to my question of whether he was okay with his firm declaration: *In this world, where body and spirit are one, how can any of us be anything but?*

Maybe he is trying to remind me.

I clear my mind of this thought, of all thought, and observe the swirl of orange energy enveloping my womb. I sit in this representation of my motherhood, the sacral chakra, for several minutes. The orange grows brighter. It travels from my belly to my heart, where it merges with the green of the heart chakra. Rather than turn to mushy brown, each color remains vibrant, albeit intertwined.

A new message emerges inside this palette, clearly from Deuxie: *Love is what I am. Love is what you feel. Love is what we are.*

Those beautiful thoughts so fill me I rise to standing. The sun has set and nobody is around, so I strip down to my bra and underwear, leave my clothes and purse on the sand, and stroll into the water. The gentle waves hug me. I step to chest level, because I want Deuxie to float. I laugh as I realize he's always floating. I guess now he's floating in water that's floating in water.

The waves are cleansing, washing away some of my grief. Not grief, I realize, since I'll never stop grieving. Grieving for a baby with a serious disease. Grieving for the life he will not have. Grieving for Don and my lost dreams for our family. Grieving that Lilah will have a dying brother.

But the anger and resistance that have barnacled to the grief since we got the results from that genetic carrier screen are slowly floating out with the tide. I hasten the process by picturing these raw emotions as red parabolas and watch them swim far, far, out to sea.

I emerge from the water as the full moon is rising. I know the moon affects the tides, and what is the womb but a private ocean? Deuxie and I appreciate this beautiful, influential orb floating in the sky.

I don't have a towel, so I dry myself with my blazer and slip my skirt and shirt back on. I grab my purse and walk towards my car, observing every step in the sand, happy to realize I'm fully returned to my body. With each footprint, Deuxie and I leave our mark, as we all always leave an energetic stamp on the universe.

There are two long roads ahead of me. One I will travel to return to Don and Lilah and my life. The other is winding and unknown. But I'm starting to feel that maybe I can traverse both without crashing.

22

My inner peace lasts exactly nine stoplights. With every mile I drive, my anxiety threatens to blossom. I almost turn around several times. Once, fleetingly, I ponder driving into the sea. Of course I wouldn't do that, because Lilah will need a mother for a very long time, even if Deuxie will not.

My mind slips to loss. Will this tragic reality cleave a fissure between Don and me? Will the early death of her brother scar Lilah for life? Will the grief of watching my baby decline cost me my sanity?

I think about all the dark chocolate and the red wine I've stupidly been avoiding since I found out I'm pregnant. *Healthy mother, healthy baby*, I used to believe. *Think positively, and only good things can come to you.* All a big joke.

After getting gas, I steer my car onto the highway that will eventually bring me home. But if home is a state of mind, mine is already in destruction. It may look fine outside, but the foundation beneath is crumbling fast.

I try to place my restless mind on my breath: *rising, falling, rising, falling.* I can't keep my attention there, because the word *falling* is fraught with toddlerhood—a state my boy may never reach. After several failed rounds, I cast about for other tools to calm me. I'm sure I know dozens, but at the moment my brain is a bucking bronco that cannot supply a single option.

I flip on the radio, sensing even a bronco is soothed by the sound of music. Bruce Springsteen is crooning about his depression, feeling lost and low. When I first heard this *Wrecking Ball* song, I could not relate. My life was so perfect—I'd met Don, made up with my mother, and found deep meaning in the spiritual universe. Now Bruce's lyrics feel as if he's peering inside my own wrecked heart. I'm too fragile for this rawness, so I flip to other stations, then give up and click the radio off.

After an hour of driving, where my terrors periodically consume me, I recall that psychological exercise Janelle had me do: singing my fears to disarm them. I realize this practice may not apply in this situation, since the fears you croon are imagined ones that never appear. That I'm the mother of a baby with an incurable disease that will kill him before elementary school is not catastrophic, worst-case thinking.

It's the truth.

I finally reach my exit and turn off the highway. I'm struck by the odd juxtaposition between the mundane actions of driving my car—recognizing a landmark, stopping at lights, stepping on the gas, turning the wheel—and the heart-stopping fact of my baby's condition.

Must I fixate on it? Worry about what's to come? It's equally true that right this moment Deuxie is happily ensconced in my abdomen, same as he's always been. It's not like he's dying today, I think, as I switch on the music again, this time to calming classical.

"Dying, dying, dying, dying, dying, dying, dying," I recite aloud, deciding it can't hurt to try the exercise of condensing my worry to a word. Then I combine my word with the music, crooning the "Dying, dying, dying, dying, dying, dying" to the rhythms of Tchaikovsky. Voicing this horrible reality actually lifts the fog.

At the next stoplight, I suddenly notice something I haven't the entire trip. Esther Hicks would say this is evidence I have raised my vibration, because it was there all along but at a frequency too high for me to access. Janelle has left a string of text messages on my phone. Don no doubt called her when he was looking for me, then circled back to deliver the bombshell. It's interesting that right after I do the exercises Janelle led me to, she enters my car, so to speak, to pep me up.

Thinking about you.

Loving you.

Loving Deuxie.

Surrounding you with healing light.

The next three are XOs and hearts. Last is a blonde angel emoji, which I gather is Deuxie, even though I've always pictured him with Don's brown hair. This cheers me enough that I'm able to drive the rest of the way in relative peace.

It's eleven o'clock when I exhaustedly pull into the driveway. The house is black but for a light in our bedroom. Through the window, I see the top of Don's head. He's sitting on the floor by the altar.

Part of me feels the urge to slap the car into reverse, because walking into our house and seeing Don may slay me. But I can't stay away from my husband and my little girl forever.

I close the car door behind me and take slow, mindful steps up the walk. I'm paying attention to my every move as if my life depends on my concentration. I'm certain my sanity does.

Don doesn't hear me open the front door. At least I think he doesn't, because he hasn't called out to me like he usually would. Or maybe he has heard and is ignoring me, hurt that I ran in both of our moment of need.

A wave of sudden nausea hits, so I bolt for the kitchen. I pull a glass from the cabinet, open the refrigerator, and remove my pitcher of peppermint tea.

I have been drinking this every evening over ice and a sprig of mint. As I sip it—sans the ice I'm sure would make me hurl—it settles my stomach. This will be the last time I can ever down this tea, now that it's forever fused with the day I learned Deuxie is on a path to perishing.

Really, aren't we all? I think, as I place the glass in the sink. I remove my shoes and drop them into the bin by the front door. Even in this horrible moment, I somehow still care about keeping my carpet clean.

I plod up the stairs. Death *is* something that's going to happen to all of us. Maybe part of why I am so unnerved is the way this news puts that front and center. Don, Angelica, Janelle, my mother, myself, even Lilah are inevitably heading beyond the veil. Of course, the idea of burying my baby before he's old enough to write his name is singularly terrifying—although I notice I no longer have the emotional reserve to feel sad.

"I'm home," I say as I enter the bedroom.

Don turns to face me. He is indeed sitting by the altar, the tears staining his face telling me he hasn't exactly been meditating. He hands are gripped around my statue of contemplating Jesus—as if he hopes to get the benefits by association.

"I'm glad you're back," he says softly. "I was worried."

"I'm really sorry. I couldn't stop myself from running. The irony is that I took Deuxie—the source of my anxiety—along with me."

"Because you can't run," he pronounces coldly. "None of us can. 'We must be willing to encounter darkness and despair when they come up, and face them, over and over again if need be, without running away or numbing ourselves in the thousands of ways we conjure up to avoid the unavoidable.'" He reaches over and holds up mindfulness master Jon Kabat-Zinn's classic, *Wherever You Go, There You Are*, from which he has memorized those lines.

He doesn't stand to greet me. I guess I was expecting him to leap off the floor and intensely scoop me into his arms. Maybe I gave up that right when I chose to leave alone, rather than affirm we are in this together—a pair, a family. Although it wasn't a choice. It was a compulsion.

I walk towards Don and sit next to him. I grasp his hand and look into his bloodshot eyes. "I really am sorry. I do want us to be in this together. I hope you're still willing."

He pauses. I watch the wrinkle lines in his forehead slowly soften. Then he hugs me fully. We both cry—loud, sobbing wails, as if the primal creature of grief I've wrestled with all evening has broken free and joined the animal in Don. Only clinging to him keeps me from being eaten.

We sit and bawl for many minutes. I can't tell if it is fifteen or fifty. Finally, I feel myself quieting down.

When I can catch enough of my breath to speak, I remember our daughter. "We're. Going. To. Wake. Lilah. If. We. Keep. This. Up," I say, between heaves.

"She's. At. Angelica's," he struggles to reply.

"Good. Thinking," I say, and we both laugh. Our cackles become as uncontrollable as our sobs had been, well out of proportion to the joke. Finally, the laughter dwindles.

Don says he needs to do something to settle his frayed nerves. I suggest our go-to: chanting.

"Do you think we have it in us?" he asks.

"I think we need to find it in there."

I turn to face the altar. Don starts a round of *"Hare Krishna,"* more robustly than I'd imagined he had the strength for. When I first heard this chant years ago at my yoga center, I worried the place was under the sway of the cult that used to hang out in airports, the one that got *Mad Men*'s Paul Kinsey to drop out of life and wear a yellow toga. Then my teacher explained it's an intonation to spirit—*Hare* and *Krishna* being two of the names for God in an ancient Indian text. I realized chanting it is a way to reclaim this ancient melody. Maybe now it will also help me reclaim my inner peace.

"Hare Krishna, Hare Krishna, Krisha Krisha, Hare Hare," Don belts. I return in kind, surprising myself. We continue with call and response. By the time we finish, I'm feeling almost human.

After agreeing to create a game plan in the morning, we ready ourselves for bed. As I brush my teeth, I recall all the mindfulness techniques I've used this evening—body scan, breathing, repeating and singing my fears, dunking into the ocean, chanting . . . Each has helped for at least a little while.

I catch the rising thought that a while is not a lifetime, recognizing that it is going to have to be enough. If I can stay mindful minute by minute—even if I lose it in some of the seconds in-between—I am doing well.

Our ringing doorbell pulls me out of a bottomless sleep. When I open my eyes, I'm surprised there's so much light streaming into the room. Don is an immobile log beside me.

I am shocked to see it's nearly noon. "Wake up," I nudge him. "Someone's at the door."

"No one's at the door," he groggily replies, eyes glued shut. The doorbell rings again. "Oh! That will be Angelica bringing Lilah home!"

He peers at his cell phone clock, then bolts upright. "She told me she had a meeting with her interfaith commission today and had to return Lilah by noon." He's running around the room now, pulling sweat pants over his boxers. The doorbell rings a third time. "I'm coming," he yells, as if they could possibly hear.

I heave myself out of bed after Don leaves. I walk to the bathroom where I glance into the mirror. There's so much puffy skin around my eyes someone could lay their head there. I splash water on my face, knowing I don't have the energy to camouflage it with makeup. I toss on my maternity yoga pants and go down to meet my daughter.

Lilah is already playing with her stuffed animals in the living room, oblivious to the news that has turned our family on its head. Her joy gives me pause. As I was descending the stairs, I thought I needed to tell her that her baby brother is going to die. Now I realize the stupidity of that thinking. Why should I ruin her happiness now by forcing her to anticipate bad things in the future?

As is often the case, my daughter has provided a crucial lesson: Why ruin *my own* happiness now, either?

"How are you?" Angelica turns to face me, care floating on her every word.

"Sometimes hanging in, sometimes not," I answer truthfully. She lets go of Don's hand, which I hadn't noticed she was holding.

"That's how it's going to be for a while." She encircles me in her arms.

"Momma!" Lilah interjects, suddenly noticing I'm in the room. "Come see what I'm playing." Angelica pecks my cheek and releases me.

"Sorry I can't stay longer," Angelica says, walking to the door. "I'm supposed to be in Trenton in just over an hour. I'll call you later. And if you need something, please, please ask." She directs this last comment to Don. It's clear she knows me well enough to understand this will be hard for me.

When the door closes, I see that Lilah has moved to her blocks and is building a large, shallow structure, which she explains is a sporting goods store. I'm guessing Angelica had to stop at one this morning. Careful not to knock over her creation, I reach out and lift her, giving her a massive squeeze. I'm hoping she'll return the gesture, but she's already wriggling to be put down.

Don joins her on the floor and follows her orders about where to place the wooden pieces. She's very specific. "The red goes *here*. That's the yoga clothes." Yup, Angelica took her, since I tend to buy my own yoga gear at Target.

They sit and play for an hour, me admiring from the couch. Twice I try to get up to make the coffee I need to energize myself, but Lilah is so insistent I not leave the room I sit back down. The first time, I did so to keep her contented. The second, I realized how joyful I am watching her play. Her happiness is my fuel.

Eventually they run out of blocks. Lilah yawns. It's past her nap time. Don carries her up the stairs, and I follow.

"I love you, Momma! And Daddy!" she says, as he places her on our bed, not even trying to get her into her room.

"We love you too, precious," we say in unison.

"I had fun with Aunt An-glel-ica," she says, adding the extra *L* that always brings a smile to my face. If I could keep her from ever learning to pronounce it properly, I would.

"So glad, darling," I say.

"I'm going to her house when my bro-rer is being born," she says, repeating the lines I've been feeding her for weeks to prepare her for the delivery, which will likely be in the hospital.

"That's right, love," Don says. I force away the thought that I'm going to have to prepare her for other, uglier things too. Why project?

I will take that on as my mantra, I think, as Lilah hugs us, snuggles into our comforter, and falls asleep. *Why project?*

Because even when the worst of it arrives, the way to honor Deuxie's life will be to keep living in the present moment.

For one thing, as Don discovered, Deuxie will be absolutely perfect for the first six months of his life. But even after he gets sick, to keep my two children—not to mention Don and myself—from being destroyed, I must not project.

I commit myself to do more than tolerate this unplanned situation. I hereby make a solemn vow to accept, even embrace, in every moment whatever comes our way.

23

After taking a week off work to get my bearings, the first three days spent largely in bed, I'm ready to go back to the office. I debated with myself how private to keep the news, but decided to be honest with everyone. I already told Jason, who was a dream, suggesting in one of several phone calls that he might be able to get me more than our company's standard maternity leave, so I can savor the time with a healthy baby.

As I dress for work this morning, Lilah plays with her dolls at my feet. Life feels so normal; I'm determined to keep it that way. I'm nearly finished with my makeup when Erin opens the front door.

Lilah and I walk downstairs. Or, to be precise, I walk downstairs; Lilah hops while squealing. She hasn't seen Erin since I left a message on her voicemail about the situation—*I have to stop calling it that*—and told her to take off until today.

Erin helps Lilah set up her favorite cooperative board game—one where all players join together to corral the horses and bring them in ahead of a storm. Before they start playing, she saunters over.

"I'm so sorry," she says, giving me a tender hug.

"Thanks." I release her grasp. "It's different than we expected, sure, but we're determined not to make it *bad*." So far, the meditation, yoga, and mindfulness I have obsessively done these past days is paying dividends.

"I have a cousin whose daughter has Tay-Sachs," Erin whispers, so Lilah can't hear.

This shocks me. "Really? I don't know anyone who's ever had this disease. And you know someone who has it *now*?"

"My dad's side is Jewish. Apparently Sara was tested before her pregnancy, but she has a rare mutation that didn't show up in the Ashkenazi panel."

"Why didn't she get the full gene sequence?"

"From what Sara said, that's just coming into vogue. Only the big labs are doing it."

I suddenly realize how lucky I am that Sally sent me to one of those labs. If my baby is going to have a terminal illness, I prefer to know. I note the irony of considering myself lucky. But in some ways, maybe I am. It's certainly helpful to view the situation—*Lorna, he's your baby, not a situation*—that way.

"Anyway," Erin continues, "I told my cousin about you. She said if you want to meet her and Justina, she would welcome it."

I picture myself walking into this woman's home, coming face-to-face with the realities of this disease—a child who can't sit, or speak, or maybe even swallow without a suction machine. I do not want this.

Down the road, as the symptoms make their forceful appearance and I have questions about how to care for my child, I'll be glad of her offer. But I'm giving birth to a beautiful boy, and I'm determined to keep his first few months as normal as possible. To do that, I can't know too much about what's to come.

"Please thank your cousin, but I don't think I want to."

"She thought as much. Truthfully, it was my suggestion. Sara thinks you shouldn't meet yet. And that you shouldn't read about what to expect. Just enjoy your early time with Deuxie like she got to do with Justina, because she didn't know." Erin walks over to Lilah and they start their game.

As I gather up my purse and blazer, my mind flashes to the popular *What to Expect* book, which details every month of a baby's development. I am reading this book with Deuxie's pregnancy as I did with Lilah's, but I take care to never get ahead of the grape or tomato or cantaloupe that is my baby's existence. *No need to look into the future,* I thought even as far back as the first time I cracked open the book.

No need, indeed.

I kiss Lilah goodbye—she seems perfectly content to have me go, as she and Erin have rounded up several stallions—and slip into my car. I'm surprised how excited I feel to be getting back to work. So many aspects of our sun-protection promotion are piling up on my desk, and I yearn to be in on all the decisions.

When I arrive, everyone seems to be avoiding me. The receptionist grabs for the phone and is talking to nobody as I pass her. Others look away as I stride down the hall. I guess

Jason told them all. Part of me is pleased he did the hard work of explaining, saving me from the task.

Still, I feel like shouting to all of them, "Tay-Sachs is not contagious!" But I stay mum. Maybe they need time to get used to the idea. I certainly did—and still do.

No one disturbs me all morning, which gives me plenty of time to make progress on my events. At lunchtime, I grab a chicken salad from the corner deli and mindlessly eat at my desk, mildly annoyed no one thought to ask me to go out.

By my third mouthful, I realize that on some level, I have been pushing them away. I'm nervous about what to say to people who know my news. Perhaps my colleagues sense this and are giving me space until I figure out how to talk about this situa—

Hurray! I finally caught myself.

After tossing away half my chicken salad—I have little appetite—I spend twenty minutes doing my favorite full-senses mindfulness practice. I start by taking in the smells, the sense I am most apt to ignore. Somebody is drinking a vanilla cola, since there's a sweet whiff coming from outside my room. I open my ears: the office is quiet. Still, I make out the whoosh of a copy machine and the occasionally ringing phone. I draw my attention to the interior of my legs, sensing how much energetic movement always takes place in them, while I'm usually oblivious.

A ripe banana, a snack I brought from home, sits on the credenza. I lean over and grab it, ready to engage my sense of taste. I tug at the peels, then take a tiny bite and squish the morsels around my mouth. My tongue clamps and swishes, resisting the urge to swallow until the pieces become mush.

I shift my gaze to the world beyond my window. I hunt down my favorite banyan tree, my eyes traveling from its solid trunk to its glistening green leaves, to its aerial prop roots launching from branch to soil. When I widen my vision, I see a small boy racing around the tree, weaving among its woody roots. He's too far to make out in detail, but from his size and enthusiasm, I peg him to be six or seven.

An age my son will never reach.

Stop projecting, Lorna. Mindfulness is the nonjudgmental awareness of what is, I remind myself. And right now, *what is* is a young boy zooming around an ancient tree. *Do not label it as bad or good.*

I return my sight to the child, while also maintaining my observation of the whirring copier, the dynamism inside my limbs, the vanilla cola smell, the lingering flavor of the banana. When my phone bell indicates the end of the session, the sound resonates throughout my body.

An hour of significant work progress later, Krista has finally ginned up the nerve to tiptoe into my office.

"You can walk in regularly," I say as she hesitantly slips inside. "I'm not a fragile piece of glass."

"I know," she replies, a crack in her voice. "You're an amazingly strong woman."

"So what's with being AWOL? Don't you need me to sign off on your graphics?"

"I'm not sure *I'm* as strong as you are." She pauses. "I guess I don't know what to say."

"How about, *glad you're back*," I say with a laugh.

"Glad you're back," she says, smiling. "But it's what to say next that has me anxious."

"I get it. I don't know myself what I want you—or any-one—to say. Maybe just 'I heard your news' is sufficient."

"I heard—"

I cut her off. "No. I don't like that. Pretend you've already said whatever you're supposed to say, and let's move on. Where are you with the signage?"

She tells me they've worked out the problems with the park regulators, and that all the signs for the events are near-ly complete. She's even lined up local celebrities to take part; people were eager, since many of them know someone who had melanoma.

By the time I leave the office at six o'clock, I'm convinced that all of the events my company will be arranging in sup-port of this product are going to be great.

I'm also sure I will not be a part of them. I love my work and my career. But this afternoon has made it clear: I need to leave my job.

My work-life balance has been precarious for several years. But for the foreseeable future, I must tip the column completely into *life*.

Several weeks later, Lilah and I are about to do partner yoga in the park. The other evening after she went to bed, Don and I did a partner class with my online subscription. He said he needed to do yoga with me because he'd had a meltdown at the office, screaming at everyone for no good reason. (Or no good *work* reason; having a diseased baby is plenty of rea-son.) The class helped, because he came home the next day pleased with how well his work had gone. This sparked the idea that I might try it with Lilah.

Now that I've stopped working, I have her with me most of the time. Erin comes two half-days each week to give me time to rest. I'm enjoying every moment with my daughter. Lilah and I have started doing yoga alongside one another, but we haven't yet done partner poses.

I roll out my mat as Lilah spreads out the one Angelica recently bought her—a bright yellow number with an illustration of Eeyore lying in *savasana*, the corpse pose. It's a posture I like to imagine suits the donkey, since the deep relaxation might coax him out of his glum state.

"Double tree pose!" Lilah shouts once I've straightened our mats alongside one another. I told her this morning about the poses we can do as "doubles." I envision the tree, where we connect our feet and touch our "branches" overhead. Then I see where she's pointing: Two trees are intertwined in front of us, doing a perfect version of the *asana*.

"Wonderful," I say. "Will we look like that when we do the pose?"

"They have more leaves," she laughs.

"That's true. Why don't we start with the double tree pose and see if we stand as straight as them."

We line up beside one another. My phone rings.

"Don't answer, Momma," she commands.

I know from the ringtone it is Angelica. I'm happy to let it go into voice mail. Angelica has left several messages since yesterday about a "brilliant" idea she's had. Apparently, there's a Caribbean cruise with Esther Hicks leaving in a month. Esther conducts her workshop sessions between the beachy ports. Angelica thinks she, Daria, Don, Lilah, and I should all go—and she and Daria offered to pay.

It's a lovely but ultimately terrible idea. With all that's going on in my life, I could hardly enjoy such a vacation.

Fortunately, when I mentioned it to Don—who'd already been invited by Daria—he told me cruise ships don't let women board in their last trimester. I guess they don't want anyone popping out an infant on the open sea. I was glad, since this gave me a gentle out.

Alas, the sisters are determined to force some sort of relaxation on us. When Don told Daria about the prohibition, she suggested we instead rent a house on the Delaware shore. Don likes the idea. I didn't have the heart to tell him those beaches are contaminated for me. Hopefully, I'll eventually be able to wipe away their association with the day I learned of Deuxie's disease. But right now I cannot go there.

"Lift your leg, Momma," Lilah orders. I realize my thoughts have been a million miles away. She's already positioned her leg into the pose, raising it slightly off the ground and turning her sole towards me. I lift my own leg a few inches—the height of her bent foot—and we press our feet together. In order for me to touch her palm, to connect the tree branches, mine stays at waist level.

"No Momma, higher," she says, eyeing my lowered arm. I raise it a few inches until she strains to stay connected. I relish the feel of her tiny foot and hand pressed against mine. Eventually, I disconnect us.

"Turtle next," Lilah says, flopping to the ground. My phone dings, indicating that Angelica has left a voicemail. Lilah gives me a stern "you better not touch that phone" look, which makes me laugh.

"What's funny?" she asks.

"I was just thinking about something funny, sweetheart," I say, not wanting her to believe I'm mocking her.

She quickly moves on. "Come to the floor, Momma."

I lower myself awkwardly onto my mat. I turn my body to face Lilah, who is facing me. I help her extend her legs wide; mine are open only a foot so hers can make contact. We thread our arms under our slightly bent knees, front to back, then lower ourselves towards the ground.

"Now come up," I say as we raise our heads like turtles emerging from a shell—or at least that's the idea. My bulging belly prevents me from lowering all the way down.

"Look Momma, I'm a turtle!" Lilah exclaims.

"You certainly are," I say, deciding I look more like a head-bobbing hippo.

Before Lilah can suggest a pose I'm no longer able to do—especially her favorite, camel—I jump in. "Let's do seated twists."

I'm aware I won't be able to rotate far, but I'm hopeful I can spin enough to make do. Lilah enthusiastically crosses her legs, and I follow. I pull her close so we're facing one another, my knees pressing against hers. She places her left arm properly behind her back, but adorably swings her right arm everywhere, apparently trying to remember where it goes.

"Take my hand," I say once I've placed my left hand behind my back and have reached it around to clasp her free hand. I extend my right hand to grab her left. She moves to intensify the twist.

"That's a good amount," I say to stop her from going farther. In partner yoga, her twists are also my twists, and right now I'm not so rotatable. "Let's close our eyes and breathe."

I land my attention on my twisted spine, then picture Deuxie smushing in my uterus. I send him a booster shot of affection before we repeat the pose on the opposite side.

"Let's do some breathing together," I say after we release. I direct her to get behind me, sitting back to back. She wiggles to get comfortable. Her breathing intensifies. I close my eyes and lengthen my own inhalations, continuing my adoration of the passenger in my womb. The love for both my children feels incredible.

Immediately and without warning, my emotion shifts to grief. *Deuxie, forgive me for failing you.*

Before I can pull my declining thoughts back where I want them, a wet drop forces my eyes open. The sun is shining, but a small black cloud hovers above. A moment later, we're in the middle of an unexpected, driving rain.

My impulse is to get up and run. But when I turn to Lilah, she's sitting still, eyes shut, contentedly smiling, and continuing her mindful breathing. I close my own eyes, and likewise embrace the cleansing rain.

24

"Are you sure the kitchen's clean enough?" I ask Don as he emerges into the living room.

"Will you relax," he says. "They're coming to pamper us, remember?"

"I won't feel pampered if the house is gross. I'll feel embarrassed."

"I should have told Daria to send a cleaning person yesterday," he laughs. "They've arranged for a chef, massage therapist, reflexologist, and who knows who else. What's one more?"

"This is so exciting!" Lilah declares, leaping down the stairs. "Auntie An-glel-ica *and* Aunt Daria!"

"Be good for them," I say, even as I know my delectable daughter can't be anything but. Lilah runs in circles around the sunlit living room, burning excess energy. She stops to scoop red grapes from the fruit platter on the coffee table— delivered last night from a local organic farm. I sit on the couch watching her move and eat—the basics of life we take for granted.

Deuxie may never be able to do those things.

Rather than allow that thought to depress me, I return to enjoying how easily Lilah does. *The human body is a miracle*, I think, as she swallows the grapes and resumes her loops.

Our sisters finally gave up trying to figure out where they could take us. Eventually they made an offer I could hardly refuse: a weekend retreat in our own home.

Angelica suggested Lilah stay at Mom's, but I couldn't do that. I barely let my daughter out of my sight these days. It's not that I worry *she* has Tay-Sachs; I was terrified after we got Deuxie's diagnosis that maybe she had the rare, late-onset kind, but we had her tested and she's clean. It's more a low-level unease that something bad might befall her. Plus I get so much joy from her innocence, which I need in spades.

The bell rings and, when Don opens the door, Angelica and Daria stand beaming, bags and boxes spilling over their arms. They've arranged to stay with us through tomorrow to oversee this massive pampering event—or, as Don has taken to calling it, Operation Mollycoddle. Despite my initial hesitation, I admit I'm as excited as Lilah is.

"Can I take that?" Don asks as Daria passes him in the foyer, balancing a box on top of three others.

"No, but you can grab a few things from the car."

"There's more?" I ask, walking towards them as my sister breezes by, arms equally overloaded.

"Lots more," Angelica says. "But none for you to take, Sis. If you think you were pampered at your Blessingway, you ain't seen nothing yet."

I try following the women into the kitchen, but Angelica shoos me away. I return to the couch. When I said *yes* to this event, I had to promise to let Angelica and Daria run the show.

"Oh good, the fruit platter's arrived," Angelica says, peeking out of the kitchen and spying the beautiful array on the coffee table.

"Last night," I reply. "It was even bigger before Lilah got hold of it."

"You sure you don't want me to run her to Mom's? I don't want your fussing over her to keep you from relaxing."

"If she were at Mom's I'd be fretting, not fussing. Anyway, she's what's keeping me sane, so I'll relax more if she's here."

"Roger." Angelica returns to the kitchen and Daria's clanging of pots and dishes.

"I thought you guys hired a chef," I shout as Don teeters into the foyer, bearing four additional boxes.

"We did," Daria says from the kitchen. "He'll be here later. But we're in charge of snacks. Starting with smoothies."

"I love smoothies!" Lilah screams. She darts into the kitchen. "Lilah can help!"

Apparently Daria hands her a banana, because she starts repeating the word over and over. I don't know what else they put in the drink, but what emerges several minutes later is delicious. I recognize the almond-butter taste and the blue-green color of blueberries and kale. But I often use those ingredients in my own smoothies and they never taste this good.

Lilah dances around, an azure mustache covering her lip. Don removes his straw so he can get a mustache too, sparking a round of giggles.

"The reflexologist will be here in an hour, followed by lunch, and then two therapists for a couple's massage," Daria runs down her list. "More treats will follow, but we don't need to overload you right now."

"I hope you two get the massage therapists after they do us," I say.

"Why didn't we think of that?" Angelica says, smiling at Daria. "Oh yeah, because we have other things we'll be doing."

"Before the reflexologist comes, I want to read you both something." Angelica pulls a hardcover book from one of her bags.

"Pema Chödrön! I love her," I say, spying the spine. "I've seen dozens of her YouTube videos."

"You make her sound like a rock star," Don laughs.

"She is. A Buddhist monk rock star."

"Close your eyes and breathe in her beautiful words," Angelica instructs. "This is from *When Things Fall Apart*."

"Appropriate," I deadpan.

She ignores me. "Lilah and Daria, why don't you sit with your eyes closed too." Daria lowers herself into the easy chair. Lilah climbs into her lap. I guess she's been missing mine now that it has completely disappeared.

"'The off-center, in-between state is an ideal situation, a situation in which we don't get caught and we can open our hearts and minds beyond limit,'" Angelica reads. She pauses, letting us absorb this wisdom.

"'To stay with that shakiness—to stay with a broken heart, with a rumbling stomach, with the feeling of hopelessness and wanting to get revenge—that is the path of true awakening. Sticking with that uncertainty, getting the knack of relaxing in the midst of chaos, learning not to panic—this is the spiritual path.'"

She stops again. Lilah rustles and start to speak, but Daria shushes her. I bask in the silence, absorbing this notion that the horror in my life is on some level my greatest spiritual teaching. I suspect my heart knows this, even if I'm not yet at a place to embrace it.

Angelica flips pages, clears her throat, and reads again. "'When we feel squeezed, there's a tendency for mind to become small. . . . We want to have security and certainty of some kind when actually we have no ground to stand on at all. The next time there's no ground to stand on, don't consider it an obstacle. Consider it a remarkable stroke of luck. We have no ground to stand on, and at the same time it could soften us and inspire us. Finally, after all these years, we could truly grow up.'" I breathe deeply, aiming to really get these lofty words.

"Nice reading!" Lilah says, immediately lightening the mood. I open my eyes.

"A remarkable stroke of luck?" Don says. "That's a bit extreme, don't you think? Anyway, what does a Buddhist monk know about feeling squeezed?"

"She knows quite a lot," I reply. "Chödrön wasn't born a Buddhist. She became one when her husband had an affair and left her."

"That is bad. But not as bad as having a dy—"

I cut him off. We haven't yet told Lilah about Deuxie. "Can we really rank our troubles? I mean, wouldn't we come up behind Syrian refugees who've had their families and homes and villages decimated? Or the parents of Sandy Hook or Parkland, who had no preparation for their loss?"

"All of them lucky," Angelica jumps in. "Not in the traditional sense, where of course these are tragedies demanding empathy. But from a spiritual standpoint. When you face down a calamity, you either shrivel or expand. And I know you two are going to do the latter."

Soon the reflexologist arrives, carrying a basin that she promptly fills with warm water and an herbal concoction. She has me soak my feet for half an hour while she rubs Don's. I didn't realize you could massage one little part of the body for so long, but Don seems enraptured.

Lilah has decided the basin is a toy; she has stepped in and out of it a dozen times, avoiding my feet by inches. Daria places a towel nearby, but Lilah still drips a trail of water. Normally this would annoy me, but in keeping with my desire to focus on the good, I appreciate that she's having fun.

When my toes are nearly prunes, the reflexologist announces it's time to switch. Don can barely exit his chair. As she rubs the soles of my feet, I see why he's in bliss. By massaging this small but nerve-filled and sensitive part of my body, it's as if she's soothing the entirety of it. I will myself to stay awake through the session so I won't miss a moment of the experience.

Next we have lunch. A local organic chef has prepared a feast featuring five main dishes—grilled tofu, free-range beef, cold salmon salad, zucchini noodles with vegetables, and Asian teriyaki chicken salad. I'm surprised Daria didn't make it all vegetarian—that would have been fine with me, since it suits my Ayurvedic type—but she said she wanted everyone to find things they love.

I do my best to sample each item, but I'm stuffed before I get to the salmon salad. I pray the chef leaves the leftovers in the fridge after he departs, which could feed the three of us all week. After lunch, Lilah plays in her room while the four adults sit around reminiscing, each sibling sharing stories of the other as a child.

I'm pondering a nap when the doorbell rings again. An attractive man and woman enter, carting their massage tables. They set up the couple's massage in our bedroom while we remain downstairs, Don and I playfully arguing about who's getting which therapist. I want the hot guy, of course, but I'm less enamored with the idea of the beautiful woman putting her hands on Don's body. Don feels equally torn. In the end, we go with our top choice—after all, pampering ourselves is the theme of the weekend.

The massage is even more delicious than the lunch. I adore lying inches away from my moaning husband, yet not being responsible for doing anything to please him. My table has a hole in the middle where my belly rests. I emit my own sighs as deep knots untangle from my back. Peppermint essential oil spills into the air from a diffuser, while soft music plays in the background. This means I can't hear Lilah, who's no doubt playing in the hallway, hoping to be let in.

When the massage is over but we're still limp on the tables, Daria and Lilah enter the room, each carrying a plush terry robe. "These are for you," Lilah says, handing the one in her arms to Don.

"You guys are too much," I say, as Daria and the therapists turn their backs while we pull ourselves up and slip on the robes.

"We aim to please," Daria replies. "You both have free time till dinner and the evening entertainment."

"You mean it's time for Momma and Daddy to play with Lilah?" I say.

"Yippee!" Lilah screams, leaping around the room and almost knocking over the essential oil diffuser.

"Yippee is right," I say to her. "Shall we bring home the horses?"

Dinner is not leftovers from lunch—although, thankfully, I do spy them in the fridge. Instead the chef has returned and prepared a new round of three appetizers and four extravagant entrées, along with a blueberry pie.

After we digest, Daria and Angelica crank up some music, and we pass the next two hours dancing. Lilah is in heaven and, frankly, so am I. Three times they play Don and my wedding song—Elvis's "Can't Help Falling in Love"—as we sway in one another's arms.

Eventually, Daria announces she's going to put Lilah to bed. After a round of hugs and kisses, she and Lilah head upstairs. Angelica says she's fixing herbal baths for Don and me, one in each of our home's tubs.

"You don't want us bathing together?" Don teases my sister.

"Nope. I want you to relax and process. What you do in your bed later is up to you."

"With you listening in from the guest bedroom? I think not," I say.

"Why not?" Don interjects, smirking at me. "Our sisters know we have sex. We're not teenagers anymore, trying to hide our sex lives from our families."

"Speak for yourself," I laugh. "I never did that."

"Oh no?" Angelica replies. "How about you and that Teddy Hamilton?"

"You knew about him?" I'm surprised to hear I wasn't as good at hiding my first love as I'd thought.

"Teddy? Tell me more about this Teddy," Don says to Angelica.

"My lips are sealed about the details," Angelica replies. "I will say I had a very good view of the side-of-the-house hedges from my bedroom window."

"This conversation is over," I announce sharply, giving my sister The Look.

"For now," Don says, smiling. "But at some point I will definitely be asking about those hedges."

Angelica has tricked out our tubs with natural bubble bath, essential-oil bath bombs, and Himalayan and Epson salts. Soon I'm soaking in our master bathroom's oversized tub, with Don in the smaller hall bathroom. The temperature is divine, and the herbal bomb has turned the water pink. I playfully swish the bubbles.

As they disintegrate, I spy my protruding abdomen rising out of the water. It's a sight I've seen numerous times during this pregnancy. But this time, the stark sight of my impending motherhood makes me cry. Within minutes I am howling, and I cannot stop. The unceasing waterworks do not feel cleansing, as I pray they might; they pull me into a deep, sorrow-filled void.

My life suddenly feels overwhelming. I cannot do this. I can't have this life, this baby, this tragedy that's about to unfold. My skin feels prickly. My brain tingles. The inside of my body threatens to break out of my skin. I suddenly want to spring from the tub, yet I also can't move a muscle. Through all this, the tears keep rolling.

This intense reaction surprises me; I thought I had processed the worst of the grief the day we got the amnio results. I want to fight it. Stuff it. Tell myself some spiritual mumbo-jumbo to make me see things in a different light. But I cannot. All I can do is suffer and wail.

Many tears later, I hear someone fussing around the bedroom. I try to stifle my gulping sniffles so whoever it is won't hear. I am obviously unsuccessful.

"You all right in there?" Angelica asks softly through the closed door.

"Yes," I eke out.

"Mind if I come in?"

I pause, unsure what to say. "I guess. If you want to." Angelica enters, then closes the door firmly behind her. Her hand holds a bottle of lavender spray. She must have been spritzing our bed pillows before my outburst interrupted. She perches herself on the closed toilet seat, takes my hand, and breathes in and out for a solid minute before responding.

"Crying is good," she says. "I know we learned from Mom not to express sad emotions—really, not to even feel them. But grief burrows itself deep in our cells. If you don't let it out, it will destroy you."

Ironically, these words stop my tears. It's as if now that they have permission, they don't need to emerge.

"I . . . was . . . doing . . . so . . . well," I say, getting a word out between sporadic breaths. "Was really appreciating . . . all the blessings in my life—including the blessing you and Daria are giving Don and me this weekend."

"And you will continue to do that," Angelica says. "But sometimes you will feel heartbroken by the gut-wrenching unfairness of it, the horrible reality of birthing a child who is likely to die—and, knowing you, the guilt you feel for giving him his genes. You have to embrace those emotions too. They're all part of being alive. Or what Jon Kabat-Zinn calls the 'full catastrophe of the human condition.' All of that has to be okay. Everything else is a spiritual bypass, the BS of people thinking they should be enlightened enough not to be affected." She pauses, giving me a moment to get in touch with my authentic feelings.

"I want to jump out of my body. Out of my life," I admit.

"I felt that way when Dad left the family."

"You did?" She and I have never spoken directly about that time, since I was too young to remember much. For me, growing up with only a mother just felt normal.

"I cried for days. Thought about running away. Mom tried to quiet me, but that only made it worse. Sorrow is something that has to run its course."

"I don't want Lilah seeing me so defeated. And once the baby is born, I don't want that for him. If he only has a short time before he goes downhill, I want that time to be perfect."

"It won't be perfect," she says, startling me with her brutal honesty. "Life is never perfect. But it can be wonderful, if you keep it real."

Despite the bath, reflexology, massage, dancing, food, company, and the delicate lavender wafting from my pillow, I sleep fitfully most of the night. Next to me, Don snores soundly. Several times I try to wake him so I won't be alone in my misery, but he doesn't budge, and I'm secretly glad for it. He can't make this better for me. He can only figure out how to get through it himself. Which is what I have to do.

But then, the next thing I know, the house is alive with morning, the sounds of people moving about. I glance at the clock; it's nearly nine. I guess I got some sleep during the early morning hours. I feel surprisingly refreshed.

As I'm tugging on my yoga pants, I burst into tears again. Embracing my emotions, I allow the stream. A few minutes later, it ceases. I dab my face with a tissue, slap on a little lipstick and mascara, and head downstairs to join the ruckus.

The day is incredible. Daria leads us in a guided walking meditation around the neighborhood—I didn't even know she knew how to do that. We watch a Wayne Dyer video, *The Shift*, about finding meaning in life. Angelica has us do another meditation, this one sitting, in the afternoon. Even Lilah is quiet, flipping through a book the entire time. (I know because I peeked, eager to see my child.) Despite the leftovers practically bursting from the fridge, the chef returns to prepare more incredible food for brunch and dinner.

In the evening, before the sisters leave, the four of us stand in a circle in the living room—Lilah sitting in the middle—and embrace in a group hug.

"You guys are the best," I say when we break the chain. "We can't thank you enough."

"We're happy to serve," Daria says.

"Very happy," Angelica adds. "Which means anytime in the next few months or years—or beyond—that you need anything from us, you will not hesitate to call."

After Don closes the door behind them, he and I remain in the foyer.

"We're going to get through this," he pronounces. "It's going to be hard. But we will do it."

"Yes," I respond. And in this moment at least, I sense that we can.

25

It hasn't even been a week and we have already taken Angelica up on her offer to serve. Don and I dropped Lilah at her home early this Saturday morning so he can hang out with some of his buddies, and I can go for a hike in the woods with Janelle.

She's standing in the parking lot of the trailhead when I arrive, but she is not alone.

"Hey there," Mandy greets me when I emerge from my car. "Hope you don't mind, but when Janelle and I were talking last night and she told me you guys were hiking, I begged to come along. I've loved these woods since my grandpa took me here as a little girl."

"When she asked, I thought it was a great idea," Janelle says. "I figure we can all benefit from Mandy's incredible spiritual connection."

"Don't be so modest," she says to Janelle. "Your connection is pretty great too."

"What about mine?" I tease, knowing I'm nowhere near the light, airy self I had been in recent years.

"Yours is a little stuck in the mud," Mandy says, smiling. "Just temporarily, though. I've no doubt you will return to your high-flying self."

"Maybe when I'm a hundred," I say.

"Nah. I give you a few months, tops. You've been dealt a big shock. It's going to take a while to get your bearings."

No wonder I love Mandy. "Part of me still can't believe it's true," I confess. "How can my little baby be so sick? I mean, I've seen his cute, perfect body on the ultrasound photo."

No one answers my query because no one can. Janelle turns to lead us onto the trail, which is already filling up with families, lovers, and Scout troops. I'm suddenly self-conscious of the protrusion from my waistband, especially since Mandy and Janelle are so fit and thin. It takes a half-mile for me to get over that—which I do when I realize I am allowing this stupid thought to mar a beautiful experience.

I notice the light sparkling on the leaves above us. It's like sun shimmering on water, animated and buoyant. Then I put my attention on my feet as they land in the soil. We're part of a machine, the three of us moving in tandem, Janelle in front, Mandy behind her, with me in the rear. When a thought—most often a worry, I admit—flits into my mind, I will myself back to this steady motion.

We walk in silence for an hour—our silence, anyway. The Scouts and families periodically passing us loudly ooh and aah over the views. Janelle suddenly turns off the trail. We follow, stepping in rhythm, trusting her forward thrust. After a few minutes, I hear water gurgling; several minutes later we're standing near an isolated stream.

"How did you know this was here?" I ask, taken aback by the sound of my voice following this period of quiet.

"Janelle knows all," Mandy jokes. "Actually, I also knew this was here. Gramps used to take me fishing in this stream, back in the day."

"I've been in these woods many times and I've never seen this," I say.

"That's the nature of the universe. There's always something new to discover." This from mystical Mandy, of course.

Mandy shucks off her backpack and opens the zipper. Out comes a blanket, chocolate, a nut spread, and apples. Janelle's pack holds a bottle of wine, and cutlery and glassware.

I feel bad I haven't contributed anything.

"Don't say it." Janelle stops me as I open my mouth. "This is our gift to you."

"You've given me many gifts already. Like the Blessingway," I say.

"And you've given us plenty too," Mandy says. "All those little presents over the years, for our half birthdays, our quarter birthdays—"

"And that's not even counting the flowers and presents for our full birthdays," Janelle interjects. "Sometimes you have to take without reciprocating."

"I'm taking," I say. "You should see how much I've been taking lately."

"Good. Now sit and enjoy our picnic," Mandy commands.

We silently nosh on the treats. I don't even care whether any of it is good for my pregnancy, let alone for my Ayurvedic type. Janelle pours the wine; I savor each sip, overwhelmed by how delicious it tastes.

When we're ready to pack up, Mandy turns to me, all serious. If I were an alcoholic, this is when I would be concerned that an intervention were about to ensue.

"What's up?" I say, seeing that Janelle has stopped gathering up the garbage and has also turned to face me.

"Have you ever heard of Anita Moorjani?" Mandy asks.

"Is she that woman who healed herself of cancer?" I ask, curious where this conversation could possibly be going.

"Didn't just heal herself," Janelle chimes in. "They were counting down the minutes in her hospital deathwatch. In a coma from her stage-four disease, she was told—or, really, she understood from her highest self—that she is part of the universe. That she could choose to live in a perfectly healthy body if she wanted. She came back from nearly dead, and within weeks shrunk her lemon-size tumors down to nothing."

"Oh yes," I say. "She wrote a book."

"It's an incredible story," Mandy says.

"I'm surprised I haven't read it." I toss a knowing nod at Janelle. The two of us seem to have tunneled through every spiritual book with more than two stars on Amazon.

I suddenly understand why they're telling me this. "You think I should be more hopeful about Lennan's prospects?"

This week, Don and I decided it was time to stop calling him Deuxie. We easily settled on a name. Lennan means *lover* in Gaelic. We know *love* is the trait we most want our boy to experience in his brief life. It doesn't hurt that I'm a big fan of John Lennon's music and philosophy—even if I'm a generation behind and am spelling the name differently. I told Janelle the news last night.

"You decided on a name!" Mandy screams, her voice echoing around the trees. "I love it! And yes, we think you should be more hopeful. I know the experts warn it's an inescapably fatal disease. I'm sure in most cases it is. But maybe Lennan could be the first not to succumb. And because *you* know we're all connected to the energy that created the universe, an energy behind every healing, maybe you can help him buck the odds. And maybe by his example help other kids do it too."

I return my attention to the babbling stream. The sound has been continuous, but I realize I stopped listening a while back. A flock of sparrows flies overhead; the three of us watch their choreographed rhythm in the sky. It takes several minutes for me to figure out how to respond. It's true that everything I've been told and have read about Tay-Sachs—thankfully not much, since I've largely avoided filling my head with all that sadness—confirms the vicious mortality of this disease. Some kids make it to six or even seven if the parents aggressively intervene with feeding tubes and such, but if we don't do that—and Don and I agree we will not—we're looking at four years tops.

Still, Mandy has a point. I know I have to get to the place of peaceful acceptance. But does that mean I can't equally be open to the possibility of more?

"You're not wrong," I say, not ready to say they're right. "I've been immersed in New Thought stuff long enough to believe we can bring things into our life when we know it and expect it." I absently fiddle with my hair. I recognize this as the nervous energy I see in Lilah when she's overwhelmed.

"But . . . ?" Janelle senses more is coming.

"But—do I believe it goes so far as to say that a death sentence can be shifted to a long and healthy life? That's so extreme. And I've never seen it happen."

"Anita Moorjani saw it happen," Janelle says. "And I bet hospitals are filled with prognosis-busting healings that doctors chalk up to some unexplainable miracle. Not many people share those stories because they know others won't understand." Daria's story of the kid with the broken arm enters my mind.

"What if you don't jump to 'miracle healing' quite yet," Mandy suggests, noticing my disequilibrium over the thought of a teenage or old-man Lennan. "What about possible medical cures? You can't know what drug might be invented in the next year or two. Many diseases were fatal until someone discovered a surgery or medication."

"There is more action on the clinical trials front for Tay-Sachs than ever," I admit. "Although the numbers—and the funding—are still paltry."

"Why not focus on that first part?" Janelle proposes. "That people are out there working on a cure that might save Lennan. It could shift your thinking enough to create a space for that possibility. At the very least, it feels better to be hopeful."

"I love you guys." I look deeply at Mandy, then Janelle, so they know I mean it. I feel their love flow back.

We pack up our stuff and begin our return hike. Mostly, we walk in silence. On several occasions one of my pals breaks out in song, and we join in. When we belt out Pink's "Secrets," some teenage girls hiking near us hum along. I love how communities like this singing sisterhood can spontaneously form, even if they quickly break apart.

Later that evening, once Lilah is in bed, I slip out to my local library. When I told Don about the discussion of Anita Moorjani, he suggested I check her stuff out. Lilah and I probably spend three days a week at this library, but when I've tried to snag a book off the adult shelves, she yanks my arm until I drop it and move to the children's section.

When I wander around, I'm amazed to see that they have expanded their New Thought shelves, with an entire section on miracle healing. Several books are by the grande dame of the genre, the late Louise Hay. Her classic, *You Can Heal Your Life,* was among the earliest books I read when I first got into spiritual teachings. I kind of brushed it off as voodoo back then—especially Hay's notion that we must take responsibility for energetically creating an illness if we hope to release it. At the time, that struck me as victim blaming.

Now as I flip through her pages, I understand what she means: "I'm not talking about having guilt, nor about being a bad person for being where you are. I am saying to acknowledge the power within you that transforms our every thought into experience. In the past we unknowingly used this power to create things we did not want to experience. . . . Now, by acknowledging our responsibility, we *become* aware and learn to use this power consciously in positive ways for our benefit," she writes.

Of course, I have no idea how this applies to a baby who isn't even born yet. Hay's famous list of the mental causes of physical diseases certainly can't apply to someone who spends his days floating around in the dark. But I do acknowledge I don't understand everything that goes on in the world.

I return the book to the shelf and snatch two others: *The Hell I Can't!*—a great title—by a guy named Terry McBride, and *A Revolution in Medicine*, by Bruno Gröning.

I've never heard of either man, but as I sit down with the books, I realize there's a world of miraculous healings I haven't been aware of. McBride writes about his "incurable" excruciating back pain, the result of a chronic infection trapped in his spine. More than a dozen surgeries couldn't fix him; he finally decided not to accept his doctors' verdict of life as a disabled man. He disciplined his thoughts towards the positive, and now he's a walking, pain-free life coach to others.

Gröning was a German healer—really, a mystic—after World War II who did energy healing in large groups, curing some people of their lifelong diseases and others of their wartime injuries. Although he's long been dead, his program lives on in healing "circles" held all over the world, where people tap into the same universal flow he did.

"Excuse me," a woman says. I look up, disoriented. I've been so enamored by these concepts, I've forgotten I'm in a library.

"Am I in your way?" I pull in my legs so they won't block the aisle.

"No, not at all. I'm sorry if I'm wrong, but are you the woman who works for that AFib app company? I was in your focus group."

It's the Anna Paquin lookalike. "What a small world." I stretch out my hand to shake hers. She leans in and hugs me instead.

"I remember you had serious cramps and had to be helped out of the room. I'm glad you and your baby are great." She releases her grip.

I want to tell her that we're not actually great, but I stop myself. Do I want to have this conversation with a stranger? I suddenly appreciate how glad I am that Lennan's condition won't be noticeable at first. I like being able to decide who to open up to. Let people coo over my beautiful newborn when I hold him in my arms.

"Have you released that app yet?" she asks. "I think it's a great product."

"Not yet."

"Well, good luck with it," she says, turning to leave. "I know it will do great."

I'm clear she means the app—which I don't let on I'm not involved with now. But I mentally shift the *it* to *him* and take her knowing as a good omen.

I glance at my watch. Don is undoubtedly eager for me to return. He's been so overprotective since our news, even though I keep reminding him he's standing in the same quicksand. But I want to flip through the Moorjani book, *Dying to Be Me*, before I leave. As I pull it off the shelf, the subtitle—*My Journey from Cancer, to Near Death, to True Healing*—soothes me further.

I bring the book to a comfy chair. Janelle wasn't kidding when she said Anita was close to death. She writes that she was comatose when she was wheeled into her Hong Kong hospital, her body riddled with cancerous tumors. Anita had avoided chemo when she was first diagnosed. I'm not sure how I feel about that. On the one hand, chemo is a toxic brew that some people die from; on the other, it's still the treatment of medical choice. *There are no easy answers, are there?*

In any event, she returned from that state. It happened after she connected with her dead father and long-gone best friend. She also claims she floated outside her body in the hospital and actually heard her doctor talking to her husband in the hallway. When she later recounted their words back to her husband, he was stunned. She's now made it her mission to travel the world, preaching of possibilities.

What I'm liking about her message is that she hasn't turned her experience into a one-size-fits-all, this-is-how-you-heal prescription. One paragraph especially leaps out at me: "I'm at my strongest when I'm able to let go, when I suspend my beliefs as well as disbeliefs, and leave myself open to all possibilities. That also seems to be when I'm able to experience the most internal clarity and synchronicities. My sense is that the very act of needing certainty is a hindrance to experiencing greater levels of awareness. In contrast, the process of letting go and releasing all attachment to any belief or outcome is cathartic and healing. The dichotomy is that for true healing to occur, I must let go of the need to be healed and just enjoy and trust in the ride that is life."

I love the idea that I don't have to demand that Lennan be healed. If I "let go and let God," as that previously confusing-to-me expression goes, and stay open to possibilities, that is enough.

Trust in our ride with Lennan. I can do that. Don can do that.

I take the book to the library checkout machine and insert my card. This book will definitely occupy top position on my nightstand pile.

26

Even though we're a mile away, I can already see the bonfire. We're heading to a farm some forty-five minutes from our home, where this supposedly renowned yoga teacher is leading a large group meditation followed by dancing around a bonfire.

Don hoped to leave Lilah home with a sitter, but I want her with us. Lilah's life is going to be upended enough once Lennan emerges—the new baby stuff at first, the who-knows-what after—so I want her to be happy now. A bonfire sounds like something she'll treasure.

Continuing to take people up on their offers of favors, Don asked Daria if she would come to watch Lilah during the hour-long meditation. I wouldn't have felt comfortable putting her out this much, but he told me about it only after the deed was done. I am a bit at war with my inner guilt for ruining Daria's evening, but also secretly thrilled with this plan. A long sujal, sans distractions, will be heavenly.

A man in a do-rag directs the long line of cars to park in the grassy area adjacent to the farm's spinach crops. When I spy those dozens of rows of greens, I'm surprised this is a working farm. The social-media ad for this event did say *farm*, but I expected maybe a small community garden.

"Look Daddy! Fire," Lilah squeals.

"Yes, love," Don replies. "Remember, we told you that after you play with Aunt Daria, we're all going to dance around that fire."

"Aunt Daria too?" Lilah asks. I appreciate how she never wants anyone to miss out.

"No, she can only stay to play with you. Then she has to get home."

"Why can't *you* play with me?" Lilah asks him.

"Dad and I are going to sujal. You know, when we sit quietly and focus on our breath to connect with spirit," I say.

"I know what that is, Momma!" she says, exasperated. She's at that age where she hates when I explain things she knows. And she knows because Don and I have been meditating in front of her since she was born. My hope is that when she's a little older she'll take to this practice herself. I was in my thirties my first time; my daughter may be five or six.

Lilah leaps out of her car seat when we finally park and spring her.

"Weeds!" she screams, running towards the spinach beds nestled behind the wood fencing.

"Those aren't weeds, darling." The plants do look awfully similar to the weeds regularly overtaking our frequently neglected backyard garden. "It's spinach."

Lilah's face twists into a knot, apparently trying to puzzle out how this can be the sautéed vegetable I put on her plate.

"No it's not," she eventually decides, walking away from the fence before I confuse her further.

The tone with which she says this almost exactly mimics what my mother recited when Don and I finally sat in her living room and told her about the genetic testing and amnio results.

"I'm sorry," she had genuinely offered at first, before quickly adding that her side was not to blame, that the baby's "sick genes" must have come from Don's family.

"No, Mom," I corrected her. "Somewhere along the line our family developed the mutation too."

"No they did not," she said emphatically, as if her brain couldn't process that her kin might be equally responsible. The remark wound Don up like a boxer, but before he could throw a verbal punch, I gave him a look that said it wasn't worth our energy. After all, my own brain still struggles to accept this terrible truth.

After we laid out the facts behind the disease, we moved on to talking about the weather, then quickly left. Since then, however, she's been nothing but empathetic, much more than I ever expected.

Tonight at the farm, we've arranged to meet Daria by the main entrance to the meditation room—a barn that's been cleaned out and filled with wall-to-wall cushions. I have no idea who owns this farm or why they allow all these strangers to descend on it, but I'm loving the location. Apparently, they do this monthly. I already sense that we'll be back.

"Hi guys," Daria yells over the din of conversation as she approaches us from the parking lot. She must have been right behind us, but with hundreds of people filing in, we didn't notice. Lilah races over to her aunt, who bends down and scoops my girl into her arms like I used to be able to do.

"Looks like people are already going into the meditation," Daria says. "Why don't you guys go? I'll take Lilah into the farmhouse. I called yesterday, and they said there's a room where kids can play."

"You're a doll," I say. "We appreciate this so much."

"My pleasure. I told you I'm happy to help. This will be another good step towards your believing that."

The two of them disappear around the building. Don and I join the stream flowing into the barn. The cushions on the floor are a rainbow of hues. I head to the purple section on the left. Don helps lower me to the floor. My instinct is to introduce myself to the people sitting near us—they'll undoubtedly be part of the army needed to raise me later—but everyone is sitting with closed eyes, getting centered.

I turn off my phone and peek around. A high-backed chair is positioned in front, where the instructor will be. Dozens of lit candles line the front of the room, with Christmassy white lights strung all over the barn. I'm momentarily reminded of that orb fiasco from my app launch, but I let that pass like a wave in the sea.

I shift my foot to get comfortable and catch some hay that has been spread beneath the cushions. I'm impressed with the level of detail that has gone into this. A woman with a large gong and a violinist stand in the corner, waiting for their cue. I'm pleased there won't be a bevy of musicians. Simple is always better for meditating, as far as I'm concerned.

A woman dressed in a basic black yoga outfit enters the room and says hello. Everyone opens their eyes and wildly applauds. I was expecting one of those model-looking yogis who teach all those online classes I've been taking—women who would have been dancers in another life, before yoga's popularity made it a desirable career. This woman, who introduces herself as Leeza, looks like me, before I got pregnant.

The violinist begins her background tune. Leeza explains that she teaches a type of meditation based on "resonant," or evenly paced, breathing, which calms the nervous system but also lets you stay alert. I'm hoping it's not one of those complicated breaths where you have to fold up your tongue or make some unnatural sound, which I always struggle with.

Leeza explains that the method has been taught to people traumatized by mass disasters around the world—everyone from 9/11 survivors to people in Haiti and Sudan. *No need to worry it will be complex; if those novices can do it, I certainly can.* I glance at Don who, like everyone except me, has closed his eyes. Leeza holds up a book that describes the breathing method. I chuckle because I'm the only one who can see it.

The breathwork is so basic I'm impressed it is so powerful. You take five breaths per minute, in and out naturally. That translates to a six-count inhale and a six-count exhale. To help us stay on track, the holiday-looking lights around the room will flash each time we're to start a new in-breath, which she says we'll be able to "see" even with our eyes closed. The gong will also make a distinct sound.

Finally we're ready to begin. Don reaches over and squeezes my hand. I squeeze back. I sense this will be great, and it is. After close to an hour, I'm feeling as well rested as after a long *yoga nidra*, or deep relaxation, but there is no lethargy to shake off. I'm so alert I could run around the block, albeit more contented and unperturbed than I was before.

As Leeza moves to end the practice, she recites a poem she has written. Apparently, nearly everyone here knows the poem—*how? from where?*—since they join in on the second stanza:

The sun shines brightly
My eyes are wide
I see a child, a bird, a loving couple
It makes my heart sing.

A cloud comes overhead
The child and bird are injured
The pair embattled
Still, it makes my heart sing.
I choose to see the light.

After several more stanzas, followed by closing "oms," everyone readies themselves for the bonfire. I ask two of the women to grab my hands. With Don pushing from the back, I wobble to standing.

"Thank you so much," I say to the women.

"Been there," one of them responds. "During my last pregnancy, it would have taken ten people to heave me up."

"That breathing was wonderful," I say to her. "Have you done this before?"

"I've been here many times, but this is the first time Leeza has led it. Usually there's an Indian man, Rajnish. He's great too."

"If she's never been here, how do you all know her poem?" I ask, confused.

"YouTube," the other woman jumps in. "She reads several of her poems in a video, with animation and great background music. It's got millions of views."

"Sometimes I feel so out of the loop of what's happening in the world," I sigh.

"I never heard the poem either," Don says, aiming to be reassuring.

"Yes, but we know you're always out of the loop," I kid.

"It's a great video. You should check it out," the first woman says before they walk outside.

I take a moment to feel my appreciation for Don: that he didn't want me to feel bad about not knowing the poem, that he was eager to accompany me here without being clear about what to expect, and that he arranged for his sister to watch Lilah so I could immerse myself in the experience. I don't have to *choose* to see the light in him. It's easy to do.

The lunacy around the bonfire is at full steam by the time we leave the barn. I turn my phone on and text Daria, letting her know exactly where we are. She and Lilah come bounding over a minute later.

"How was it?" Daria asks, at the exact moment Lilah starts sharing all the things she's seen. "Cows! Plants! Hay!"

"Sounds so fun," I say to her, "and it was wonderful," I answer Daria. "A really powerful breathing practice. Calming *and* energizing. We'll have to show you sometime."

Daria agrees she'd like to learn and then says her good-byes. The three of us walk to the bonfire; the party around the fire is already in full swing.

Several people twirl neon, glow-in-the-dark batons. Others perform gymnastics moves. There are hammocks hung between trees, where people are swinging and laughing. A dozen yogis do poses on mats arranged in a starburst, colorful lights lining each one. And the single violinist has joined a half dozen musicians, playing rousing tunes from a makeshift stage. There must be three hundred people dancing.

Lilah is eager to sample everything, and so am I. (Except the gymnastics, which I could not do even before I had an off center of gravity.) During the evening, the three of us leap from one activity to another, dancing, twirling things, and doing our favorite family yoga poses. With a food table overflowing with finger foods and nonalcoholic drinks, we eat to excess.

We end the evening by making ice cream sundaes from the elaborate fixings. Lilah deviates from her typical vanilla ice cream with chocolate sprinkles to douse her creation with cookie bits, strawberries, caramel sauce, and chocolate stars. I don't care how many calories are in my own creation—which is similar to Lilah's but with hot fudge instead of caramel—or how bad all this sugar is for me. I relish every mouthful.

Lilah falls asleep minutes after we place her in the car. I get behind the wheel to drive home, moving the seat back from where Don had it earlier. He and I are contentedly quiet for much of the drive. At several points, I notice Don do the breathing exercise we just learned. Since it didn't dull me, I suspect I could safely do it while driving, but I decide not to chance it.

"Everything's good when we stay in the present, isn't it?" Don says, suddenly breaking the silence.

I know exactly what he means. We had so much fun tonight, I didn't once think about Lennan's illness. I'm sure Don didn't either.

"Yes. And we're going to try to stay in the moment as much as humanly possible," I vow, as much to myself as to him. "That's going to be the gift of Lennan."

"The gift of Lennan. I like that," he says.

Lilah lets out a loud snort from the back seat, and we laugh.

"The gift of Lilah, too," I say. "Toddlers don't let anything get them down."

I tell Don about an article I found online today. It was written by a guy who learned he has a disease that will make him blind; maybe in days, maybe not for decades. There is no way to know.

"He wrote that somebody who was also going blind shared some powerful wisdom with him." I pause to recall the exact words but can't, so I paraphrase. "You can't spend your life preparing for future losses, because it insults all the blessings you're receiving now."

Lilah snorts again. Don and I glance at one another, aware that we have plenty to feel blessed about.

27

The next morning, Lilah mercifully sleeps in. This gives me time to do the resonant breathwork with the even breaths, plus a few hatha yoga poses, and a little reading—including from Anita Moorjani's mind-blowing book.

I take a moment to intend for the great day I have planned with my daughter. She's sleeping late, so I noodle with our household budget, which without my paycheck must be cut to the bone. My car and Netflix are already on the chopping block.

My cell rings and I answer immediately, thinking it must be Janelle, who always calls in the morning.

"Yoga mission field," I say brightly.

"Huh?" a voice responds.

"Sorry. This is Lorna. Who's this?" I pull the phone from my ear to check the number. It's Krista from the office.

We exchange pleasantries. She tells me about the beautiful Samoyed puppy she recently rescued. I tell her about Lilah's newest adorableness: playing hide and seek by running into the corner and facing the wall while cupping her hands over the sides of her eyes. Lilah thinks if she can't see us, we can't see her.

"I'm sorry to bother you at home," Krista says, clearly gearing up to ask a favor.

"It's no bother."

"The team's been trying to decide whether to have a big opening event in *each* city where we do the sun-protection carts, or just in the major ones. I'm hoping you can weigh in. You're such an expert."

It amazes me how quickly our priorities can shift. I don't mean this in a bad way. Getting excited about a big work project, and especially a special event, has fueled me for years. But since I've left my job, I hardly remember what I did there. Things that were pressing weeks ago are barely a blip in my brain.

"What does Jason think?" I ask.

"He thinks a big opener is nice but not necessary. That we should pass in some cities, since we're short on—" She stops herself.

"Short on staff. You can say it: My leaving so close to the events put you guys in a bind. I know that."

"I didn't mean to imply you shouldn't have left. All I'm saying is I think a celebrity event is more valuable than Jason gives it credit for, in terms of media attention."

I marvel again at my lack of investment in a project where I was all in so recently. "I agree with you. But I also agree with Jason. If you don't have the people, you'll kill yourself trying to do too many."

"But *you* would do them everywhere if you were here, because they're important, right?"

Important is a relative thing, I want to tell her. *Leaving a war-torn country is important. Having enough food to eat is important. Giving my son a good life before he begins the process of dying is important.*

But then I remember the purpose of the S-Check app is to protect people from lethal skin cancer. That's important too. Anyway, even my previous job, bringing attention to our ice cream, was important to me. And to all the people who love ice cream. Importance isn't something you can grade.

"I would," I respond. "Still, you're doing events in the most important cities." *Ha, that word again.* "If you'd like me to mull it over with Jason, I'm happy to."

"I appreciate that." She pauses. "It's not the same here without you."

"But you *were* there without me before. You predated me."

"And it was fine. But then you came, with your great ideas. You made my job better."

"It means a lot to hear you say that, especially when I'm just here juggling my bills."

"I doubt that's all you're doing. I'm sure you're shoring up your spiritual arsenal. Those practices are going to serve you well."

"Yes, there's that. I admit I haven't thought much about the office. But I do miss you and the other people there."

Krista promises to stop by my house sometime, and we hang up. Not two seconds later, Lilah awakens and calls me to her bed.

After she and I dress and eat breakfast, I drive us to a local kids' gym that's having a special "parent-and-me" event. (Hoboken is such an egalitarian town; they'd never call it mommy-and-me, even though nearly all of the stay-at-home parents are female.)

They're having a famous kids' singer, characters from popular movies, and arts-and-craft activities. Lilah ruminates nonstop about the trampoline, which she barely got off the last time we went to this gym. I tell her there will be special things there today, but the trampoline is the only object capturing her imagination.

Until we arrive. Standing just outside the door is a group of people dressed as movie characters, including a home-made version of Olaf.

"Olaf, Olaf," Lilah yells, racing into his arms. He hugs her tightly and she is overjoyed to be here, even though we haven't yet walked through the front door.

We've arrived before the crowds, so we have our pick of things to do. Not surprisingly, Lilah races to the trampoline.

"Why don't we make an art project first? Before that area gets crowded," I suggest, pointing. "Look, they're making Disney puppets."

She ignores me and keeps running. I take one more stab, knowing that later the craft tables will be mobbed. "We can make Olaf and Elsa puppets. After we can go to the jumps."

She snubs me again, and soon she's climbing onto the trampoline. When this girl sets her mind to something, there's no talking her out of it—actually a good trait, I remind myself. She hasn't been socialized to please other people at her own expense.

Lilah leaps up and down, bounces on her bottom, falls on her back and springs back up, squealing all the while. She even attempts a midair flip—which doesn't quite work out, although she's a great sport when she crashes onto her belly.

Soon, another little girl climbs onto the next trampoline. They begin synchronizing their bounces and imitating one another's arm gestures. The girl's mom moves towards me.

"Aren't they precious?" she says.

"They certainly are. I'm Lorna."

"Jennifer. Congratulations." She points to my massive abdomen.

"Thanks." I leave it at that. I have no desire to get into the details of my baby's medical condition.

"Look, Momma," Lilah says, as she and the girl twirl between bounces.

"Look, Momma," the other girl shouts, and Jennifer chuckles.

"She doesn't ever call me that. I'm always Mommy."

"My mother was Mommy when I was younger. That's why I went with Momma," I say, surprising myself with my candor.

"Not a great childhood?"

"Not great. But not horrible. I just want to be a different kind of mother."

"My mother was this paragon of virtue, which isn't always so great, either. A tough standard to live up to."

"Does she make you live up to it?" I ask, curious.

"She passed a few years ago. It's me who wants to live up to it."

"I'm so sorry for your loss."

Suddenly, Jennifer starts weeping. I place a consoling arm around her waist. She roots around her purse, searching for a tissue, which she doesn't find. "I have one," I say, fishing the packet out of the backpack diaper bag I always keep handy and passing it to her.

I expect her to wipe her eyes and gain control, but she snivels more intensely. Her daughter is immune, as if she's seen this movie before; she keeps jumping and spinning with Lilah. I'm confused about Jennifer's reaction, since she said it had been several years.

"I'm sorry," she says between tears.

"Nothing to be sorry about. Crying is cathartic."

"I guess I can't hear the word *loss* yet. My twin sister left her body two months ago."

I add my other hand around her waist and pull her into a hug. More mothers and tots have come into the gym, and some stare as they pass. I barely notice.

When Jennifer gets a grip on herself and releases my embrace, I'm stumped about what to say. It strikes me that this is the position other people will be in soon enough with me.

I stand by quietly, giving her the opening to say whatever she desires. She remains silent. That's when I realize it might help her to share my own story. Because what will comfort me is the knowing that everybody experiences tragedy and loss, with all its accompanying messy emotions.

I tell her about Lennan. She's familiar with Tay-Sachs, but says she thought it was a Jewish disease that's been eradicated through genetic testing. I guess this is something else I'm going to hear plenty of; the facts about this condition are not well known. I don't know why I want to educate her, but I do—about how Lennan will be fine at birth but that slowly lipids will build up in his brain because his body lacks the enzyme to remove them, and eventually he'll reach a tipping point where he'll visibly decline.

"Is there no cure? No possibility of a cure?" she asks, horrified.

"No cure now. But you never know." I'm pleased I'm starting to believe in the possibility.

"There's always a chance," she says, confirming my prior statement. "Things can shift in the direction we're wanting, if we keep our focus on it."

I have a sense I'm right about something, but it feels weird to ask. Still, I go for it. "Are you familiar with the teachings of Abraham-Hicks?"

She looks as if that's not a question she's ever been asked. "I am! I love them. I thought about saying my mother and sister *croaked*. I love how Esther Hicks uses that word to imply we don't die in the sense we think, that we simply move to another dimension. But you can't say that in public. Still, knowing they 'croaked' doesn't make it less sad for me not to have them here."

"So true," I commiserate. "I know that on a soul level Lennan will be fine. But it's hard to picture him leaving our family so soon after he joins us."

The girls finally have their fill of the trampoline. They run towards us, holding hands. "Dancing time!" Lilah yells. The four of us head for the singer and his band set up in the corner. He's singing about appreciating the air, the sky, the flowers, the trees. It's simplistic, but I like the message.

"It's so great finding another Abraham fan," Jennifer says once the kids have settled into their dancing—or, really, their jumping up and down, which doesn't look much different from what they were doing on the trampoline.

"I know there are a lot of us," I say. "I've always joked to my friend Janelle that we should have a secret handshake. Or all wear lavender bracelets or something, to tip off other people that we're open to these spiritual teachings. I bet there'd be other lavender bracelets even in this gym."

"Have you been to her workshop? Or her cruise? I've been dying to do the Caribbean cruise: beaches, piña coladas, swimming with dolphins, and workshop sessions right on the ship! Obviously, that's going to have to wait a while," she says, pointing to her daughter, whom I've learned from Lilah's shouting is named Serena—the name of a spiritual radio host I used to love listening to before she moved to cable television.

"The cruise does sound enticing. My sister actually suggested it recently, but I was too far along to go. Obviously at this point I'm going to have to wait a while too. Maybe we'll go together. Like in a decade," I smile.

"That means we're going to have to stay in touch during the decade, which I'm all for. I'd love to have playdates with our daughters. And, once Lennan arrives, I'm happy to take Lilah off your hands when you need."

People are more amazing than I've ever given them credit for, I think as the girls race from the dance area to the crafts. Lilah blows me off when I ask if she wants to make a puppet together. "I'm making one with my new friend," she says, garbling the word friend as she usually does so it sounds like *fiend*.

"She *can* be a fiend," Jennifer jokes. "But she's a nice fiend, like Shrek."

"Shrek puppet," the girls yell together. My heart drops when I realize I'll never watch Lennan make a puppet—or make a new friend.

Or maybe I will. If I keep myself open to all possibilities, who knows what the future will hold.

Four exhausting hours later, Lilah is ready to leave. "Thank you for being so understanding about my meltdown," Jennifer says.

"Thank you for being so understanding about my baby," I reply.

"Thank you for being my new friend," Serena says to Lilah.

"Thank you for being fun," Lilah responds.

"That sure sums us up," Jennifer says. "Come, Serena. It's time to go. I'm sure we'll see your new friend again soon."

As they walk to their car and we to ours, I realize how perfectly my vision for this day has unfolded. We had fun. We made friends.

And I've found another gift of Lennan: a well of compassion for other people that is deeper than any I've experienced before. No doubt many other gifts are going to follow.

28

We're sitting in the living room watching a rerun of Oprah's *SuperSoul Sunday* when a contraction wafts over me. I reach over and squeeze Don's hand. He's deeply into Oprah's interview with Eckhart Tolle, so he doesn't respond. I squeeze again.

"I know—this discussion is amazing," he finally says, eyes fixed on the TV. Lilah sits at our feet, building an elaborate farm, spinach and all, with her blocks.

"That's not the only thing that's amazing," I say firmly. Don finally looks at me. I smile and nod.

"You think it's time?" he shouts. Lilah inexplicably starts crying.

"It's okay, precious," I say, wondering if what got to her was Don's strong voice or the fact that a newborn is about to share her place at the center of our universe. Lilah bolts into my arms. I hug her as another contraction hits.

"I feel baby kicking!" she shouts, pointing to my abdomen.

"Not just kicking, love," I say. "Lennan's getting ready to come out and say hello to us."

"Now?" She backs away startled, as if he might slither out of my body this instant. I have explained numerous times the process of a baby's birth and we've read dozens of books, but she hasn't grasped it. It's hard enough for an adult to comprehend that a new being can slide out my tiny hole. "You said next week," she says, as if I've purposely fed her faulty information.

"Remember, I told you he could come anytime. That Sally said he was in position for next week on his official due date, or before that, or after."

"We should time the contractions." Don is racing around slightly crazed, probably trying to locate his cell phone to start the timer. After a minute of spinning he discovers the phone in his pocket. "We should call Sally," he adds more calmly.

"Not so fast. Sally said to call her when the contractions are regular. So far I've had two. Hardly regular."

"The baby is coming! The baby is coming!" Lilah dances around the room. I guess the answer to my earlier query is that Don's booming vocals made her cry.

"He'll be here sometime today or tomorrow," I tell her. "It will take a while."

Lilah rushes upstairs to her bedroom for who-knows-what purpose. Don and I appreciate our moment alone.

He sits down next to me and clasps my hands. "So this is it. The beginning of the most wonderful and most difficult time in our life."

"Let's stay focused on the *wonderful*," I reply. "Our baby will be born the same as any other healthy child. Remember our promise to enjoy that."

"I remember. But we also promised to be honest with our emotions."

Lilah is tromping around her room. I can usually discern what she's doing by the sounds. But this time—*plop, flop, stomp, slam*—I am clueless.

Don plucks a book off the end table that we've been reading together the past week: *Smile at Fear* by the late Buddhist master Chögyam Trungpa.

He flips to a dog-eared page and reads: "'Often, when someone tells us not to be afraid, we think they're saying not to worry, that everything is going to be all right. Unconditional fearlessness, however, is simply based on being awake. Once you have command of the situation, fearlessness is unconditional because you are neither on the side of success nor on the side of failure. Success *and* failure are your journey.'"

"That's our journey," I repeat.

Lilah finally emerges on the top stair landing, tugging a half dozen of her favorite stuffed animals, toys, and T-shirts, which she has deposited on her blanket.

"These are for Lennan," she announces breathlessly as she lugs the lot downstairs. "He can play with them. Maybe they will help him feel better when he is sick. And my animals can help him sleep good, like me." She points to her favorite teddy and the two stuffed otters she now snuggles with in bed. These have thankfully returned her to the all-night sleeper I desperately need her to be.

"That's so sweet. I'm sure Lennan will love them," Don responds, lifting Lilah into his arms. "But you can *share* them with him instead of giving them to him. When he's born, he'll be too little to play with them without your help."

"Because he can't sit or walk," she says, pleased with her knowledge of infant development, thanks to the big-sister books we've been reading. "Until he drinks enough milk from Momma's nipples, like I used to."

"That's right." Don plants a sloppy kiss on her cheek.

"Daddy!" She pulls a hand from around his neck and grandly wipes her face.

"Remember what we told you, that he won't be sick for a long time," Don says, taking one of her hands into his and waltzing her around the living room.

Don and I had gotten up early two weeks ago, the day we planned to tell Lilah about Lennan's Tay-Sachs. We were so anxious about how it would go that we centered ourselves for nearly an hour. I don't know whether it was the ease with which we were able to deliver the message, or the fact that she's comprehending with a two-year-old brain—I suspect both—but she took the news in stride.

As they circle the room, Lilah babbles on about the coming of her new brother.

I'm hit with another wallop. I double over.

"Is that the rushes, Momma?" Lilah asks, as they stop dancing. Don places Lilah on the floor and looks at his phone stopwatch. In his notes app, he jots the time between this contraction and my last: seven minutes.

I smile at Lilah's use of the word *rushes*. Since I decided to give birth at home, I've been reading all the granola birthing books Sally has in her office lending library, starting with the grandmother of the movement, Ina May Gaskin.

Her 1970s *Spiritual Midwifery* first put homebirths on the map. In an attempt to downplay the pain, Gaskin termed contractions *rushes*. I didn't love that word when I first read it, since it sounds right out of the sixties hippie scene that Gaskin was an integral part of. Now I'm hating it more, since it doesn't do justice to being ripped apart from the inside. They're not rushes, they're explosions.

It's a full minute before the pain ceases.

"You sure you're going to be able to do this?" Don asks, concerned.

"A little late for that, isn't it?" I joke. "The time for me to decide that was before you put this baby in there. Now he's gotta come out!"

"Funny. I mean delivering at home. Without the option of an epidural."

"Absolutely," I say, still amused by my little funny. "I've never been so sure of anything. Everything that's happened has convinced me this birth should be a beautiful experience, and what's more beautiful than our own bedroom?"

"And you still want a water birth?"

"I'm going to *labor* in the water. That's all I'm committing to. Most likely I'll get out before he comes."

"Can I go in the tub too?" Lilah has been excited about the birthing tub since it arrived in the mail. I can't blame her; it looks more like a blow-up wading pool than a medical gadget, although it's got high walls, a cushioned seat, and handles for me to hold. Much to Lilah's dismay, I haven't let her play in it so I could keep it sterile.

"No honeypie, you can't go in," Don answers. "We told you, this is a special tub for Momma when Lennan wants to be born. It will help her rushes." Don smiles as he says the word, knowing how I feel about it.

"Well get in the tub, Momma! Lennan is coming!" Lilah jumps up and down, conveying her urgency.

"That's a great idea. Let's go to the bedroom and start putting in the water," Don says to her, instructing me to clock the next few contractions. After they head upstairs, I hear rustling noises—covering the birthing tub with the liner and connecting the hose to our faucet, I suspect—then water flowing.

When I told Sally I had decided to give birth at home, she asked why I chose this option. I told her truthfully: I'm not afraid to take chances anymore. Lennan's Tay-Sachs made me realize you've got to seize every adventure life puts in your path. Not that birthing at home is even risky. I've read all the studies on home births, and for healthy women with the right caregiver, they're actually safer than a hospital.

Relishing a moment of solitude, I sit up straight on the couch and do a short meditation, aiming to observe my chest rising and falling. I give up after a minute, accepting there's no way I can keep my focus.

I allow my mind to leap to the memory of the overwhelming, unconditional love I felt when I first held baby Lilah. Connecting to a being who just emerged from the world of spirit, and feeling that same lofty energy inside me, was life-altering. I'm eager to experience this again.

My thoughts jump to the heartbreaking image of a memorial I glimpsed on a Tay-Sachs website last week, as I was looking for a recommendation for a local pediatrician famil-iar with the condition. I'd done a good job staying away from projections of what our life with the disease might entail. But the memorial scene this dad made on his home mantel was impossible to overlook. There was the child's tiny footprints, his favorite rattle, a piece of the tubing from the suction ma-chine that had cleared his mucus-filled lungs, a collection of heart-shaped stones his older brother gathered, and a photo of the toddler a few weeks before his death—head and body limp and nearly lifeless.

I can't shake that vision, so I step back to watch it mind-fully, as if it were a cloud passing through the sky and I am a child looking up from the grass. The image floats away.

I place my hand on my abdomen and send deep love to Lennan. He rewards me by bringing on an especially intense contraction.

Once it subsides, I pull out my phone and text Janelle and Angelica: *BABY COMING!*

Angelica phones me not ten seconds later. "Ooooooh! So exciting! When did the *rushes* start?" She emphasizes the word like Don did, because I've complained to her about it too.

"The rushes are painful as hell—as you well know. I'm go-ing to call them volcanoes. And my first volcano was not long ago. I've only had four."

"Are you timing them? Should you be calling Sally?"

"You sound as anxious as Don. I thought you'd be chill."

"Sorry. I'm excited to be an auntie again. I'll be better." She pauses. "When are you going to call Mom? And are you sure you want her over me?"

"It's not her *over* you. But I think it's a big step in my forgiveness and appreciation of Mom to have her do it."

Last week I asked my mother if she wanted to be at our house for the birth, to watch Lilah. At first, she replied exactly as I expected, railing about how birth should be done in a hospital and maybe I wasn't thinking straight because of the "disease thing," as she has taken to calling it.

After we hung up, she evidently realized this was not the path she wanted for us—I give her props for that. She called back and said *yes*. I'm a little concerned how it will go down, but I'm also eager to share this monumental experience with a mother, even if mine doesn't always live up to the title.

"I'm not calling her yet," I tell my sister. "It could be hours before my labor gets going, then more hours before the birth. I don't want her here much longer than necessary."

"I understand," Angelica says. "In the meantime, I'm going to cut off my ribbon bracelet and light my candle from your Blessingway. I'm also putting out word to my prayer group for your birth to be easy and wonderful."

"You don't really believe their prayers are going to determine that, do you?"

"No. It's you and your higher self that determines that. And Lennan's. But us praying gives your higher self easier access to that idea."

My phone beeps. "Janelle's calling. Mind if I take it?"

"Go ahead. Please keep me in the loop. I love you."

"I love you too." I disconnect my sister's line and click on Janelle's.

"Hi mom-very-soon-to-be!" she greets me. "Is it really happening or a false alarm? Actually, it better be real. My bracelet's cut off."

"Oh it's real. Fake contractions can't hurt this badly. This is the yoga mission field to the extreme."

"Shall we take a moment to set intentions? For an easy, beautiful birth?" she asks.

"I'd love that."

"Good. Start by centering yourself. Sit up straight. Feet flat on the floor, shoulders back and down, jaw relaxed, eyes closed." I follow each instruction. "Let's start by doing some of that resonant breathing you've taught me. I'll time the inhalations and exhalations by ringing my Tibetan bell when it's time to switch."

We do this breathwork for about four minutes. I'm heading for the magical state of alert bliss when Lilah bounds down the stairs.

"Momma, the tub's almost ready!" she shouts. Don races after her.

"Not quite ready," he tells me. "Probably another ten minutes."

"Great," I reply to both of them. "I'm on the phone with Janelle." I nod in Lilah's direction, and Don takes the hint.

"Come, honey," he says. "You and I are the official tub fillers. We need to stay in the bedroom till it's finished."

"Can I be in charge of the tem-om-eter?" she asks, adorably.

"Yes, you can be in charge of the thermometer, so the water is a perfect temperature for Momma and Lennan." They head back up.

I return to the phone. "Sorry about that."

"Don't apologize for that adorable creature. Since time is short, maybe we should cut the breathing and move on to the intending."

"Good idea."

"You're going to have a quick and magnificent labor in that cute blow-up tub," she starts. "Sally and her assistant will be efficient, generous, and caring. Lennan will come out easily and effortlessly." I summon all this, feeling the excitement well up.

After a moment, she continues. "Your home will be filled with your loving husband, who will rub your back and bring you water to drink; your daughter, who will periodically give you kisses; your mother, who will be helpful and kind. . . . " She pauses here, no doubt awaiting my reaction. I'm not going to let the idea of my mother disconnect me. I happily moan, so Janelle knows I'm with her.

"You will eat and drink wonderful things during labor if you want to," she continues, "while listening to your favorite chanting music and smelling your fragrant incense." She pauses again. I think she's waiting for me to take this in, but then she adds: "And your devoted friend Janelle will be there with you, helping in any way you want her to."

I laugh out loud. "I didn't even know you want to be here."

"I didn't want to intrude. But now that your mother is coming . . . and it's Sunday, so I don't have to work."

I ponder this idea. It would be lovely to have my girlfriend with me. But I already told Angelica she can't come, and she'd feel slighted if Janelle did. Not to mention Gretta.

Plus, Don wants the moment of the birth to be as bonding between him and me as Lilah's was.

"We'll text you right after he arrives. You can come then. I can't guarantee it won't be in the middle of the night, though."

"It won't be." I can feel her smile through the phone. "Remember, we envisioned a short labor."

"I'm not officially in labor. My contractions haven't been that regular ye—YOW!" I scream as I'm seized by another volcano. *Rushes*, I correct myself. *They're just rushes.* Maybe Gaskin is onto something—that thinking them smaller will make them feel so.

"Picture a serene setting at a lake, and breathe the moist air in, slowly and deeply," Janelle says—but at the moment I want to tell her where she can shove her imagery. Once the contraction peaks, though, I'm glad I had explained to Janelle that Sally suggested I get through the contractions with visualizations. No doubt it will benefit me to remember this image.

"I think you're officially in labor, sweetie," she says. "You should get Don to time those suckers."

"I should. And I probably need to call my mother so she can do her full rosary before coming to assume Lilah duty. I'm going to need Don full-time soon."

Five hours later I'm in the birthing tub in our bedroom. Sally is sitting on a chair on one side, Don on the other. Right after that call with Janelle, my contractions starting coming so hard and fast it was Don who had to call my mom. He also rang Sally and gave her the contraction times. She and Madison raced over. Madison has periodically taken my vital signs, but otherwise she's been largely invisible.

"Argh!" I shout, as another volcano—*screw that rushes idea!*—detonates inside me.

"Try moving around, maybe put your legs up a little more," Sally instructs. "Like you're doing a boat *asana*."

My cell phone chimes from its perch on my dresser. I use that app's sound this time, as I have for months, to remind myself to focus inside my body. It helps settle me.

I raise my legs into a V and press my feet into the springy tub. Instinctively, my hands go to the sides of my thighs like when I do the boat.

"Don't let go of the handles," Sally cautions with an even tone, although it feels I'm being admonished. I return my grip to the handles while keeping my legs up. This new position does make the next contraction more bearable.

I had requested earlier that Don light sandalwood incense, but now the scent nauseates me. I ask him to stub it out and he happily complies, eager to have something to do. I sense his helplessness watching me suffer. For a few contractions, I tried stifling my reaction so he wouldn't feel bad, but that made it hurt so much worse. I'll never make it through if I don't react authentically. And that means yelling and growling.

Lilah and my mother are playing hide-and-seek in her bedroom. I can hear my mother periodically shout, "I can't find you, dear!" even though I know Lilah is hiding in plain sight. I'm impressed my mother is going along.

Madison appears out of nowhere with a cup of coconut water. She places the cup under my mouth and instructs me to sip. This makes me realize how hungry I am. I haven't eaten since breakfast.

"Can I eat something?" I ask Sally. I remember reading that eating during labor is verboten in hospitals, although I can't recall why.

"Sure. Anything you're in the mood for."

"Anything?" I thought she'd restrict me to something light. "What if I'm in the mood for a steak?"

"I kind of doubt you'd be in the mood for steak while you're in active labor." I realize she's right. Something light isn't a bad idea. "Although I did once have a lady order a pepperoni pizza. She had several slices."

I decide on half a turkey sandwich on sprouted-grain bread. Don and Madison fight each other for the right to make it. Sally decides Don should stay, especially when, during a roaring contraction, I beg him to hold my hand. Madison returns from the kitchen and, between contractions, I scarf down every bite, followed by a chaser of blueberries with whipped cream.

My skin is getting pruney, so I drag myself out of the tub. This gives Madison a chance to add more hot water so the temperature stays cozy. I so appreciate both of these women, whose only desire is to keep me as comfortable as possible and ensure I deliver a healthy baby.

Well, a healthy-for-now baby. Which is the best I'm going to get.

After I dry myself, I lower my bottom onto my large exercise ball, which Sally is calling a birthing ball. *Does she expect me to deliver on it?* I decide not to ask, since I'm trying to stay in the moment, and in the moment I'm angling to find ease between these damn contractions. I will deal with the birth later.

I got the ball after reading *The Essential Homebirth Guide,* which has indeed been essential. Bouncing during my next volcano proves better than sitting on the bed, but it makes me appreciate the tub. Two contractions later I climb back in.

I move from position to position with each contraction. None sufficiently soothes me. Don asks if I want to try laughing yoga. I've never heard of this. He admits it is something he occasionally does when no one is around.

"You're hiding something from me?"

"Not hiding, exactly. I prefer to do it alone because I know how ridiculous I look."

"But you want me to do it here, in front of Sally and Madison—and my mother?"

"You already look ridiculous, howling and shrieking. What's a little laughter?" I take this the way I know he means it, as a loving tease.

Apparently, laughing yoga really is a thing. "I know it sounds crazy, but I agree with Don," Sally says. "I've had other laboring mothers do it. It sends endorphins through your body and takes your mind off the rushes."

Don starts by guffawing as unabashedly as he can. I immediately understand why he does this in private. "Join in, Lorna," he says through his cackles.

"Ha ha ha ha ha," I roar. For the first few rounds I'm faking it, but eventually the ridiculousness of the moment causes true chuckles to come. Don and I laugh in unison. Soon Sally and Madison join in.

Lilah runs into our bedroom, followed by my sheepish-looking mother, rosary beads in hand. My mother looks so uncomfortable I pray she'll quickly leave the room. I know she has seen a naked, pregnant woman in labor before—after all, she has two daughters—but this scene is so far outside her comfort zone.

"What's so funny, Momma?" Lilah asks.

"Nothing really, darling. We were just laughing to make the rushes feel better."

"Want my rubber ducky?"

I have no idea how she came up with that non sequitur, but that's the beauty of a young child's mind. "I'd love it."

Lilah runs into her bathroom, returning with the ducky. She places it into my hand as the next rush comes over me. Still holding one handle to reassure Sally, I squeeze the duck tightly. Coupled with the residue from the laughter, it helps me get through the pain.

"Are you done . . . um, um . . . laboring?" Lilah asks, proud of herself for remembering the word.

"Not yet," Don interjects. He turns to me before continuing to answer her. "I'm hoping it's soon. I'm not sure I can take much more of this." He smiles coyly, since of course *I'm* the one bearing the contractions. Still, his discomfort at my discomfort is part of what I love about this man. Apparently realizing she's not going to see the baby wiggle out yet, Lilah skips out of the room, my relieved mom right behind her.

"*Am* I almost finished?" I beg Sally. "I really can't take much more."

"Come out and I'll check you," she responds. I exit the tub, dry off, and lie down on my bed, which has been covered with disposable pads to keep the sheets clean. Madison appears with a cup of juice, which I sip even though I am no longer the tiniest bit thirsty or hungry.

"Drink it all down," Sally says. "Then I'll do a dilation check." I do as I'm told—I'd swallow a live octopus if it meant Sally would tell me I'm nearly done.

Don wraps our teal blanket around my legs to keep me warm, and places a microwaved sock filled with uncooked rice around my shoulders—a tip he no doubt garnered from the homebirth book I've seen him read. I finish the juice and hand Madison the cup. Sally tucks a pillow behind my back, then slips her gloved hand under the blanket.

"You're there!" she announces. "Ten centimeters." Madison scurries in the background, arranging items I can't see onto a tray. "Do you want to deliver in the tub, on the ball, or on the bed?"

"Or our birthing chair," Madison interjects, holding up a seat that looks like a toddler's preschool perch.

"I'll start on the bed." I'm concerned—unnecessarily, Sally has assured me—that Lennan might drown in the water. And I'm certain I'll collapse off the ball or such a tiny chair during these contractions. I yank the blanket Lilah loves so much off my legs and place it over the rice sock around my shoulders. Sally bends my knees and tells me I can push with the next contraction.

I glance at my beautiful altar. All the candles are lit, including the one I got at my Blessingway, which is ringed by my ribbon. Last week, in preparation for the birth, Don added items to the bottom shelf: a porcelain statue of a baby angel; a moonstone, supposedly a symbol of fertility; and a drawing of the baby Lilah made, which makes Lennan look like a spider. Taking in all these items fortifies my strength.

Good thing, because at the next contraction the urge to push is undeniable. I give it all I've got, which is apparently a lot. That happens one more time. Then another. And another.

"I see something," Don yells.

"The top of the head," Sally explains.

"I want to see!" I demand. Madison produces a mirror, which she positions at my pelvis. Glimpsing a small patch of black amidst my folds overwhelms me; a monsoon of tears gushes down my face.

"Let me see!" Lilah bursts into the room and runs to the foot of the bed. Apparently, she's been listening so she wouldn't miss the birth. This time, my mother does not follow. Don places his hands on Lilah's shoulder and shifts her out of Sally's way.

A few more pushes, tears spilling the entire time, something soft and slimy thrusts out of my body. Sally grabs Lennan and immediately places him face-down on my abdomen. Lilah takes a step towards him, but Don pulls her back—a job that's supposed to fall to my mother. Fortunately, at this moment I'm too ecstatic to care.

I'm transported out of myself. My body has lost its tonnage and is floating around the top of the room. Lennan is with me, weightless and wonderful. Somewhere in my brain I know there are people below us, including my beloved husband and daughter. But at the moment I am oblivious.

I am merged with my son, with the angel he is and the world of spirit I can see, via shimmering silver threads, he is attached to. He doesn't need to tell me not to worry—there is no possibility of that emotion here. The love all humans are made from infuses each of us completely.

After a while I watch the silver threads dissipate, while the love confines itself inside both our hearts. We float gently back to the bed.

"He's born! He's born!" Don shouts, as I feel my body, heavy with Lennan on top of me. Don pauses. "It is a boy, isn't it?"

Sally lifts Lennan a few inches, and we all see that indeed he is.

After a while, Sally cleans and checks him and me. Lennan is wrapped in a blanket and joyfully placed into my arms, then Don's. When Don lowers him to show Lilah, she gives him a loving lick on his forehead.

Angel, beauty, cherub, delicious, entrancing, fantastic, gorgeous, hopeful, important, juicy, kissable, loving . . . The alphabet process of summoning positive emotions flows effortlessly. My heart feels so full, I begin to sob again.

"What's wrong, Momma?" Lilah asks, concerned.

"Absolutely nothing," I reply, knowing at this moment that is more than true.

Suddenly Angelica, Daria, Janelle, and Gretta are at my bedroom door. Each holds her burning candle from my Blessingway wrapped in the yellow ribbons.

"How . . . how did you get here?" I stammer.

"They've been here for hours," Don replies. "Janelle called so many times I finally told her she could sit downstairs as long as she was silent."

"Then he realized, and rightly so, that the rest of us would be upset if we found out Janelle was here and we weren't," Gretta adds. "I'm glad to know we were quiet enough that you didn't hear us. We were chanting for a successful birth."

"Softly," Daria adds. "Almost whispering."

"I'm so happy to see you guys. Look at my baby boy!" I point to Lennan, as if they wouldn't otherwise know who I was referring to. "He's such a blessing!"

"He certainly is," Angelica say, stroking his head in Don's arms. "And your task," she looks first at Don, then me, "is to stay in the moment these next years so you remember that."

Lennan screams. Sally deftly takes him from Don and places him at my breast. He suckles immediately.

My mother finally enters the room. My impulse is to cover my exposed body with the sheet, but I override it. This is birth, in all its bloody glory.

"You have a grandson!" I announce.

She looks at my face, avoiding my body, but I look down at Lennan until she can't help following my gaze.

"A grandson," she beams. "How wonderful."

Suddenly I feel inspired, and the words tumble out of my mouth on a plume of unconditional love. "I think we should have him baptized. I know it's important to you—and maybe even to us—to acknowledge our heritage." I shoot Don an apologetic look, but he's in such bliss he doesn't react. "Lilah too. We should have done it when she was born."

"Thank you, Don and Lorna." My mother leans over to hug me, but thinking better of getting so close to my nakedness, she touches my arm instead. "I love you."

"I love you too, Mom." At this moment at least, when she who gave birth to me is witnessing my giving birth to another, I sincerely mean it.

Lennan sucks loudly, pulling my attention back to him. As I watch him, I'm clear that the experience awaiting Don and me will change us to our core. But, with all the spiritual work we've done and will continue doing, I know the change can be magnificent, even as some aspects will inevitably be tragic.

As Eckhart Tolle wrote in *Stillness Speaks*, "Your unhappiness ultimately arises not from the circumstances of your life but from the conditioning of your mind."

I glance from Don to Lilah, to Sally and Madison, to my sisters, my friends, my mother, and ultimately to my baby. I have magnificent people and circumstances in my life. But if everything changes, if the conditions grow dire, I will strive to keep my inner contentment and my happiness. That will be the ultimate blessing—and the legacy—of Lennan.

I focus intensely on him: seeing his soft skin and matted hair, feeling his little mouth press onto me, smelling his newborn scent, hearing his little slurps.

Tolle has also written, "Now is the only place where life can be found."

If that is true, and I know from the core of my being that it is, my life is spectacular indeed.

Books mentioned in *Warrior Won*

Meditation for the Love of It
Sally Kempton

The Amazing Power of Deliberate Intent
Esther and Jerry Hicks

The Science of Mind
Ernest Holmes

The Universe Has Your Back
Gabrielle Bernstein

Awaken the Giant Within
Tony Robbins

Clippings from My Notebook
Corrie ten Boom

Ayurveda Beginner's Guide
Susan Weis-Bohlen

Happiness
Zelig Pliskin

The Power of Now
Eckhart Tolle

Merton's Palace of Nowhere
James Finley

Interior Castle
Teresa of Avila

Loving What Is
Byron Katie

Tao Te Ching
Lao-Tzu

Get Out of Your Mind and Into Your Life
Steven Hayes

*Prayers of
Teresa of Avila*
Edited by
Thomas Alvarez

*Dark Night of the
Soul*
St. John of the
Cross

The Blessingway
Veronika Sophia
Robinson

*Wherever You
Go, There You
Are*
Jon Kabat-Zinn

*When Things Fall
Apart*
Pema Chödrön

Dying to Be Me
Anita
Moorjani

*You Can Heal
Your Life*
Louise Hay

The Hell I Can't
Terry McBride

*A Revolution in
Medicine*
Bruno Gröning

Smile at Fear
Chögyam
Trungpa

*Spiritual
Midwifery*
Ina May
Gaskin

*The Essential
Homebirth Guide*
Jane E. Drichta
and Jodilyn
Owen

Stillness Speaks
Eckhart Tolle

About the Author

Award-winning writer **Meryl Davids Landau**'s prior books include the novel *Downward Dog, Upward Fog*, a finalist in the *Foreword Reviews* fiction-book-of-the-year competition, and *Enlightened Parenting*, a book of essays.

Her work has been published in *O: The Oprah Magazine, Prevention, Parents, Vice, HuffPost, Glamour, Self, Good Housekeeping, Redbook, Everyday Health*, and many others. Meryl has won many writing awards, including a nomination for the prestigious National Magazine Award. She is a certified yoga teacher and a moderator of the Yoga Folks group on Goodreads. Meryl blogs about yoga and spiritual topics at *Medium.com*. She lives with her husband in South Florida.

Connect with Meryl
on her website: MerylDavidsLandau.com
on Facebook: Facebook.com/MerylDavidsLandau
on Twitter: @MerylDL

Acknowledgments

Readers have asked me for years to write a sequel to *Downward Dog, Upward Fog*, but I could never figure out what might be big enough to cause Lorna's hard-won inner peace to wobble again. Then, a few years ago, I met a pregnant woman who told me that her doctors feared something might be wrong with her baby, and my heart broke for her. I never did discover how things turned out (I pray all is well), but I owe this stranger my gratitude for planting the seed for this novel.

All books require research, and for their insights and expertise my heartfelt appreciation goes to Lauren Propst, a Chicago genetic counselor; Diana Pangonis and Monica Gettleman, the director of family services and a board member, respectively, of the National Tay-Sachs & Allied Diseases Association; and Piero Falci, Margaret DeAngelis, Lisa Kelly, and Miranda Gray. Of course, any factual errors in this book are mine alone. Also, thanks go to Andrea King Collier, for keeping me writing early on.

I greatly appreciate the people who read early drafts and provided invaluable feedback: Jessica Topper, Penelope Love, Nichola Veitch, Michelle Dry, and Stacy Rodriguez.

Thanks, too, to my wonderful copyeditor Sophia Dembling (who was going through her own health challenges while reading about Lorna's) and my proofreader Kelsey Landau. And to my publicist and all-around sweet person, Carina Sammartino—you're the best.

I also want to acknowledge the wonderful people in the various creative and writing organizations who inspire my work, including the Boca Raton branch of the National

League of American Pen Women, the Florida Writers Association, the Association of Health Care Journalists, and the American Society of Journalists and Authors.

A mindfulness-based novel like *Warrior Won* is possible only because of the spiritual journey I myself have been on for many years. Special thanks for expanding my horizons over the decades go to the spiritual leaders and members of: the Integral Yoga Institute in New York; the Yoga Research Foundation in Miami; the Center for Spiritual Living in Boca Raton; Temple Adath Or in South Florida; and our long-running (but now sadly defunct) Tuesday Night Spiritual Book Discussion Group (here's remembering you, Bob), especially member and now dear friend Leslie Lott.

There are also so many teachers who have moved me with their books and retreats, a number of whom I have cited in this novel. Special shout-outs go to Esther Hicks, Neale Donald Walsch, and Eckhart Tolle for their amazing messages.

My love knows no bounds for my beloved husband Gary, my children Richard and Kelsey (and their wonderful significant others, Karla and Leo), my parents Joyce and Joe and mother-in-law Sylvia, sisters Fern and Andrea, and all of my terrific friends.

Finally, I have immense gratitude for you, my readers. I hope this novel inspires you to bring more mindfulness into your life in a meaningful way, and to take time to appreciate *all* of the people and experiences that have made you who you are.

Reading Group Questions

Meryl Davids Landau is happy to Skype into your book group. Contact her via her website (MerylDavidsLandau.com), Facebook (Meryl Davids Landau) or Twitter (@MerylDL).

1. At the start of the novel, Lorna has difficulty maintaining her practices of yoga and meditation the way she did before her child was born. Does her struggle strike you as genuine? Have you had a similar experience of life getting in the way of your daily practice? How did/do you deal with it?

2. Lorna loves her boss and her job, and is obviously good at her work, yet her mind occasionally flips to worrying about whether her boss is unhappy with her. Why does she do this? Why do we all do this sometimes? How can we stop our minds from catastrophizing for no reason?

3. From the moment Lorna faints, she becomes concerned that something is wrong with Deuxie, even though for many months there is no medically proven problem. Did you feel that Lorna was worrying about nothing at the time, or was she right to trust her instincts? Have you ever sensed a problem before it happened? What do you attribute that to?

4. Don is a key source of support for Lorna for much of the novel. How did you feel when Lorna hears the news about Deuxie's diagnosis and runs out of town without him? Do you like how Don handles her return? What about how he manages his own reactions to their reality?

5. Lorna has a group of tight, spiritually aware girlfriends who aim to lift one another up. Do you find yourself drawn to some of the women more than others (and if so, which),

or to all for different reasons? In your own life, do you have a friend, or group of friends, who fills this important role?

6. Continuing a theme from *Downward Dog, Upward Fog*, Lorna has a fraught relationship with her less-than-perfect mother. How does Lorna eventually come to terms with her? Do you have a difficult relative you might try to view in a different light?

7. What do you think about the Blessingway, and that it pampers and honors the mother rather than the baby? Could you see yourself throwing one for someone in your life?

8. Lorna has a mixed view of the conventional medical community. She respects doctors and their proven treatments, but at times denigrates them. How do you feel about her reactions? How do you reconcile any tension you might have between Western and Eastern medicine?

9. Lorna (and author Meryl Davids Landau) is an avid reader of spiritual nonfiction books. Have you read many of the books Lorna does? Which are your favorites? Which had you not known of that you're now inspired to discover?

10. *Warrior Won* includes many spiritual practices that Lorna uses to maintain her center. Which ones included in the book have you personally tried? Are there practices that are new to you that you want to explore? (The practices include "sujaling," as Lorna terms it, which can be a sitting or walking meditation; hatha yoga; various types of breathwork; appreciating people; consciously intending what you want in the next segment; focusing inside your body; engaging all of your senses; bringing a "smile" to your body; eating mindfully; singing about your worries; rapidly repeating your worries; challenging your worries; attending meditative musical events; and reading spiritual books.)

CPSIA information can be obtained
at www.ICGtesting.com
Printed in the USA
FSHW022216230419
57494FS